Country At Heart

Andrea J. Graham

D1711960

Published by Reignburst Books, 2020.

COUNTRY AT HEART

First edition. November 10, 2020.

Copyright © 2020 Andrea J. Graham.

ISBN: 978-1393598312

Written by Andrea J. Graham.

To My Mother, Debra Ann Hatfield, 1956-2014.

"Awake, you who sleep, Arise from the dead, And Christ will give you light." (Ephesians 5:14b NKJV)

Chapter 1
Saturday, August 10, 1996

"WHOA!" SUSANNA FLAILED, unbalanced. The steep, downhill trail rushed up. She dove sideways and tumbled down into the wooded ravine.

At the bottom, she sat up, clutching the ground. The world spun. Her elbows and right knee smarted. She felt around her right foot's white Reebok sneaker, checking the ankle just recently freed from a cast. Thirteen-year-old younger sisters could be so careless, when determined to win at all costs.

Cara ran up and knelt beside her. "Are you all right, Sis?"

Susanna blinked and squinted ahead at the huge fallen oak, refusing to die. Its head lay caught in the canopy above her. Its trunk stretched down at a fifteen degree angle across a creek to roots pointed skyward, leaving a huge hole behind it. Why was everything so blurry? Her hands flew to her face and she gasped. "My glasses! Cara Bethlyn McCoy!"

Cara stiffened. "I didn't do it! You're the clumsy one, always falling."

After bullies shoved her. Susanna glared, her left hand on the pocket of her size-14 women's carpenter jeans, below her purple tie-dyed T-shirt. At almost fifteen years old, she'd long since lost all hope of being skinny like her dad rather than plus-sized like her mom. "I didn't clobber into myself."

"As if!" Cara laughed. "For reals, I didn't mean to knock you down."

Susanna turned over on her knees and peered around her at the rocky dirt path, but those darn frames blended into the background. She groped for them. "Just help me find them."

Cara started up the hill. Something crunched underneath her platform Dr. Martens. "Uh, I think I just did."

SUSANNA FOLLOWED HER sister up the sun-speckled one-lane gravel road to their campsite. Salty sweat trickled onto her brow. She wiped it away. In the dog days of August, the woods provided no relief from the humidity.

The sisters reached the rusted 1980s swing set near the edge of their lot, in the gravel lawn before a deck and their white Nomad travel trailer. A wood bench painted red, a matching chair, and a picnic table sat out on their deck. They entered the front door, to the right of the dining booth across the head of the trailer, currently still lowered down into their unmade double bed.

Their auburn-haired mom looked up from washing the breakfast dishes and put her hand on her ample hip. "Susanna, where are your glasses?"

"They broke." She dug in her pocket then handed over the pieces and held her breath. Even if her dad could tape the arms on and bend the frame back in shape, the scratches on the thick lenses rendered them useless. That might be a godsend—if her folks didn't kill her. Cara better appreciate this.

Her mom shifted through the remains of Susanna's glasses, shook her head, and dropped the deceased in the trash. "Any chance you obeyed us and kept your old pair so you'd have a spare?"

The huge Steve Urkel glasses, held together by tape? Lost, in the trash. Susanna shuddered. The penalty for her stuff getting broken or lost was the item not ever getting replaced. Surely her mom would be kind and replace the brand-new, broken glasses even though she didn't at all deserve that.

Eyes closed, Mom took frustrated breaths to calm herself. Looking up, she said softly, "I will walk down to the payphone and call the eye doctor. You're off the hook for now, kiddo, but be more careful. We can't afford this."

Susanna sighed with relief. Thank goodness her mom didn't punish her. Bad enough she now had to endure a fuzzy world where numbers and letters vanished five inches past her nose. Procrastination was her family's hobby, so she'd be lucky if she got new glasses before school started. She rubbed at her aching temple. This was not going to be fun.

"What's for lunch?" Cara asked.

"Nothing. We ate a late breakfast."

"But, Mom, we're starving!" Cara batted her eyelashes. "Pretty please? How can you deny a growing girl a meal?"

"Oh, all right." Her mom grabbed a bill from her purse and handed it to Cara. "Here, go get something to eat."

Cara and Susanna rushed for the door. "Thanks, Mom!"

They headed back to the shortcut through the ravine, walking this time. Susanna glanced sideways at Cara. "I can't believe you got away with that."

Cara beamed. "It comes with the territory."

At the Glenshire Campgrounds Office, the sisters grabbed ice cream bars from its convenience store freezer. They took them to the register on the L-shaped front counter. Cara passed the five dollar bill to the gray-haired Phill Durant, who owned Glenshire.

He peered at Susanna. "What happened to your glasses?"

"They broke," she said.

"Oh, I see." Phill rang up the ice cream and gave them a grandfatherly smile. "Will that be everything, girls?"

Cara leaned forward. "We'll take two mini-pizzas, too, please."

Phill finished ringing up the order. He slipped a quarter into one of his fists and held out both. "Pick one."

Why couldn't Susanna be anywhere else?

Cara pointed at Phill's right fist. Phill laughed, opened the empty hand, and tossed Cara her quarter before heading to the freezer. The girls moved to the side counter. Behind it, Phill pulled out what Susanna assumed was their four-inch pizzas and stuck them in the microwave.

Amy and Krystal raced out from the game room, giggling, and headed over. Both preteens wore shiny pink jelly sandals. Amy's overalls hung from one shoulder over a florescent Lisa Frank screen-printed shirt, an outfit that did zip to relieve her pudgy, baby look. Butterfly clips held back her blonde-streaked, brown bob. Krystal's hot pink short-shorts peeked out below her baby doll tee, and her dirty blonde hair was feathered.

Susanna sighed. In the absence of girls her age, she could either hang out by herself or tag along with the immature middle schoolers.

Amy sent the sisters a wide smile. "Hi, Cara Beth. Hi, Sue-Ann. Did you get contacts?"

"I'm not allowed contacts. My glasses are broken."

The microwave dinged.

Phill took out their pizzas and slid them across the counter. "Here you go, girls."

"Thanks." Cara and Susanna took their food over to the orange booth in between the game room's entry way and the office's main double doors.

Krystal and Amy slid onto the bench across from them. Between bites of pizza, Cara said to Amy, "I told Susanna what you said about the cute new kid. It's her bet Jordy is a snob."

Krystal snorted. "Please, being filthy rich and from a major city doesn't mean he's a snob."

"Whatever." Susanna waved. City boys like Jordy would be nice to pretty little things like Krystal, but at best they ignored girls like herself.

Once the sisters finished their lunch, Amy stood. "I have to find Ricky. Somebody come with me."

Cara and Krystal slid out of the booth.

"We're coming," Krystal said.

"Susanna," Phill called, "could I talk to you a minute?"

"Ooh, you're in trouble." Krystal giggled.

"Not." Susanna wrinkled her nose. "Go on ahead, I'll catch up later." Fat chance. She and Cara had known the brothers Nate and Ricky since Ricky and Cara were in kindergarten. But both brothers now ran with Boo's gang. Five rowdy, noisy teenage boys, all in one place, and clearly not keen to be chased by three oblivious middle-school girls? Not adding to that crowd.

After Cara and her friends had left, Susanna joined Phill at the counter and leaned into it. "What's up?"

Phill sighed. "I suppose you've heard Jordan's on board?"

"You could say that," Susanna said dryly. Krystal's most outrageous tale held Phill's son was an ex-con, which she'd clearly made up. Her more likely story claimed Jordan was an architect turned bum. Both stories involved his rich daddy bailing him out. Evidently it never occurred to anyone Phill might like to retire some time this millennium. "Cara's interested in your grandson, but I doubt it'll be mutual. She heard Jordy's much older than us?"

Phill shook his head. "Junior just turned sixteen last Memorial Day. I'm warned he got his license over the summer and is dying to hit the road."

And of course he wouldn't get special treatment and be allowed to drive in the park despite Phill's rules against minors driving. Susanna bit her lips together to keep that bit of sarcasm to herself.

Phill cleared his throat. "Jordy's lived around Chicago his entire life, and he's been hiding in his guest room since he got here. So I want someone who knows the park like the back of her hand to give him the chef's tour."

"In other words, you want me to introduce City Boy to nature."

"Oh no, Jordy spent seven years in the Scouts. He knows the woods."

"Sure and I'm not a country hick." She'd seem so, to a Chicago boy.

"Does tomorrow at noon work for you?"

"We're not leaving until later that afternoon."

Phill beamed and patted her shoulder. "Great, see you here tomorrow."

"See you." She turned and left out the main double doors.

Just before the gate to the permanent campers' area, she stopped in her tracks. Did she promise Phill that she'd give his stuck-up grandson a tour of the park? Oh gosh, she did. Her cheeks warmed. If anyone found out, she'd never hear the end of it.

She glanced back at the office. Just a fuzzy, brown rectangular blur. She sighed. No, she couldn't take it back. How could she ever get through this? What if she tripped over something? Okay, so she'd gone back up the hill and down through it again without another incident. If she could navigate that, she shouldn't have any problems elsewhere in the park, either.

But if she went along with this and anyone saw them . . . . She shuddered but stomped around the gate and back toward the woods. It wasn't fair. She shouldn't have to face such humiliation. Not here.

She laid her index finger beside her right eye, passing through the space her glasses should have filled. A slow smile came over her. Maybe she didn't have to play dead this time. Maybe, for once, she'd get the upper hand—and teach City Boy a thing or two.

AROUND NOON ON SUNDAY, a white 1993 Suburban roared past Jordy and stirred up a dust cloud. He coughed and picked up his pace, mentally cursing at the rude driver.

Once in the clear, he stopped to knock any lingering dust out of his hair, which the sun had bleached to an irritating dark blond. He preferred "light brown," like it said on the license Gramps' dumb rules had rendered useless. At least his blue Tommy Hilfiger shirt and his cargo shorts looked okay. And his chain was long enough that it never popped out of his loose-fitting shirts and got him asked questions about his sparkly jewelry's significance.

Jordy got moving again, albeit at a turtle's pace. He eyed the gatehouse coming up on his right and glanced to the camp office built into a distant hillside ahead. Like the party house he'd already passed, both needed a fresh coat of paint. Cracks laced the foundation of the gatehouse. Moss grew on the roof. One broken window looked like some kid put a baseball through it, and no one bothered to board it up, let alone replace it. Beside the gatehouse, a quaint, dusty payphone booth waited for Superman to change clothes in it.

Jordy reached a crossroads before a tent camping area and took the road leading toward the office. He shook his head. Gramps' idea of fixing potholes seemed to be dumping rocks on the roads, and he hadn't done that recently. Maybe with Jordan here, this place would get some much-needed repairs. Jordy had no intention of sticking around long enough to find out. With any luck, his mom would soon get here and take him back to Chicago.

His so-called father was too far gone—by three years. Jordan had yet to acknowledge he'd never again be the dad that Jordy loved and missed. Jordy had spelled it out for his so-called father, who only insisted his name was still "Dad," and that he'd rather be in Chicago, too, but he had needed a job this badly. If that garbage were true, then why hadn't Jordan been in Chicago?

And why had Jordy's mom suddenly shipped him off to here? What was keeping her, anyway? She made it sound like she would follow by car within a couple days. Surely the drive here didn't take this long.

Likely, his parents were making their split official. His mom had been hiding something for months. Her secret better not involve an engagement ring in her future. Not even a cleaned-up Jordan could ever replace his dad. He just wasn't the same. Nothing could ever be the same again.

At camp office's hillside walkway, Jordy groaned. No more delaying the inevitable. He took the steps uphill two at a time and let the screen door bang shut behind him. He glanced over the deserted store. The tacky, brightly colored T-shirts on sale all declared "I'm a happy camper!"

Frowning, Gramps tapped his fingers on the L-shaped counter's white linoleum. "What'd you do, boy? Get lost? We've been waiting half an hour."

Jordy approached his grandfather, almost tripping over a snag in the gray carpeting. "Gees, Gramps, it's only a quarter after. It's not my fault you got here early. What's the big deal?"

A snort beside the counter drew his eye to the girl standing there. If she was a girl. She was around five-seven, four inches shorter than himself. Her long, reddish-brown hair was pulled back in a ponytail too snarled to tell if it was straight or curly. She'd paired a moth-eaten violet, tie-dyed T-shirt with the filthiest carpenter jeans he'd seen on a girl over ten.

Oops, his eyes had strayed to her well-padded hips and her rather nice pear-figure. He sheepishly moved his gaze back to where it belonged. Okay, she was definitely a girl, and looked to be the same pants-size as his last ex-girlfriend, who he had liked the most. The high cheek bones also hinted that a pretty girl hid beneath the dirt, but it seemed she was a real-live hick.

She shook her head. "Figures. Keeps a lady waitin' then wonders what he did wrong. Come on, City Boy, where's yo' manners? Thought he wouldn't need 'em so he left 'em in Chicago." She snorted. "Ya bitter go and get 'em, even hicks will want respect."

Jordy arched one eyebrow at the way she'd said Chicago. She spoke with a country twang and mocked the way Chicago natives spoke? That took gall.

Gramps said, "Jordy, you owe us an apology. We're waiting."

He rolled his eyes and mumbled a sorry.

"What was that?" She all but purred, smirking. "You'd bitter speak up, we can't understand mumbo jumbo."

"I'm sorry I kept you waiting! Satisfied?"

"Ya don't need to shout." She had flinched like his noise was painful and now turned to face Gramps. "Well, Phill?"

"What? Do you need anything else?"

She stamped her foot. "Ain't you goin' to introduce us? I ain't takin' no stranger 'round."

Gramps laughed. "Oh, right." He turned to Jordy. "This here's Susa—"

"Sue-Ann McCoy." She extended her hand. Her scornful cat-green eyes dared him to take it. "And you are?"

Gramps scrunched his brows. "She's been here twelve years. Sue-Ann will be in the tenth grade when school starts."

While Gramps spoke, Jordy stepped forward and shook Sue-Ann's hand. Surprise flashed through her eyes before she lowered them.

"Jordan Walker Durant, Jr. My friends call me Jordy."

She backed away, shifting like he'd violated her comfort zone. So much for friendly hillbillies.

"But, you can call me Jordy anyway." She'd better, anyway.

Sue-Ann rolled her eyes. "I bet ya'd rather me call you Master Durant, like I'm some sorta servant. I got news fur ya. You ain't no bitter than me."

Gramps leaned over the counter and whispered to Jordy, "I'd behave, if I were you. She is as sweet as raspberry pie. But she was born with fire in her soul. And that attitude of yours is pouring on the gasoline."

Sue-Ann shifted her weight. "Let's get started. Ya wanna start with the business stuff or the fun stuff first?"

Like anything was "fun" about Glenshire, especially if all the girls acted like this. "I'll take fun."

"Good." Her eyes brightened. "By the way, welcome to Glenshower. First stop's the game room, then the pool, then we'll be headin' o'er to the lake."

He shrugged. She continued, "The game room's this a way, through the big doorway."

Jordy followed her through the door on the right. He surveyed the game room—one pool table, three ancient video arcade games, a pinball machine, and foosball table. The pool table was located near the main entrance and ought to play decent. Not much to say for the atmosphere. The beige walls begged for a fresh coat of paint.

"What'd ya think?" Sue-Ann asked.

What could he think? This place was decrepit, just like the rest of the campgrounds. "Not bad. Though, I've seen better."

"I bet ya have. Come on, this-a-way to the pool." She headed for the exit on the south wall.

Before they reached it, four guys came in with a middle-school boy. The tallest, oldest guy had a ponytail and swaggered like the BOSS emblazoned in camo letters across his hunter green shirt. The guys all sent curious glances at Jordy and started a pool game.

Sue-Ann shook her head. "Ya can play with Boo's gang later."

Had he heard that right? "Boo? How do you spell that?"

"Don't ask me. I ain't his ma." She escorted Jordy out to the cement area surrounding the deep end. He blinked at the pool smiling with crystal-clear depths and a trace of chlorine on the breeze. A diving board and a slide stood guard. On three sides, healthy grass stretched out beyond the cement patio, with a chain-link fence on the right and the left. The swimming pool, at least, beat the one he'd used in Chicago hands down.

She waved. "That buildin' out back used to be a restroom, but now it be the laundry. It takes coin, of course. Showers and restrooms be down under the camp store. Ya ready to move on?"

Jordy sighed. "I guess. Not that I wouldn't mind staying here all day."

"Ya can play later. We best keep movin', I reckon." She took him down a ramp leading from the pool to the putt-putt course, and then slid under the railing and down to the ground.

Jordy hesitated but followed. She headed back toward the office.

"Where are we going?" he asked.

"To the lake. There be a clearin' up ahead. Figured ya wouldn't want to jump o'er the crick."

Crick? She said *crick*. "Whatever."

Sue-Ann turned onto a dirt path leading through some trees. The path opened up at the bottom of a grassy hill with a steep incline.

Jordy stopped. "I don't see a lake."

Sue-Ann pointed up the hill. "It's up there."

Might as well see if she knew how to have fun. "Race you."

She eyed him sideways. "Okay. Ready, set . . . ." She took off running up the hill. Near the top, she shouted, "Go!"

"Hey!" He sped after her. At the top, he found her standing on the grassy shore of a fishing pond large enough to be blue. This would be a lake—to a preschooler. He ignored an urge to steal her cute nose. "You cheated."

"Ever hear of the survival of the fittest?" She laughed with joy shining in her beautiful green eyes. She raced around her so-called lake.

"Come back here!"

At least ten yards ahead, she stopped and turned to face him. "And why should I?"

"So I can throw you in the lake!" He kept his tone lighthearted.

Chuckling, Sue-Ann grinned back playfully. "Gotta catch me first!"

Chapter 2

BY THE TIME JORDY CAUGHT up to Sue-Ann, she'd climbed up a tree-lined, rocky path leading away from the water's sandy bank in this spot. It would've been fun to find out if a pretty girl was hiding under all of that dirt, but it was for the best. He'd never earn her good graces, if he actually pulled that stunt.

She cleared her throat, and the playfulness melted away. "This be the lake. Folks like to fish while lil'uns play on the shore. Kids like us often take walks up here. Some permanent campers like me prefer the lake. Now, 'cept for the hill, that's the fun stuff, so on to the business. Well, first I bitter show ya the other side. Come on."

Jordy followed her around a bend with a semi-circular thicket of trees hugging the lake shore. On this side, it looked like the pond that it truly was with green water, algae, and cattails.

Sue-Ann turned and took him up still another grassy hill, this one with a gradual slope. At the top, she stopped on the road. "This be called the front. The first two roads come together and swing on by the lake here to hook up with the third. On the other end, the main road crosses all three then turns to meet the three roads into the woods. It dead-ends at the overflow, which this road will take us to. Walk with me and see."

Her verbal portrait left his head spinning, but around the next bend, two roads split off from theirs. They continued on back into the woods, crossing a wider road before hitting a clearing, which the path looped around.

They headed up the left side. The empty sites in the middle must be what she'd meant by the overflow. He said, "So, you've got a full map of this place inside that brain of yours."

"Just don't ask what the road names be. Those signs were just put up in July. If ya really wanna know, we can check. Officially, the roads be lettered and the lots numbered. Mine is 41C, for instance. Be sure to look us up. Cara Beth be tickled pink."

Would "Cara Beth" be the only one? He looked Sue-Ann over, but her face revealed nothing. Man, this girl could put on a show. Well, so could he.

Sue-Ann rushed on, "Ya'll notice lots of folks have signs on their sites sayin' who all lives there. That was Dad's idea. He made ours first and when new folks moved in, they got one, too. My dad even helped some. It was the same with the dog run. Folks with dogs saw what he done with Ginger and said, 'hmm, that be a good idea,' and the rest be history."

He decided not to tell her people did that stuff in Illinois, too. The poor girl seemed to think her daddy invented campgrounds.

They reached the end of the road, turned left, and hit a fork in the road. He glanced at the road sign. "Wait—they're both Road C?"

Sue-Ann turned to the right. "It loops, like the overflow."

"Oh. What's to the left?"

Sue-Ann stared at the gravel road. "My lot's that a way. It's nothin'. Ya need to see this road."

They walked down the twisting back road. What was so important down here to make her lot nothin' all of a sudden?

When they came up behind a Nomad, Sue-Ann winced.

Out of it dashed a cleaner, younger version of her, with a dark tan and without red in her brown hair. "There you are!" The younger sister's almost-black eyes took in Jordy. She smirked. "Who's your friend?"

Red flooded Sue-Ann's ivory cheeks. "Phill roped me into showing Jordy around, Sis."

Jordy blinked. What happened to her accent? Her younger sister spoke normally, with a mid-western accent. And, all of a sudden, so did Sue-Ann.

Her sister squealed and tugged on her hands. "Oh, please let me go with you! Mom and Dad are driving me crazy! Come on, cut through the site."

Sue-Ann sighed. "We might as well."

They headed across to the Nomad's site, headed toward the ashes in the rustic campfire ring, surrounded by four rugged benches. Each consisted of a weathered board slapped across two stout logs. Nice, for what it was.

Sue-Ann waved at the younger girl. "This is my sister, Cara Beth. She's thirteen and is starting the eighth grade. Cara, this is Jordy. I'm sure the Gossip Queen here knows more than I do."

"Of course," said Karen, or whatever Sue-Ann had just called her sister.

The sister stopped by the campfire ring, with Jordy and Sue-Ann right behind her. Sue-Ann sent a nervous glance toward the Nomad.

Her sister asked, "How did you like Chicago, Jordy? Have you been to Columbus yet?"

"Chicago is awesome." Or Chicagoland was. His opinion of the city itself was none of their business. "I can't wait until my mom comes to her senses and I can go home."

"Oh, I see. Homesick, huh?"

This was also so none of their business. Jordy caught movement in the camper out of the corner of his eye.

Sue-Ann waved and headed off though a circle of young trees growing closer together than usual here. "Come on, we need to get going."

Jordy and Sue-Ann's sister ran to catch up to her out on the gravel road.

The younger girl fell in step with Sue-Ann as they turned left onto the next road. "Where are we headed? To the office?"

"Where else is there?" Jordy asked.

The younger sister turned onto a path matted with dead leaves. Sue-Ann put her arm out. "I'm not taking City Boy down the hill. It rained last night."

Cara Beth glanced at Jordy's Nike sneakers. "I see. Silly boy has got his good shoes on."

Oh? He jerked his thumb at her new-looking Dr. Martens. "Nice shoes."

"Yeah, my new school shoes are all that and a bag of chips! What of it? My mom made an exception to the rules just this once."

"To stop your whining," Susanna grumbled, rolling her eyes.

"Whatever. *His* momma would kill us, if we bring him back filthy." The spoiled, silly girl giggled. "Especially considerin' where it came from."

Jordy narrowed his eyes. "Where?"

Mischief twinkled in Sue-Ann's eyes. "The sewage tanks empty into the creek running through the ravine. Everyone under twelve loves to play in it. We used to come back covered in gunk and my parents would be furious. We still hang out down there, but we've outgrown playing in the creek."

In an open sewer rather. Jordy wrinkled his nose. "That's disgusting!"

The girls laughed, in the way meant to exclude the ignorant outsider.

Hint taken. If Sue-Ann wanted to play it like that—fine. He would shut his trap for once and keep his distance.

THANKFULLY, SUE-ANN, Cara, and Jordy passed behind Krystal's campsite without incident. They'd also made it past Amy's and Nate's places, but Nate and Ricky had spotted them in the game room along with Boo, Greg, and Ty. Why couldn't the boys have gone home already? Whoever heard of playing pool at 12:30 on a Sunday?

Sue-Ann glanced at her watch. If they walked Jordy all the way back, their parents would come looking for them. She'd already narrowly escaped introducing them to Jordy once. She pointed to the left, down the main road to the gate separating the permanent campers' area from the weekenders' area. "That'll take you back to the office. You should be able to find your way from there, okay?"

Jordy nodded.

Susanna turned and fled down the path into the ravine. At the bottom, she headed for the fallen tree, the one which soared over the creek at about a fifteen degree angle. It remained caught in the trees atop the steep hill on the other side of the ravine. She used the tree's vertical root like a ladder to climb on its back, favoring her right ankle, and settled down.

Cara pulled herself up on the tree beside her. "Should you be climbing trees on your bad ankle, *Sue-Ann*? Especially after the tumble yesterday."

Susanna rolled her eyes. "And whose fault was that? Relax, I know what I'm doing. I don't need my little sister babying me."

"Whatever." Cara leaned in. "Why did Jordy call you Sue-Ann?"

"Probably because I told him to."

Cara narrowed her eyes. "What are you up to, Susanna Quinn McCoy?"

"What do you mean?" She kept her tone innocent by using her last four years of theater arts classes to become Sue-Ann. "I'm up to nothing."

"As if! You hate that nickname more than we hate it when Dad mortifies us by loudly singing 'Susie Q' at you."

Her sister was lucky that her song, "Every Breath You Take," wasn't old enough to be on the oldies station yet.

"I'm waiting." Cara folded her arms.

Sue-Ann sighed. "I didn't want City Boy to miss out on getting pranked by his tour guide, so I gave him our hillbilly routine. He fell for it, too."

Cara's jaw dropped. "My sister, conning Phill's grandson? How long do you think you can keep this up?"

"Oh, you've blown the accent, but a guy like Jordy Durant would never pay attention to me anyway." Susanna jabbed at her sister's midsection. "But don't you go spilling the rest. I'd rather not be around when he figures out that Sue-Ann is an improv role played by Susanna of Columbus, Ohio."

"Um, okay, he won't hear about it from me." Cara glared a moment, lips pursed, before she poked Susanna's gut. "So, what did you think of him?"

Susanna jumped down. Sharp pain shot up her right ankle. She winced. Oh yeah, still healing. "We need to get back."

Cara hopped down and grabbed Susanna's arm. "Oh no you don't. Spill."

"Hey!" Their dad shouted at the top of the hill, on the trail back to their campsite. He wore a blue windbreaker despite the heat and clownish plastic glasses. He waved with his whole arm. "Cara, Susie Q, we've got to go!"

"Coming, Dad!" the girls called in near unison.

Susanna jumped over the creek, favoring her sore ankle.

Her sister followed her. "We'll finish this later."

Susanna shook her head. Not on her life.

ON TUESDAY AFTERNOON, Jordy sat on his guest room's made double bed upstairs at his grandfather's house. Two new Chicago Bulls posters featuring the Jordan named Michael "flying" made a lame attempt to dampen the "you don't belong here" being screamed by the preppy, earth-toned décor clearly chosen to please married, wealthy, adult guests.

At least Gramps had tried.

Jordy tossed a pair of socks at the basketball hoop laundry basket on the closet door. The socks landed short. He retrieved his socks from the floor and tried again. All net. This gift was sweet, but he was bored out of his skull after an entire week of activities this exciting.

His mom was still MIA, along with Jordy's not-packed Nintendo game system. His so-called father kept planning the bonding rituals Jordy's mom loved to drag him through, but Jordan kept rescheduling, thanks to Gramps.

Someone knocked on the door. He called, "It's open."

His father entered and thrust a paper bag at him. "Could you take this to your grandfather? He's at the office, son."

Son. Grr. He'd save the battle armor in case Jordan ever tried to call him Junior, though. "Sure, I don't have anything better to do."

"That a boy. Why don't you go see if your grandpa will give you the keys to the truck? I'm sure you could use more driving practice."

"Cool." He smiled—Jordan hadn't offered his keys. At least something hadn't changed. His dad had always been overprotective of his car. Gramps would probably likewise baby his truck, but it was worth a shot.

In the deserted camp store, Jordy called, "Gramps? You here?"

"Back here!"

Jordy followed the sound of his grandfather's voice to a back office. He set the paper bag on the cluttered desk. "Here. Jordan said to give you this."

Gramps looked up from the forms before him. He frowned and put his pen down. "J.J., why are you calling your dad by his first name?"

"Don't know," Jordy lied. "Just do."

Gramps peered at him skeptically. "Right. Thanks for bringing this over. I'd love to chat, but I have to fill out this paperwork."

"Okay, when can I have the keys to the truck?"

Gramps laughed. "When you know the park like Sus—" Gramps shook his head. "Like Sue-Ann does."

Jordy's jaw dropped. "But she could find her way blindfolded."

Gramps grinned. "Then you better get practicing."

Seemed Gramps had no intention of ever letting him drive. "Isn't there anything to do around here?"

"Of course there is! Follow me."

Jordy followed Gramps over to the main exit. Gramps opened the door, which screamed for oil. Gramps gestured down the grassy slope's pathway to the pine trees that stood guard at the bottom. "I'm gonna dig this all up and put in a parking lot." Gramps pointed at the lawn in between the gatehouse and the road here to the camp office. "Over there we'll put in basketball and volleyball courts. We already have the putt-putt."

Jordy snorted. "Terrific. How about right now?"

"Teenagers. Aside from putt-putt, I recommend the lake. You can fish, take a walk, explore. And there's the game room and the pool."

"Great. I can go skinny dipping with Sue-Ann."

Gramps' hard stare said he didn't have a sense of humor.

Jordy laughed nervously. "Gramps, I'm kidding."

"You'd better be," Gramps grumbled, before saying, "You couldn't if you wanted to. The McCoy girls aren't here."

"Aren't here? Where else would they be?"

Gramps sighed and shook his head. "Haven't you learned yet?"

Doh. "Permanent camping is the middle-class, rental version of owing a vacation home?"

Gramps nodded. "A handful of employees do live here in RVs, but most families with kids are only here on the weekends. Sue-Ann and Cara talk like they live here, but they don't. They've just been coming so long, it's a second home to them. Don't let Sue-Ann fool you. They live on the East Side."

East side of what? Not Chicago surely. "Whatever. You know what they say. Don't send your kid to the pen and expect to get back an angel."

ON FRIDAY AFTERNOON, Jordy dropped his last quarter in the game room's Pac-Man machine. He pretended the ghosts were the grandfather stealing all of his money. Okay, so that wasn't Gramps' intent, but it was the end result of making Jordy filter requests for money through Jordan. He'd rather stand barefoot on live coals than ask his father for anything, so he was now dead broke until his mom decided to show.

On Pac-Man's last life, his father entered the game room's doorway into the office. "Could you come here a minute, son?"

A ghost ate Pac-Man. Stupid distraction. Grunting, he followed the jerk into the store. "What's up, Gramps?"

Gramps looked up from the till he was counting. "There's a ravine in the woods at the end of the main road. The camp kids like to play down there on a huge, uprooted white oak."

"Would it be close to an open sewer that gets mistaken for a creek?"

"Yeah, the oak crosses the sewer alongside an unofficial trail through the ravine. Boards provide a safe crossing on the ground. The unsafe crossing is over the oak. Don't attempt that. But do go make sure the oak hasn't decided this is the year it surrenders to death; it is somehow still alive. If it does look unstable, go tell your dad, and we'll take care of it."

"Sure." Jordy shrugged. The undead oak did explain the attraction to a sewer, but no way would he ever admit that now.

"COME ON, SUE-ANN! I want the dirt! You've been mum all week!"

Grr. Susanna picked at the fallen white oak's bark, perched sidesaddle on its trunk, facing the hill. She rubbed at the ache above her right eye. Cara wouldn't let up until she gave in. "There's nothing to tell, Cara."

"No way. You got to meet him. You actually talked to him!"

Susanna laughed. "So did you."

"Not like you did. Come on, what's he like? Is he as nice as he is cute?"

"Nice? Please! City Boy's a jerk. And cute? Hardly."

"Don't lie to me, Sue-Ann. I've seen him. Of course he's cute! Sandy hair and those blue eyes. I know you like those blue eyes."

Ha. Without her glasses, dark shadows hid his eyes behind a raccoon-like mask. Not that she minded, that made it easier to look at him—from a safe distance. "Strange, I seem to recall a certain someone . . . ."

Cara groaned. "I'm sorry! Okay, I forgot. But, he can't be as bad as you thought. I think you're lying so you can keep him all to yourself."

Yeah, right. "Can we *please* change the subject already?"

Cara's hands flew to her mouth and her cheeks turned pink.

Behind Susanna, a guy said, "Oh no, go right on ahead. A guy just loves to hear how fabulous he is."

"Hey!" Sue-Ann whirled to face Jordy. He was leaning against the white oak's vertical roots, too close for comfort, though he did still have raccoon eyes. She scooted back from him. "What are you doing here?"

"I live here," Jordy said. "Too bad you can't say the same."

Sue-Ann smirked. "You assumed that I lived here? Assumptions can be dangerous, City Boy."

"How long have you been back there?" Cara asked from behind her.

"I heard that you've been pestering your sister about me all week," Jordy replied. "Doesn't anybody take vacations around here? Man, as bad as this place is, it's worse during the week. There is no one here."

Sue-Ann covered her mouth and snickered. Poor City Boy, all alone in the big woods.

"My friend Krystal's living here this summer," Cara said. "Next week is her last. Can you believe we have less than two weeks before school starts?"

"Yeah, hopefully, I'll be back in Chicago."

Huh? Chicago was an awfully long commute. Susanna resumed picking at the white oak's bark. "Your parents will want to stay close to Glenshower. You'll probably get a place in Columbus."

Jordy snorted. "Terrific. School in a cow town."

"It's not a cow town! Columbus is a big city."

"Yeah, right. Chicago's a real city."

Figured. Sue-Ann chortled. "Have you been to Columbus yet?"

"Well, not exactly—"

"Go, and then tell me it is a cow town. Cities come in more sizes than just NYC, LA, Chicago, and Smallville."

Jordy crossed his arms. "Fine, I've got more important things to do than argue with a couple hicks."

Cara frowned. "Excuse me? You just wait until everybody is gone. We'll see who's a hick."

"By Monday, everybody else will be gone, all right." He pointed his index finger at Cara. "Including you."

Sue-Ann sniffed. "For your information, Mom and Dad are on vacation this week. We'll be here every day, except for Tuesday and Wednesday." Sue-Ann resisted the urge to stick her tongue out and add, "so there." Her mom surprised her by calling her eye doctor last Saturday, but he wasn't able to get her in until that coming Wednesday afternoon.

Jordy brushed dirt off his shirt. "I'll be so busy next week, I won't have time to hang out, but if you're lucky, I might be able to fit ya in."

Oh, he was not going to play that game here. "If we're lucky? You'll be lucky if we let you hang out with us, City Boy."

"Well, I have work to do." Jordy patted the tree's back. "I have to secure old Betsy here. Can't have her falling on innocent kids, now, can we? So, if you girls would scram . . . ."

Cara jumped down beside Jordy, fury contorting her face.

Must intervene. Sue-Ann stood up on the tree and laughed. "City Boys. You don't know nothin'. Can't you tell when a person's tryin' to get rid of ya? This old tree ain't goin' nowhere."

Jordy groaned. "Don't. Crossing the 'creek' up there is too dangerous."

"For a girl? Watch me." Arms out like the cross, she walked up the fallen tree's trunk as if on a balance beam. Her heart pounded hard. So cool.

Over the dry creek bed, Sue-Ann peeked down. So high up, and the thick branch ahead of her, leading down to the ground, was so steep. Her stomach lurched to the left and the ground wobbled. She jumped to safety and landed on the far side of the creek, on her good ankle. *Thank you, Jesus.*

Cara hugged her, squealing. "You did it!"

"Thanks." Sue-Ann glanced back at City Boy. "What I tell you? Come on, Sis, let's get out of here."

The sisters turned on their heels and marched up the hill.

At the top, Susanna glanced back. Jordy stood where they'd left him. His shoulders drooped, and . . . was that sadness on his blurred features? Her gut said he'd missed her last week. But, that was crazy. She could barely see him and hardly knew him. So why did she still think he missed her?

Chapter 3

LATE SATURDAY MORNING, Susanna walked outside her trailer. Her sister squatted in front, overturning the bricks around it with one hand. The other hand held an empty, wet seasoned salt shaker.

Susanna leaned down and tapped her sister's shoulder. "Cara Beth, what are you doing?"

Cara glanced up. "Looking for worms to go fishing. You wanna come?"

"Yeah, let's go."

Cara pulled up another brick. Several worms squirmed and tried to dig under the dirt. Cara shrieked with delight, picked them up, and put them in the plastic shaker.

Susanna wrinkled her nose. "Aren't those things slimy?"

"Only when they're dead."

Yuck. Susanna pretended to gag.

"I have enough. I'll get a pole, then we can go." Cara stood, rushed into their white shed, and returned carrying over her shoulder a fishing pole as rusted as their shed.

Later, while the sisters descended the slope to the shallow, green end of the lake, Susanna asked, "Do you plan to fish on this side?"

"I'm gonna try the beach where the goose was last June."

The girls rounded the thicket of trees growing right along the lake. They stopped at the top of the path down to the beach. A couple weekenders had already taken the spot they wanted.

"The dinosaur egg, maybe?" Susanna smiled with nostalgia.

Cara giggled and nodded. "That'll do."

The girls took the trail around the lake until the rocky beach gave way to the grassy hilltop, which curved along the bank. A young maple tree grew next to a boulder shaped like a giant chicken egg. Susanna climbed up on it and leaned back against the maple tree.

Cara put a worm on a hook and cast her line into the lake. She pulled her line back in and tried again. After repeating this all again, she set the pole down and joined Susanna on the boulder. "Can you believe how obnoxious Jordy was yesterday? Telling us to scram. Did you see the look on his face when you told him off? It was classic."

Susanna laughed. "I can't believe City Boy fell for Phill's lame excuse to get rid of him—and then had the nerve to boast about it!"

"I'm glad you did something. I was about to get ugly."

"You looked like you wanted to push him in the creek."

"That's because I did want to! Would've served him right."

"You should've. I can just see him covered in gunk." Susanna chuckled. "Now, that would've been classic!"

"We could shove him in the lake instead. That's him over there." Cara pointed across the lake.

Susanna squinted at the fuzzy blur standing about half-way around the lake. "What makes you think it's City Boy? It could be anyone."

The blur headed in their direction.

Cara rolled her eyes and snorted. "Any sixteen-year-old male with sandy hair. Not a whole lot of options around here, Sis."

Oh, right, her sister could see clearly from that far away. "Point taken."

Cara jumped down from the rock and grabbed up her fishing pole. "It's moving! There's something on the line!"

Susanna jumped down and ran over. Cara thrust the pole at her. "Take it! You're stronger."

"Whoa!" Susanna gasped at the pull on the line. What had Cara caught, Jaws? Susanna jerked on the line and fought to reel in Jaws, but if anything, the line went in the exact opposite direction than she wanted it to.

A few moments later, strong male arms grabbed the pole from behind Susanna, enwrapping her. Jordy said in her ear, "Steady! Keep that up, and the line will break. Take deep breaths now, and bring it in slowly. It's the fish running out of time, not you."

Jordy reeled the line in slow and steady, his hands firmly over hers.

After what seemed like hours, the former boy scout reeled in a foot-long trout. Sue-Ann let go of Cara's fishing pole and sucked in calming breaths as told. Oh gosh, where was she? She ducked out of Jordy's arms, being careful to focus on her gaping sister until she was a safe distance from him.

Cara picked up Jordy's discarded fishing rod and switched with him. The foot-long trout twisted at the end of Cara's pole, as if glaring at them, but powerless out of its element.

Jordy rubbed the back of his head. "Just when I was starting to think there weren't any fish in there."

Cara pipped up, "Sue-Ann said that when she came up empty-handed last time."

Sue-Ann glared. Why did God curse her with such an embarrassing baby sister? "He's just too much of a city boy to catch a fish."

"Really? If not for me, that fish would've snapped that old pole in two. If that's all the thanks I get, you can take your fishing pole and shove it." Jordy stomped down to the beach.

Cara removed the fishhook and gently put the trout back in the lake. She wiped her hands on her shorts then turned back to Susanna. "You know, he helped us, and instead of thanking him, you insulted him. Not only do you still need to thank him, you now owe him an apology."

Whose side was Cara on? Susanna pursed her lips. Why had she said something so mean, so obviously untrue? "Guess some habits are hard to break. Besides, you didn't thank him, either."

"You only met last weekend, Sue-Ann."

Don't remind me. Susanna grunted. "Let's go for a walk."

Cara stood there, watching her.

Susanna blew her breath out. "This way." She started around the hill in the opposite direction than the one Jordy had gone in.

Cara caught up. "Why this way? Right now, all I want to do is go home."

"You're just upset because of City Boy. Let's start over. Pretend we never saw Jordy today."

"Who? Oh, the totally cute but obnoxious guy we ran into yesterday? I haven't seen him today. Have you?"

Susanna bit back a smile. "No. Wouldn't that be the worst?"

"I'm sure it would be." Cara smirked.

Susanna put her right hand on her hip. "Why, you wouldn't be hoping we might run into him again today, could you?"

"Who me? Never!" Cara flicked at her. "*You*, on the other hand . . ."

Susanna's cheeks burned. "City Boy can drop dead for all I care!"

"Then why are you blushing?"

Her cheeks grew even hotter. "I am not!"

"You are too! Your face is the same color as your hair!"

"My face is brown?"

"No, it's red and so is your hair. You know it's a bright red in the sun."

They stopped behind two trees growing on the edge of the lake. One had a low horizontal branch hanging over the water, perfect for walking on.

Cara faced Susanna and patted her shoulder. "Sis, seriously, what is up with you and Jordy? And why are you pretending to hate each other? Don't lie to me. Today, your body language said something different altogether."

Susanna shook off the feel of his arms around her. "Not possible, Sis."

"I'm not losing it!" Cara's voice climbed childishly. "I've never seen you like this with a guy. Mom thinks you're gay, but she said to not say anything, in case . . ." Her eyes danced. "Hmm, is that it? You are fourteen-going-on-eleven and finally growing up? So sweet, Baby Sis. I remember the 'starting fights with my first crush' phase. For reals, I did that back in fifth grade!"

Don't take the bait. Susanna growled and walked out on the branch over the water while gripping an overhead branch for balance. "Get real, Cara."

"You get real. This isn't the first of the weird-for-you behavior. Don't you remember that hurt puppy look on his face when we left yesterday? His eyes said, 'I missed you' and your eyes replied, 'I missed you, too.' And that's so crazy. Two seconds earlier, you guys were ready to kill each other."

Grr. "We didn't miss each other. We do hate each other."

"No way. It could've been 'I'm scared,' but not hate. I know you, Susanna Quinn McCoy. The anger was gone from your eyes."

Susanna whirled to face her sister. "You wanna know the truth? Fine. Boys like Jordy never like girls like me, so why should I ever like him?" She jumped down from the branch and stomped past Cara, in the direction of the tunnel-like, grassy passage back to the other side of the lake.

JORDY STORMED UP THE trail to the lake's shallow end. *The gall of that girl!* Instead of thanking him, she had insulted him, and what had he done? Nothing but save her ungrateful hide, that was what. The snottiest, wealthy kid from Chicagoland had nothing on the country girl named Sue-Ann.

He stopped and watched the dragonflies buzz around the cattails. Skater bugs stirred the algae lapping up in between the graceful plants. He glanced up at the road. Nah. He'd stay. This seemed like a good spot for thinking.

Why did he bother to help her in the first place? He crouched and picked up a stick. He poked with it aimlessly at the grass.

Probably thanks to Scoutmaster Fuller. Fuller had drilled it in that it was his duty as a scout to always help others whenever he could. Fuller would've expected him to help Sue-Ann without seeking praise. He could hear Fuller scolding him for doing the right thing, for the wrong reasons.

Sue-Ann's words had cut like a knife. Was he getting too city-oriented? Were his parents right to drag him back into the woods? It wasn't like he'd wanted to move out of the suburbs, into the city proper. He hated their dinky apartment. Moving again would be tempting if it meant living in a real house with a real backyard with flowers, maybe a vegetable garden . . . . Whoa. He was supposed to be mad at Sue-Ann, not dreaming of home.

Speaking of Sue-Ann, did they ever have a conversation where she didn't insult him? Yeah, once, during the initial tour of Glenshire when she showed him the lake, their race up the hill. She cheated, sure, but it'd been all in fun. And her laughing eyes were filled with joy instead of scorn and distrust.

He was dreaming again. She'd been doing her job. She was supposed to be nice to him, so she'd been polite. Now, her obligations were over, so she could show how she really felt.

Smart girl. The brainy ones always hated him. He stood and tossed the stick into the lake. It floated. She hated him. Why couldn't he hate her back? Why were the girls put-off by his antics always the ones that sincerely turned his head? Guess he'd have to settle for neutral. That much he could manage. He just had to keep focused on her poor grooming and not on how pretty her eyes would be, if they didn't regard him as pond scum.

JORDY FOLLOWED THE curve of the lake around to the other side. Might as well give the fish another shot at being dinner.

Brush sprang up on both sides of a narrowing passageway and blocked his view of the lake. Red chokeberry shrubs bowed to each other, forming a low, green ceiling. Yuck, those were bitter raw and caused diarrhea in large quantities. He crossed over the rocks and broken bricks stuck in a crevice to cover a lake runoff. Bushes of edible, wild raspberries also lined the tunnel-like path, their aroma all too much like the pies his mom used to make.

He picked several berries and started to shove them in his mouth.

Sue-Ann appeared around the corner with her sister and slapped them from his hand. "Don't eat those! They might be poisonous. Oh and these." Sue-Ann tugged at the chokeberries growing into a low ceiling. "Don't even touch these. I know these are poisonous."

Her sister giggled. "She got sick on 'em when she was little. Had to go to the emergency room and have her stomach pumped."

"So?" Sue-Ann blushed and glared at her sister. "I was three. City Boy was about to do the same and he's sixteen."

Since I can tell edible wild berries apart from the toxic and the simply gross. He found himself instead saying, "You have nothing better to do than to follow a guy around, worrying about his health?"

Sue-Ann's jaw dropped. "What? Us following . . . ."

Jordy smirked. "It's okay, I'm well used to girls chasing me. What's two more? Hey, if you're lucky, maybe I'll even give you my phone number."

Fire ignited in her cat-green eyes. "And if you're lucky, maybe I won't puke all over your fancy City Boy shoes."

The sisters pretended to gag, drew their index fingers across their necks, and then brushed past him. Their laughter rang in Jordy's burning ears.

He grunted. *Flirting, with Sue-Ann? Dude, what were you thinking?*

NEAR SUNSET, SUSANNA sat at her trailer's booth-style table, with her feet propped up on the opposite bench's brown cushions. She squinted to make out the words of a Lurlene McDaniel novel. She'd have finished it already, if a migraine-sized headache hadn't sent her to bed early last night.

Cara slid onto the bench across the table from Susanna and knocked her feet to the floor. "Can you believe that guy? Just when you start to think he is halfway decent, Jordy resumes acting like a jerk. I can't figure him out."

Susanna put her book down. "Cara, I'm trying to read here. I don't want to hear any more about City Boy. He's just a jerk, okay? Go complain to Amy and Krystal already and leave me alone."

"I'm obviously not appreciated around here!" Cara stormed out.

Susanna's mom bustled out of the bathroom, went into the bedroom in the back of the trailer, and shook Susanna's dad awake. "Come on, Elliot. It's seven o' clock. You need to take me to bingo."

He grumbled incoherently but sat up on the edge of his bed, rubbing his bright green t-shirt, which claimed he was a happy camper.

Ugh. Susanna hid her nose in her book and didn't look up until her mom stormed in hours later. Her dad had forgotten to pick her mom up again, and this was somehow Susanna's fault rather than his fault.

After soothing her mother with an apology for her apparent thoughtless selfishness, Susanna put the table down and made up the sisters' bed for the night. She curled up on her side, near the wall, and returned to the story.

Around one a.m., Susanna finished her novel and put it at the bottom of her stack of library books on the counter behind the bed. She settled beside her sleeping sister. Her dreams had so better not star City Boy as the sullen, cancer-stricken young man from her story.

"SUSANNA, GET YOUR LAZY bones out of that bed!" called her mom.

Mid-morning sunshine streamed through the curtains. Susanna groaned and groped behind her. She bolted upright. "My glasses!"

"You broke them, remember?"

"Oh yeah. We'll get me new ones before school starts, right? Can I get contacts?" Wearing glasses seemed dreadful now that she was awake.

"It takes two weeks, so you may have to go without for a few days. Now, put the table up. Your breakfast is in the microwave."

After Susanna finished her Egg McMuffin, she swallowed and drummed her fingers on the table. "Mom, about those contacts . . . ."

"Maybe when you're older."

"That's what you always say."

"When you're ready, I'll let you know."

Susanna rolled her eyes. Mom always said that, too. "Where's Cara?"

"She went swimming with Amy and Krystal."

"Change and go swimming, too," her dad called from the porch.

"Nah," Susanna said, "if she wanted me there, she'd have asked me."

"You were asleep," her mom said, "you wouldn't get up."

Susanna shrugged and grabbed *the Giver* off her stack of library books.

Her dad let Ginger in. The Doberman-Rottweiler mix jumped up on the bench beside her and turned in a circle. Susanna petted Ginger's head. The dog licked her in the face.

Ew. Susanna laughed. "Silly, if I want a kiss, I'll ask, okay?"

Ginger lay down, gazing sorrowfully up at Susanna.

"Oh, is that it? You thought I was asking? Sorry, next time I'll make it clearer." Susanna got a bag of doggie treats down from the loft and took a treat from the bag. "Want one?"

Ginger sat up and barked, so Susanna gave her the biscuit.

The cat mewed from on top the space heater under the refrigerator.

"Sorry, Misty, these treats are just for doggies."

Misty slinked off the heater and jumped up into the loft to explore the remains of her last meal.

That afternoon, Susanna's dad approached her. "If I give you a buck, will you go away?"

Susanna kept her nose in her book. "Make it five and I'll think about it."

Her dad held a five dollar bill under Susanna's nose. "Remember, you have to go away."

Wow, he went for that? Sweet. Susanna put her book down and took the five. "Deal."

As Susanna entered the office, awkwardness stole over her. Who was the man on duty? Maybe it was only her poor eyesight, but nothing about him registered as anyone she knew. And a stranger on duty didn't sit well.

She circled the store area, selected cheese puffs and an ice cream bar. She swallowed and approached the main counter. Yep, she didn't know this man, though something seemed familiar about his crew cut, or the wet-sand color of his hair rather.

She slid her purchases across the counter.

He rang up the items. "Will that be everything?"

"I'll take a pizza pocket, too, please."

He finished ringing up her order and then grabbed what must be her hot pocket out of the freezer and put it in the microwave. He returned to the cash register. "That'll be 3.75, miss."

She handed over the five and got her change back. So cool to not have to guess which hand held her quarter, like she was still a child. "Thanks."

Smiling, she moved to the side counter to wait for her order.

The man returned to the microwave. He drummed his fingers on the counter. She peered at him. Why did he look so familiar? "Um, sir?"

"It's Mr. Durant, miss, but you might as well call me Jordan. Everyone else does, even Junior." Jordan cleared his throat. "But that's another story."

Oh. Duh. That sure explained things, but why would Jordy call his dad by his first name? She said lamely, "I'm sorry, Mr. Durant."

The microwave dinged.

Jordan took her hot pocket out and slid it across the counter. "Careful, dear, it's hot."

"Thank you." She took her purchases over to the only dining booth and moved a beach towel someone left behind. She sat with her back to the game room, so she didn't have to watch Boo and Jordy shooting pool with Nate and Ricky. Maybe she should look for Cara. By the time she found her, the boys should be gone, and they could play a game or two.

While Susanna ate, a young blonde girl in a pink bathing suit came in and snatched the towel. Her obvious relief gave away she was a weekender. A permanent camper would know Glenshire still followed the code of honor kindergarten teachers try to imprint upon their pupils—don't take what isn't yours, for instance. Someone once lost a bike down the hill, and no one ever took it. It got moved out of the path, but otherwise it'd stayed down there, rusting away as it waited for an owner who never returned.

Susanna threw away her trash and approached the front counter. "Have you seen my sister, Cara McCoy? She has shoulder-length brown hair, dark brown eyes, and is about five four."

"Check in the game room," Jordan said. "She and two other girls were in there earlier. Jordy or one of the other guys should know."

Susanna smiled weakly. "Right."

Best to forget about finding Cara. Did she really want to run into City

Boy again? No, that was what Susanna would do. This was Sue-Ann's turf, and she had as much right to be there as the next permanent camper.

Inside the game room door, a furtive glance revealed Cara wasn't there. Asking for her might be taken all wrong. Ignoring the four guys playing pool, she crossed through and headed for the exit.

"Hey, Jordy," one of the guys said, laughing. "There goes your girlfriend, not gonna say hello?"

Sue-Ann whirled around. Just her and the guys. That had to mean her. Jordy's "friends" waited for a response while a red-faced Jordy tried to stare a hole in the floor. Her heart pounded. *Voice, work.* "I'm sorry, my ears must not be working right. I thought I heard you call me somebody's girlfriend."

"You heard me," Boo answered.

Her face flamed. "I wouldn't be caught dead with City Boy."

Jordy snorted. "Dude, I don't have a clue why she keeps following me, but no biggie. I'm used to girls following me around like puppy dogs."

Sue-Ann seethed. "You're the only dog here, Jordy! And the sooner you get back to Chicago, the better!" The air thickened and turned green. She had to get out of there, before she completed her mortification by fainting. She disappeared around the corner but unfortunately not out of earshot.

"Man, what'd you do to her?" Ricky asked. "She's the last person you'd expect to go off like that."

One of the others snickered. "The lovebirds had themselves a fight."

"Hey," Jordy snapped, his tone a tad off, "Sue-Ann can take a long walk off a short pier, for all I care, so drop it."

What? Stomach tight, Susanna stumbled away from the door. No.

Cara got out of the pool and ran up to her. "Are you okay? You look like you caught Misty eating Lucky."

Their goldfish. She'd rather be facing that. "I just need to be alone."

"Sue-Ann, what's going on?"

"Nothing, I'll see you later." She slid under the putt-putt ramp then ran into the woods and over the creek. She stumbled up the hill where she had raced Jordy. Competing thoughts and emotions swirled within but only one stood out. It made no sense, but her heart thudded with the certainty born of the same gut instinct that warned against two-faced bullies' deception.

Jordy had lied. He *did* care, at least enough to value her life. How? Why?

Chapter 4

LURED BY THE SCENT of frying bacon, Jordy entered Gramps' yellow and green country kitchen that Monday. Jordan stirred scrambled eggs at the gas stove. Jordy blinked. "I didn't know you cooked."

His father turned off both burners then spooned the eggs onto two paper plates with the spatula. "When you're on your own as much as I've been, you learn to make do. And I took Home EC in high school."

"You? Home EC?" Jordy snorted and flopped at the round glass table. No way. He couldn't picture his dad in an apron, even at his age.

"They stuck me in there because woodshop was full. Mrs. Henderson wouldn't let me drop it." His father dished out the last of the bacon. He set one of the plates in front of Jordy before sitting down with the other.

His father bowed his head. "Lord, we thank you for providing this meal, and we ask your blessing upon it. In Jesus' name we pray, amen."

Upon the first we, Jordy jabbed his fork in his eggs and shoved a forkful in his mouth. His mom did this at every meal, but his father lost that right three years ago.

They ate in an awkward silence Jordy rather enjoyed.

Once they finished eating, he rose to run.

His father extended his hand and waved for him to stay. "So, son, what have you been up to?"

"In the last three years? Oh, not much, just busy growing up while being abandoned by my so-called father. How's life been for you, Jordan?" Jordy spat the name out while still standing, his arms crossed.

His father flinched. "Son, my own father, your mother, and both of our counselors advised being triply sure that I've got my own shattered life back together before bringing you out here. I haven't spent enough time with you, since, either, I know. I'm sorry, it can't be helped."

"Hey, no biggie. A guy gets used to being abandoned. He makes his peace and, in his mind, it's like his dad's dead also. After all, he might as well be. On the bright side, at least Mom isn't driving me crazy. She works extra hard to bond with her son in an attempt to make up for the fact he no longer has a dad. Speaking of Mom, where is she, or do you no longer care whether she's dead or alive, either?"

His father shifted in his chair. "That's something I need to talk to you about. What your mom's up to, I mean."

He might as well help him. "Look, I know what's going on."

"You do?"

"It's obvious you're making the total abandonment official and getting divorced." What if this was more than Jordan's way of saying adios? "That's it, isn't it? You've gotten divorced and a judge says I have to live with you."

His father hesitated. "Actually, we've been working toward restoration for some time. Your mom wanted to be sure that I wouldn't disappoint you, before telling you that we are getting back together."

"But, Dad, that's good news! Where's Mom?" Jordy fell back into his country dining chair. What had just poured out of his mouth? What was he thinking? This changed nothing.

His father relaxed. "The rest of the news is I have loyalties here now. We need to stay within driving distance."

Jordy's eyes widened. "She's getting us a place in Columbus?"

"Yes, how did you know?"

"That's what Sue-Ann said you'd do. Man, how did such an ignorant girl manage to be right?"

His father cleared his throat. "Yes, well, what do you think?"

"Do I have to?"

"Financially, we don't have a choice."

Jordy swore.

His father said, "Don't cuss, young man."

"Since when do I still have to listen to you? Since you've decided to be my dad again? Forget it, Jordan. You can't expect everything to be the same. It doesn't work that way."

Understanding filled his father's eyes. "Do you have any questions?"

Jordy stared sullenly at his empty plate.

"It's a blue house. A house, not a cramped apartment like in Chicago."

Jordy's head snapped up. "How would you know? You were never there.

And if wasn't for you, we wouldn't have been there in the first place."

His father winced as if punched. "There's only one bedroom, but it has a great finished basement dying to be a teenager's room, and there's a pool in the backyard. Your mom says the school offers lots of Advanced Placement courses. It's called Easthaven, home of the Trojans."

"Peachy, we're still ignoring our real issues," Jordy sneered.

His father sighed and spread his hands out on the table. "I hear you, but you're not ready for apologies, or to forgive, so what can I say? I know you're hurting, and I'm sorry our lives exploded. We'll never be the same, and I hold myself responsible. I can't imagine how hard this move must be for you, after everything. It's just . . . I need to do this. We have to be here."

"We don't have to do anything. There is no we anymore. Why do Mom and I have to be here?"

"You don't like it here?"

"Like it here? I hate it here! I want to go back to Chicago! Back to Isabel. I have to get back. She won't talk to me. Brandt's taking her out, I know it. The scumbag is stealing my girl. I have to get back to claim her."

His father arched his eyebrows, the alarm in his eyes almost mirroring the reaction his dad would've had to him dating. That passed like an illusion and gave way to a shake of the head accompanied by a thin smile. "Jordy, a girl isn't an object for you to claim, and her heart isn't a sports trophy for you to win. If she went with him, she'd split sooner or later anyway. The longer you keep such a relationship going, the harder it is when it's over."

What part of "forget it" did Jordan find so difficult to understand? He had as much right to give advice as he had to say grace on Jordy's behalf, which was none. "So? I still hate it here!"

"Haven't you made friends? What about the boys you played pool with?"

"They're okay, but everything gets on my nerves. Like that Sue-Ann." He shook his head. How could he put that frustration into words?

His father smiled. "The oldest McCoy sister? Dad's had a lot to say about her. I got to meet her yesterday afternoon. She seems like a sweet girl. Those green eyes, though . . . they're so much like Christine's."

Jordy leapt up in his father's face. "Don't you dare say that name! I've got enough problems without you tearing me open again. And I don't care about that girl!" Jordy stormed out and slammed the door behind him.

JORDY RAN BLINDLY UP Glenshire's drive, his face scrunched from fighting his threatening tears.

Near the gatehouse, he clobbered into the last person he wanted to see and knocked them both onto their backsides in the dirt.

Opposite him, Sue-Ann sat up and snapped, "What was that for?"

"Nothing, I wasn't looking where I was going." He stood and offered her his hand automatically, as if he were still the model boy scout.

She hesitated as if considering whether to slap him.

Please, no. He bit his lip. He was already too close to bawling in front of her, and that was the worst thing he could imagine. He'd never live it down.

Gentleness softened her face. She took his hand and let him pull her to her feet but didn't quite meet his eyes.

Her hand was warm, soft, and surprisingly dainty, given it belonged to a full-figured, curvy girl. He made himself look away and let go.

They stood awkwardly a moment.

"Sorry." Jordy took off toward the lake.

Once he reached that area, he jogged up their hill. He flopped down on the bank's grass on his stomach. He wouldn't cry. He wouldn't.

The lake called out with a soft breeze, washing him with a tinkling song as if to soothe his pain. The beautiful tranquility mocked the storm within as much as it calmed. He had to think about anything but the memories Jordan had stirred up. All that came to mind was that last incident with Sue-Ann. What had just happened? He didn't understand.

Why did Jordan have to point out her eyes? Yeah, he liked green eyes. Every girl he'd been at all serious with had green eyes. Patti, Vera, Isabel . . . .

Isabel. Of course she'd go with Brandt. That was how he met her in the first place. She'd admitted upfront she'd started hanging around because she had a huge crush on Brandt but found Jordy much easier to talk to. Not that this admission had phased him. In retrospect, it should have.

He sighed. Why did he ever let himself get mixed up with Brandt's kind of girl? He should've known better, but now that he was seeing her, he'd like to get through this without playing her—or getting played. But what could he do about it? With Jordy stuck in Ohio, if Brandt noticed Isabel, she would go out with him. He was the one she'd really wanted.

And now Sue-Ann. Every time he turned around, there she was. Was she following him? No, she had made it clear she wasn't. Then someone else was setting them up. Now, that burned. If he hated nothing else, it was having someone forced on him, but who was behind it? Jordan? Didn't he start it by bringing her up at breakfast? Said he ran into her yesterday . . . .

Wait. Yesterday afternoon, while Jordy was shooting pool with the guys, had Jordan sent Sue-Ann in? Maybe, but he had just met her. He couldn't have set the other stunts up.

The new fishing pole. When he had to try it, no one would join him. Or would they? Jordan wanted to, but Gramps put him to work so he couldn't. The old fox knew Jordy's scout training demanded he please him by taking it out to the lake. He couldn't have known Sue-Ann would show up, though. If Gramps was conspiring against him, he had luck on his side, big time.

One incident Jordy could pin on him—the tour. Gramps could've asked any of the guys to show him around, but he chose Sue-Ann.

A girl giggled. Her high-pitch felt like a pick ax through his skull.

A shiver of annoyance flashed over Jordy. He stood and whirled around.

The giggle belonged to a middle-school girl only about five feet tall with a mop of dishwater blond hair and dull gray eyes. His face warmed over her bare mid-drift and her denim underwear. When he was her height, no adult he'd known would've let any of their daughters dress like that.

"Yes?" he purred at her forehead.

Another giggle burst forth. "Just introducing myself. I'm Krystal."

"Jordy Durant." Maybe rudeness would get rid of her.

"I know." She giggled again. "Do-ya-have-a-girlfriend?"

To get this pest to buzz off, he'd have to be honest, if anything short of engagement would work. "I do have a green-eyed honey in Chicago."

"Chicago's awful far away. Sure you're not interested in someone a little closer? A McCoy girl, maybe?"

He glared. "Are you one of Sue-Ann's friends?"

The giggler eyed her nails. "Cara and her sister do often share their stuff, so I guess you could say that, but I think I get on her sister's nerves."

Shocker. He rolled his eyes. "I can't possibly imagine why."

The young girl started giggling again.

"Stop that!" He snapped as he impulsively slapped his right hand over her mouth. "Giggle one more time, and I swear I'll—"

The brat chomped down on his hand. He yelped and jumped back.

"Jerk!" She waved her clenched fist. "I don't care who you are, you're a fat creep! And I am gonna make sure everybody knows it, too!" She spun on her jelly heels and marched down to the beach.

Jordy groaned. Really? His stomach sank. *Fat* creep? Oh no. What had he done? Forget that, what had an actual fat creep done? How could he help, after his foul-up? His own reputation hardly mattered; he was quite good at ruining it himself. Besides, the only high school girl here was Sue-Ann, and she already wouldn't give him the time of day.

Someone cleared their throat.

Jordy jumped and whirled around. "You're Sue-Ann's sister, right?"

She nodded. "It's Cara. They call me Cara Beth, too."

"Right." He glanced to the beach and watched the giggler escape up the rocky path to the other side of the lake. Poor kid, what had she been though?

"Don't worry, Krystal is all talk. We're friends, but she is a spoiled brat who tells mean stories and can't keep them straight. Folks ignore her when she makes stuff up. Besides, you're a Durant. She couldn't touch you."

Poor kids. He kept his face neutral. "How old is she? Eleven?"

"Twelve, actually."

"Same difference." What was wrong with this world, that any girl in it believed reporting a creep wouldn't make a dent? Jordy watched the cattails waving by the trees on the other side of the lake. The breeze rippled across the azure surface. Dark shadows flickered below the depths.

Cara followed his gaze. "It's so beautiful here. Walk with me?"

Hmm. This one was too young for his tastes, but he didn't have anything better to do or a polite way to ditch her. At least she wasn't giggling nonstop. He nodded and turned to the right, following the curve of the lake. Sue-Ann's sister fell in step with him.

Birds chirped. Dragonflies buzzed. "This place isn't all bad." If he hinted he needed to be alone, would she pick up on it and leave? "I'm sorry, I'm not good company today. My parents dropped a bomb on me this morning."

"Oh, sounds painful. I'm surprised you're still here. Heck, I'm surprised

I didn't see it. Bombs can take out entire cities."

So much for that. He groaned. "You know what I mean."

They reached the tree with the limb hanging over the lake.

"My sister was right? You're moving to Columbus?"

Jordy shrugged. "She should've been wrong. My dad left us almost three years ago." Months after their lives first "exploded," as he'd so aptly put it. "I thought my parents were getting divorced and Jordan drug me up here to say adios. I mean, why else would he suddenly want to see me, after dropping off the face of the planet? He doesn't even know me anymore."

Sue-Ann's sister stepped up on the low branch and walked out over the lake like an Olympic gymnast on a balance beam. That trick likely would've gotten her in trouble, in his scout troop. Hadn't she learned anything from her sister's stupid stunt in the ravine? "You could fall like that."

"I won't. I know what I'm doing."

Like they knew what they were doing with the berries and that fish?

She stopped two-thirds of the way out and spun. "Come on up."

"And if I fall?"

"You won't. Unless you're afraid."

That didn't leave him any choice. He stepped up and grabbed one of the overhead branches. Fuller definitely wouldn't let both of them on it like this, but the limb did hold.

"Told ya you could do it," she said.

He shrugged. "I wasn't sure if it could hold two."

"Of course it does. We've done this lots. Sis always holds on, just like you are." Mirth faded from dark eyes. "Is it okay to ask you something?"

"Depends on how good you are at keeping your mouth shut."

"Pretty good, but I wouldn't hide anything important from my sister."

So she planned to squeal to Sue-Ann. Terrific. "Shoot."

"How close are you and my sister?"

"Gee, not very." He kept his face straight. "I can't even see her right now, but sometimes we're so close, we're actually in the same room."

"Jordy, I'm serious!"

"Really? With who?"

"That's not what I meant, and you know it!" She took a long breath and let it out again. "I was wondering how much you like her."

"What makes you think I do?" Surely that was not a waver in his voice.

Cara picked at the bark on a branch hanging down from above them. "To tell the truth, I don't know what is going on between you two. You're always biting each other's heads off, yet I keep picking up on something else. I asked my sister, but she gave me the runaround. She ended up on the end of this branch, turned away and refusing to answer me."

Uh-huh. "And you thought I'd escape out here, too, so you walked out to attempt to block me."

"I swear that was not what I was thinking."

He stepped closer. "You know, I could push you in."

She wetted her lips. "I'll tell my sister."

Like she hasn't already figured out to keep me at arm's length. Jordy laughed uncomfortably. Why did he care?

"You know she'll never forgive you. She'll hunt you down like a dog."

Jordy snorted. "And do what? Kiss me?"

Sue-Ann's sister smiled wickedly. "Don't you wish."

Why did his temperature shoot up ten degrees? "I don't, I repeat, don't care about Little Miss Country. I mean it. I really don't like that girl."

Her sister just stood there, nodding.

Jordy snapped, "Really! I don't!"

"Then why did you say it four times? Everybody knows if you say it four times, the only person you're trying to convince is yourself. All you got to do is say it once or twice, but if you got to do it four times, you're lying."

He rolled his eyes. "Right."

"When I, uh, happened by, Krystal was asking you if you were interested in a McCoy girl. You thought she meant my sister, didn't you?"

"Who else would she mean?"

Sue-Ann's sister nodded, smirking. "Me. Yesterday, Krystal claimed you liked me, no doubt hoping I'd buy it and make a fool of myself. I knew better than to believe her, but she made a bet of it." Sue-Ann's sister leaned in and added confidentially, "Actually, I think she had a crush on you herself and was only looking for an excuse to get close to you."

"So I gathered. To be honest, I'll never get used to giggling school girls."

"You never did answer my question about my sister."

"Why does it matter? You know as well as I do Sue-Ann hates me."

Her sister blinked at him. "First off, I doubt my sister is truly capable of hate. She's too forgiving for that. If anything, she's afraid of you."

That chilled Jordy. He frowned. "She's afraid of me?"

Chapter 5

AROUND THREE IN THE afternoon, Susanna's sister stormed in their trailer, banging the screen door behind her. Misty ceased purring and dug her claws into Susanna's stomach before leaping into the open cabinet overhead, but Ginger continued snoring, curled up on Susanna's feet at the bottom of her parents' bed. Susanna gripped her paperback and kept her nose buried in it, opened toward the back.

Tennis shoes landed hard inches from her head. Cara barked, "Put those on. We're going for a walk."

Susanna glowered at her sister. "And, pray tell, why should I?"

"This is not a conversation you want to have in front of the folks."

Susanna pulled her feet out from underneath her dog and sat up. "This had better be good, sister dear."

Cara smirked. "Oh, but it is."

What was she up to? Susanna put her shoes on and followed her sister out the trailer's screen door. "Mom! We're going down the hill!"

"All right, try not to get too dirty."

"We won't," the girls chimed.

Down in the ravine, the sisters hopped up on the fallen tree, straddling it to face each other. "Okay, Cara, spill it. What have you been up to?"

Mischief danced in her sister's dark eyes. "Ran into Jordy?"

Susanna's cheeks burned. Cara saw that? "No, he ran into me."

Cara leaned back. "When?"

"When you were on the payphone this morning. Remember? I got bored and split? Well, City Boy came out of nowhere and plowed right into me then had the nerve to try to be a hero and help up the lady in distress." Susanna crossed her arms. "I didn't need his help. I wanted to slap that stupid hand of his."

"Wanted to? Why didn't you?"

Susanna let her arms drop. Good question. "I don't know, it felt wrong.

Actually, he seemed so upset, I was afraid he'd start crying. I wanted to ask what was wrong, but he ran off before I worked up the nerve."

"I did see him heading for the lake, but didn't think anything of it. Then Yoli had to go, and I spotted Krystal following Jordy, so I followed her."

"What happened?"

Cara flicked an ant off the fallen oak. "They got in a fight and Krystal ran off swearing revenge."

"So you were left alone with him?"

Cara eyed her nails. "We had such a lovely conversation."

Uh-oh. Susanna groaned. "Cara Beth! What did you do?"

"You wouldn't tell me what was going on! I had to!"

"There's nothing going on. And even if there was, it wouldn't be any of your business!"

"You never let anything go on. You know what Jordy told me? He thinks you hate him!"

"Maybe I do!"

"That's not true, Susanna. Knowing you, you're afraid of him, and for no better reason than he's a boy. You've never even had a boy friend, let alone a boyfriend. But Jordy is different than the other guys, when he stops showing off and gets real. He's only a jerk to you because of the way you treat him."

Susanna opened her mouth to protest.

"Don't you get it? You're mean to him because you expect him to be. So, you think you're protecting yourself while he thinks you hate him and reacts negatively, which in your mind proves your first assumption."

Okay, time to change to Cara's favorite subjects: boys and Cara. "Exactly what did you two talk about that put such talk in your head? Did you find out why Jordy looked like his goldfish died?"

Cara pointed at her. "Ah ha! So you do like him!"

Susanna groaned and stared at the fallen oak they still straddled. "No, I—I was just curious, after all, he did literally knock me off my feet. I'm owed an explanation."

"He'd gotten in a fight with his parents. They are moving to Columbus."

"I love being right! What else did you find out?" Her cheeks warmed. Why should she care? "After all, knowledge is power."

Cara snickered. "His parents have been separated. He thought they were getting divorced but I think they're getting back together. I asked how close you were, but he cracked jokes and threatened to push me in the lake."

"What? He pushed you in? I'll kill him."

Cara waved. "He was teasing. He never touched me. Besides, I said I'd tell you and you'd hunt him down. You should've seen the look on his face. He clearly valued your opinion of him, but he tried to laugh it off. His actual response was, 'And do what? Kiss me?' So I said, 'don't you wish.' "

Oh no. Susanna's stomach sank. "Remind me to kill you someday. I bet City Boy wanted to die. What did he have to say to that?"

"Uh, that's not important." Cara glanced away.

Susanna glared. "Cara . . . ."

Cara sighed. "He said he didn't like you four times."

Susanna stuffed all emotion into her mental lockbox. "Oh, well, I guess you were wasting your time, huh?"

"I knew you would be impossible. If they say it four times, they're lying. And believe me, it was four times. I counted."

"Cara Beth, that's a kid's tale."

"Anyway, the other day, Krystal bet me that Jordy liked me and tried to get him to say he did. Only, he thought she was talking about you!"

Sisters. Susanna growled. "And I suppose you think he likes me?"

"At the very least, he would, if you'd give him a chance." Cara leaned in close, her dark eyes scheming. "So?"

"So what?"

"Do you like him?"

Susanna picked at the bark on the tree. "Like who?"

Cara swore. "Do you or don't you have a crush on Jordy?"

"Do you have a crush on Jordy?"

"This isn't about me! Just answer my question!"

Susanna tapped her face near her right eye. "I'm half-blind, remember? Ask again after I get my glasses. Maybe City Boy will seem nicer when I can see him clearly without having to get so close I'd touch him if I sneezed."

"You've been close enough. When he saved you from the killer fish."

Susanna shook off the phantom arms Cara's words evoked. "Thank you so much for that marvelous observation. It wasn't my idea. And, why bring it up? He was standing behind me, so I couldn't see him, anyway."

"That's true, but . . ."

Amy came bouncing down the hill. "Hi, guys, what's up?"

Cara and Susanna twisted to face her.

"I thought you went home?" Susanna asked.

Amy shook her head. "Nah, my folks didn't have to work today. I have a couple hours yet. So, what are you up to?"

"Just talking. What about you?"

Cara added, "Meet any cute guys lately?"

Amy squealed.

"Who is it now?" Susanna asked, "Billy-Bob, Jimmy-Bob, Bobby Joe?"

Amy giggled. "No, silly, Jordy Durant. Sandy hair, dreamy eyes, isn't he to die for? Oh, sorry, Susanna, your glasses are broken so you can't see him. Poor baby! Boy are you missing out! He's so fine. Don't you think, Cara?"

"He's okay."

"No, he's gorgeous. His eyes are better than Boo's ponytail!"

"So I've heard," Susanna said dryly. "I'm glad I can't see Jordy. This way, I could keep my eyes on his personality, instead. Believe me, he's—"

Cara elbowed her. "Jordy's a really nice guy, right Sue-Ann?"

Take a hint. Susanna sighed. "Maybe I'd think so, if I could see him."

Krystal appeared on the trail from the front of the campgrounds. "See who? And don't lie. I know you're talking about a guy."

Amy clasped her hands. "The fly prince of Glenshire, Jordy Durant, the subject of every girl's fantasies. And about how poor Sue-Ann can't see him."

Gag me. She rolled her eyes. "Poor Sue-Ann really doesn't care."

"Sure, Jordy's simply divine." Krystal's voice dripped with sarcasm.

Amy squealed again. "Just remember, he's mine."

Susanna raised her eyebrows. "Does Jordy know that?"

"No." Amy squirmed. "But I saw him first. Look, but don't touch."

Someone needed to give this flat-chested, just-turned-eleven-year-old a reality check. Susanna sent a "you tell her" look at her sister at the same time that she got one from Cara. Both continued the staring contest.

Amy snapped her fingers. "Hey, I know! You ain't totally blind, are you, Sue-Ann? If you got close enough, you could see him, right?"

"If he was like, five inches away."

"How about we come up with an excuse for you to get that close."

Cara giggled behind her hand. "Yeah, I could push her in the lake while he's watching, then he could pull her out and give her mouth to mouth."

"What?" Susanna and Amy both exclaimed.

Susanna took a breath to calm down. "Wouldn't work."

Cara put her hand on her hip. "Why not?"

"One, I'm bigger than you, so you pushing me in isn't logical. Two, I can swim, so I can't drown. Three, if I faked it, I wouldn't swallow any water, so I wouldn't need mouth to mouth. Four, if he tried it, I'd kill him."

Amy pouted. "You'd have to get in line, girl."

Cara put her hands out. "Can't you guys take a joke? I was only kidding."

Sure, to get a rise out of her. "I don't know about you sometimes."

"This is totally stupid." Krystal flipped her hair over shoulder. "All she has to do is drop something, they both reach for it, and he's in range."

Cara grinned. "That's perfect! Don't you think so, Sue-Ann?"

Whatever. Susanna slipped down from the tree and fled up the hill.

At her camp site, she let herself inside of their trailer, took aspirin, then collapsed on her parents bed and grabbed her paperback.

Cara came in huffing. "Why did you take off so fast?"

Susanna buried her nose in her book. "Don't know, just felt like it."

"Oh, really?"

"Yes, now leave me alone. The subject is closed. I'm not talking about this anymore. Period."

"Fine, I'm outta here." The door slammed behind Cara.

AFTER DINNER, JORDY sat in the brown leather wingback chair in Gramp's wood-paneled, cozy den, staring at the black, corded landline so old, it had a rotary dial. Should he try to call Isabel again? Yeah, he definitely had to talk to her, after the tempting ideas put in his head by Sue-Ann's meddling sister. He sucked in a breath and dialed.

Isabel's voice stunned his ears. He usually got her mother, who'd claim Isabel was washing her hair. "Hi, it's Jordy. I'm so glad . . ."

"No se un Isabel. No hay un Isabel aquí. Isabel no vive aquí. Tienes el número incorrecto."

He called, "I know it's you, Isabel. Please don't hang up, Isabel! Isabel!"

A recording of a female operator came on the phone. "If you would like to make a call, please hang up and try again. If you need help, hang up and dial your operator. If you would like to . . . ."

Jordy slammed down the telephone.

A pair of female hands covered his eyes. "Jordy, guess who."

It was his mom, but he said, "Um, let's see . . . Isabel?"

"No, your mother, silly!" She slapped his shoulder playfully.

"Only kidding." He twisted around to face his mom. She wore her golden curls pulled back with a claw and wore a white T-shirt under her floral cotton slip dress. Hope shone in her green eyes. He grinned. "I missed you."

"I've missed you, too, son. Sorry I couldn't get here any sooner. I have so much to get done at the house, and your dad is so busy here, when he does make it down, he's often too tired to help much."

So that was where his father had kept disappearing to, leaving him alone with Gramps. Jordy stared, numb and chilled. This was for real. They were moving. "We're doing fine on our own, Mom. Why are you uprooting us from everything we have left for Jordan?"

"Honey, I love your dad. And he loves us, believe it or not. He's worked hard to get us back. Why can't you give him a chance?"

"I can't forgive him so easily, Mom. I don't see how you can, either."

"The same way I've endured through a trial that knocked my guys down. Christ upholds me. He'll restore you, as he has your dad, if you let him."

If only. He glanced away from his mom. No way would he reply to her nagging. The last time they had this discussion, his mom invoked Christine. His day had been bad enough without another reminder of how grieved *she* would be, if *she* knew he'd spat in the Lord's face.

His mom side-hugged him. "I want to spend time with you tomorrow. Guess where we're going. It'll be just the two of us. Your dad has to work. It'll work out, you'll see."

"Disneyland?" He wished.

"Close! The Ohio State Fair!"

"Uh, great, but I'll need spending money."

"I've got that for you." She pulled three twenties out of her purse and handed them over.

"Thanks." He pocketed his money and headed for the door.

"Where do you think you're going?"

He stopped facing the door. "Game room."

"I haven't seen you in a week, Jordy."

"And you'll have me all day tomorrow, but tonight I have a date with a pool table." He blew his mom a kiss and walked out. Once upon a time, his dad would've grounded him for this, but Jordan wouldn't do a blessed thing even if his mom tattled.

GOLDEN EVENING SUNLIGHT beamed down as Susanna and her sister passed behind Krystal's campsite. Krystal climbed out of her hammock and strolled over. "Hey, Bobbsey Twins."

"Don't call us that," Susanna said, "you know we hate it."

Krystal waved. "Whatever. What's up?"

Susanna looked up. "Some tree branches and the sky."

Cara snickered. "We're going to play pool, wanna come?"

Krystal shrugged. "Sure, but it's odd."

"Then you don't need me anymore. See ya!" Susanna waved and whirled to take the shortcut through the ravine back to her site.

Cara called, "Hey, Sis! Wait. Don't go! We'll figure something out."

Susanna sighed and followed her sister and Krystal.

Inside the game room, they found Jordy setting up a solitary pool game. Krystal opened her mouth to speak, but Sue-Ann cut the wench off, placing a hand to her chin. "Ooh, a tough game. Jordy vs. Jordy. I wonder who wins."

His head jerked in her direction. "Cute. What are you girls doing here?"

"We were going to play pool," Cara replied.

Krystal wrinkled her nose. "We still can. I don't see anybody else in here who deserves the privilege to play."

Jordy put his hand on his chin. "I wonder if the owner would agree." He waved. "Oh, silly me, it must've slipped my mind. Gramps owns this place. Of course I have every privilege that his grandson deserves. At the least that would be the same as the peasants. And I seem to remember a rule among ordinary folks. Now, how did that go? Would it be first come, first serve?"

"True," Cara said, "but they also say, ladies first."

"That's right, sister," Sue-Ann said. "But, I'm a fair person. I say we play for it. Winner gets the table for the night."

Jordy laughed and pointed at her. "Okay, you're on. Me against you."

Susanna gasped. "What?"

"Not fair." Cara jerked her thumb at herself. "I want to represent us."

"Yeah," Krystal said, "we vote for Cara, not Sue-Ann."

Jordy grabbed a cue stick from the rack. "Hey, Sue-Ann made the bet, Sue-Ann plays the game. The rules are the rules."

"But, she . . . ." Cara started.

No. Sue-Ann shook her head. "It's okay. I'll play him."

Cara frowned. "Are you sure?"

No way could she win without glasses, but neither could she get out of it without revealing her weakness to Jordy. "Positive."

He reached for a fuzzy blue object dangling from one corner of the pool table and rubbed his cue stick on it. "I break."

"Be my guest. Cara, bring me a stick."

Cara retrieved another cue stick and handed it to Sue-Ann. Krystal and Cara hopped up on two bar stools by the arcade games.

Jordy leaned over the table and took his shot. Colorful spheres whirled in all directions. Three clunked into the pockets. "I'm solids. Thank me for the stripe later."

Sue-Ann flinched. She was in trouble. "I see you've played before."

"Our apartment complex had a rec center with four pool tables. I play all the time."

Okay, she was toast. "It's City versus Country, isn't it, City Boy?"

"And we'll see who wins this one. Just take your shot."

Humiliation, here I come. She peered at the pool table in an attempt to make sense of it. Her eyes saw two fuzzy, solid balls of every color plus one black ball and one white ball. She leaned low over the table, pretending to set up her shot. Stripes. Why did it have to be stripes? Like it mattered. She took a breath and shot. She hit several balls but none went in.

Half an hour later, somehow, only the eight ball remained on the table. Jordy took his shot. It went in.

Pointing at him, Cara jumped to her feet. "You didn't call your shot. That means you lose!"

Jordy whirled around. "No way, I had the game nailed."

Krystal shook her head. "Sorry, Jordy, 'the rules are the rules.' You said so yourself."

Susanna bit her lip. She hated it when this happened to her. It wouldn't be fair to steal his table on a dumb technicality. And with Krystal, their group had an odd number of players. They needed a fourth anyway. "Why don't we play doubles? Me and Cara against Krystal and Jordy."

"No way!" Krystal jumped down from her stool. "I'm so not playing with that sleazeball. I play on Cara's team or I don't play at all."

"Fine," Cara said, "me and Krystal VS. Jordy and Sue-Ann."

Sue-Ann glanced at Jordy. Surely he wouldn't go for that.

He shrugged. "I'm game if you are."

Well, she asked for it. "Oh, all right. No offense, but why do I always get stuck with him? Is fate conspiring against us?"

"I don't believe in fate," Jordy replied.

"Oh, really? Then, how would you explain why we are surgically joined at the hip? And don't you dare suggest I'm following you."

Jordy shrugged. "Maybe you're just lucky."

She laughed. "I'm lucky? How is luck different than fate?"

"Luck is random chance. Fate is a divine power decreeing where we will go and giving us no choice in any of our actions in getting there."

"Would that much control really be necessary? Aren't we limited by our characters? Without any way to know all of the consequences of our actions, how can we change ourselves and thus our destinations?"

As she spoke, Jordy went from staring with his eyebrows raised up high to closing his eyes and pressing his lips together tight.

Krystal snapped, "Hey, we came here to play pool already."

Jordy cleared his throat. "My team goes first. Sue-Ann, you'll break. If we're going to figure out what you're doing wrong, I've got to see your game."

Uh-oh. She glowered. "Why do you care all of a sudden?"

He raised his hands. "Hey, I want to win, and if we're going to win, I've got to fix your game and fix it fast."

Cara put a quarter in the pool table and then racked the pool balls. "Just break, Sis. You ask too many questions."

Sue-Ann gripped her cue stick so tight her nails dug into the flesh of her palm. She leaned over the pool table and attempted her shot but missed the cue ball. Jordy came over with an air of reluctance. From behind her, he took hold of the cue stick, not nearly shy enough about touching her. "Here, hold it like this." He moved her right hand back on the cue stick, loosened her left hand's death grip, and demonstrated how to aim through her fingers.

Trying to ignore the musky scent of Jordy's aftershave and the nearness of his person, Sue-Ann clamped down.

His sigh tickled her ear and made her tremble. Jordy again loosened her grip on the cue stick. "Sheesh, girl, no wonder you can't shoot straight, you're shaking like a leaf. You've got to relax and concentrate on the game."

Cara snickered. "How can she, with you breathing down her neck? Any closer, and the two of you will be kissing."

He dropped the cue stick like it was on fire and headed to Cara. "I'm tired of your mouth! Nothing's going on. And nothing should be going on. I have a girlfriend, for crying out loud. There. Are you happy now?"

Sue-Ann winced. Why did those words hurt? Stranger still, why did he sound so fake to her ears? "No more lies, Jordy. For once, tell the truth!"

Jordy fidgeted. "I haven't a clue what you're talking about."

"Oh?" Sue-Ann put her right hand on her hip. "Then what's her name?"

"Isabel Herington."

"Where does she live?"

"In Chicago!"

"And how does she feel about you moving two states away?"

Jordy's cheeks turned pink.

"You haven't told her, have you?"

"It's not my fault, she won't take my calls! For all I know, she's going out with my so-called best bud." Jordy clasped his hand over his mouth.

Ha. Sue-Ann smirked and walked out. If there was one thing she hated, it was a liar. But exposing the truth sure felt good.

Chapter 6

WHILE SITTING ON THE edge of her bed in the trailer on Tuesday morning, Susanna slid a wide-tooth purple comb through her still-wet hair. The comb caught a bit but she didn't slow down as the last of the tangles came out. She lifted the right half of her tresses to inspect the results of her labor. Already, the lovely waves the vigorous combing had straightened were springing back. She flipped her hair back over her shoulders. *Please don't frizz up. I want to look nice for the Fair today.*

Cara opened the bathroom door and squeezed out past her mother. She sat on the bed beside Susanna. "What was that all about?"

"What was what about?" Susanna replied, removing the soggy scrunchie from her wrist. She wrapped it around the comb's handle so it wouldn't get lost, and then laid the comb on the shelf beside her.

"You know, you and Jordy last night."

The unbidden memory rose of his arms around her. Susanna's cheeks grew warm. "He was lying through his teeth. You know I hate liars."

"But how did you know? I didn't notice until you said something."

Her family wouldn't understand. "I just knew, okay?"

Their mother handed them each a fork and a plate of bacon, eggs, and toast. "Eat up, girls. We have a long day ahead of us."

"SUSANNA! LOOK! WE'RE almost there!" Cara cried, awakening Susanna from the sound sleep only a vehicle in motion could evoke.

Susanna stretched and put up the back of her red van seat. She blinked out her window. Sure enough, blurry florescent flags rose in the distance.

A few minutes later, they reached the fairgrounds. Attendants in neon-orange vests showed them where to park with bright yellow sticks.

Everyone climbed out of the van. Cara pointed at the screaming white dots flying in circles overhead. "Look! Seagulls!"

Susanna peered at the white blurs in the sky. "What are they doing here? Lake Erie's not around the corner."

Her dad said, "They must've wanted to go to the fair, too."

Their mother shook her head. "Don't be silly. They want the food."

Cara sniffed. "Yeah, doesn't it just fill you with anticipation?"

Susanna arched her left eyebrow. "I guess you could say that."

She spun toward the fair. Jordy Durant climbed out of a car one row up from them with a small black object in one hand.

Gasping, they pointed at each other and cried, "You!"

Cara stared at them. "What in the world?"

"Do you know that boy?" their dad asked.

Sue-Ann laughed. "Why, if it ain't the Jordan Walker Durant, Jr. Come down to the Fair to spend time among your subjects, Your Highness?"

Her dad squinted. "Huh, is that Phill's grandson? It is a small world!"

Jordy crossed over to where they were and extended his hand to her dad with the airs of a young aristocrat. "Please, call me Jordy, sir. It's a pleasure."

"Uh, same here, kid." Her dad shook his hand. "Where you from?"

"Chicago, sir," Jordy said.

Face warm, Sue-Ann glared at her dad. *Stop it.*

"Chicago, huh? I had a feeling you were from out of state. Chicago's a big city, even bigger than Columbus."

"Yes, sir, only NYC and LA are bigger cities than Chicago."

How did City Boy keep a straight face and respectful tone while her dad was so—so her dad?

Her dad cleared his throat. "So, you're from the city. Did you enjoy it?"

"As your daughter refuses to let me forget."

Sue-Ann had a feeling those raccoon eyes were shooting her a dirty look.

Her dad laughed. "I see you two have met. Don't worry about her. She's a big tease like her mother."

Face blazing, she suppressed a low growl. At least Jordy had the sense to not respond. "Dad, let's go. We came to see the fair, not to talk to City Boy."

Her dad opened his mouth to protest.

Her mom said sweetly, "Honey, she's right. Let's get moving."

"Sure." Her dad faced Jordy. "So, Jordy, is it? Who are you here with?"

Jordy turned pink. "My mom. She forgot her camera and sent me after it." He held up the small black object as if for proof. "I'm meeting her inside."

Her dad nodded. "Walk to the gate with us. You don't want to be caught out alone in this crowd."

Jordy shrugged. "Not like I got any better offers."

Cara shifted impatiently. "Whatever. Let's just go already."

They finally started heading toward the crowd at the gate.

Jordy fell in step in between Sue-Ann and Cara and eyed Sue-Ann. "Is this thing any good?"

She shrugged. "It's awesome, as far as fairs go. But Cedar Point is better. The fair doesn't have any real coasters."

"How's the midway?"

Cara said, "Your average rip off."

"Peachy," Jordy replied.

Cara giggled. "You sound like Sue-Ann. She says that a lot."

"I do not!"

"Whatever," Jordy said. "What makes the games a rip-off?"

Cara shrugged. "All I ever won was a goldfish."

"Oh? I wouldn't think fish would mix well with camping."

"They don't. Lucky stays at home."

"Where do you live, anyway?"

The sisters eyed each other. Sue-Ann bit her lower lip. "Uh, about half an hour or so south of Glenshower."

"Why do you keep calling Glenshire that?" His glance flicked to her dad and focused back on her.

Sue-Ann's cheeks burned still again.

Cara said, "Habit. We couldn't pronounce it right when we were little."

By the time Sue-Ann and Jordy reached the gates, she was all but racing him and both were well ahead of her family.

She clutched her knees, catching her breath, an ache in her side.

"Sorry." Jordy touched her back lightly, beside her. "You may not want to hear this from me, but please listen. It's disrespectful for a man to call any girl a tease, but his own daughter? So wrong. You deserve way better."

What? She stared as his feet strode on ahead. She rose as he showed a gatekeeper his stamp and went on through. Whoa. He was still the boy scout.

Whatever her dad meant, hopefully Jordy had misunderstood, but whoa.

Her family caught up, and the four of them had to wait in a long line.

She shifted on her feet, tantalized by the shouts of those spinning on the carnival rides. Err, why did her vision have to reek? Half the fun of the fair was seeing everything.

She thrust her hand in her pocket and fingered the half dozen aspirin tablets she'd dropped in there before they left. She'd need every one of them before the day's end.

Once inside the Fair gates, they stopped near a flower garden below the end of the sky lift. "Now stay together, girls," her mom said, "but if for some reason you get lost, meet us back here, okay? And Susanna, whatever you do, don't lose your sister. I still say we should've waited until we got her glasses before coming."

Her dad shook his head. "By then, our vacation would be over. She'll be fine. She's not blind, Denise. And she knows our voices."

Must he talk about her as if she wasn't there? "Don't worry. I'm almost fifteen. I can take care of myself."

"If you say so," their mom said.

Cara asked, "Do you think we'll see Jordy and his mom?"

Their dad unfolded the fair map the gate attendant had given him. "With this crowd, it wasn't likely we'd run into him once, let alone twice."

Susanna waved this off. "I'm always runnin' into that boy."

Her mom smiled. "Maybe he likes you."

Susanna rolled her eyes. "Please, Mother. Guys like City Boy don't care about girls like me."

Cara added, "And they don't get along."

Mom shrugged. "Love and hate are opposite sides of the same coin."

Susanna groaned. "Mom, that's what you said about Ken. I never could stand him. I was thrilled when he moved."

The sisters spent most of the morning waiting in line for carnival rides. Most of them were well worth the wait.

Standing in the grass, Cara pointed up at the pirate ship ride. "Oh look! They got that here this year! Come on, Susanna!"

The ship swung up until it was nearly vertical in the sky.

Susanna gulped. "I don't know."

Cara dragged her by the arm. "Come on, scardy-cat. You rode the Mean Streak with Dad. This is nothin' compared to that."

Half an hour later, Susanna found herself seated next to Cara at the very back of the pirate ship. It had neither seatbelts nor a lap bar or anything else whatsoever to keep her securely on their bench in the pirate ship.

The ship swung her up. Susanna screamed. Any second now, she would certainly fall out and plummet to the earth so far below. The ship swung back down again. She breathed a sigh of relief. The ship swung her up again.

Her rear end left the seat. She shrieked in terror and squeezed her eyes shut, praying. *Jesus, please don't let me fall out. I don't want to die.*

Eventually, the rocking death ship stopped trying to buck her off of it and slowed to a stop. Susanna peaked her right eye open. Safe. "Thank you, Jesus," she whispered. She willed her jelly legs to follow Cara off the ride.

As she passed by those foolish souls waiting for their turn to sign death's dance card, someone tapped her shoulder. "Hey."

She spun. "Jordy!" He just had to see that, didn't he?

"That's a way to greet a guy." Jordy laughed and leaned further over the railing between them. "Was it me, or were you freaking out up there? Don't tell me Sue-Ann's afraid of heights!"

"No!" Susanna snapped, then said a bit sheepishly, "Just of falling." She ran to catch up with Cara.

Outside the ride's gates, Cara said, "Wow. Dad was wrong. We did run into Jordy again."

"Sort of," Susanna said.

Cara added, "Wasn't that a blast?"

Why did folks enjoy almost plunging to their deaths? Susanna grunted.

Their dad whistled from several yards down the midway. He jumped up and down while waving his arms. Mom stood beside him.

They hurried to their parents.

"Having fun?" their dad asked.

The girls nodded.

"Why don't we go see the animals?" Their mom shuffled away from the noisy midway to the farm animal contest barns.

The animal exhibits were so cute, but her folks insisted on going through the Horticultural Building too. Susanna shifted her tired feet. What was with her parents' fascination with vegetables?

"Can we go yet?" Cara whined.

Their dad pointed to the wood stairs headed up. "We're eating lunch at the Smorgasbord."

After her family got a table at the restaurant upstairs, Susanna spotted Jordy in the buffet line and froze. He turned around—and waved at her. Face warm, she fled into the women's restroom. After waiting ten minutes, she got in line and hurried to get her food.

Jordy reappeared, heading back to the buffet.

She took her half-full plate and fled to her parents' table. Hopefully, he'd take the hint and not follow. The last thing she needed was another awkward encounter with him and her folks. Last time, on top of her dad's painful idea of small talk, he had come close to enlightening Jordy about the location of their permanent address. If Jordy ever realized his country girl was from the city, too, he'd hit the roof.

JORDY STARED AT SUE-Ann's retreating back. Chew him up and spit him out, that he was used to, but turn tail and run? That didn't jive with her style. Though, she hadn't chewed him out at the pirate ship, either, and in general, a remark like that would put him at the top of her hit list.

He crossed the room and slid into the booth across from his mom.

She raised her eyebrows. "Chasing complete strangers now, are we?"

"Lay off, will you?"

His mom's eyes narrowed. "Will Isabel lay off?"

So his mother had missed Isabel's premeditated murder of his ego last night. "Long distance isn't her cup of coffee."

"Now there's good news if I ever heard it, but must you repeat history?"

"Relax, Mom." He looked to where Sue-Ann was eating with her family on the other side of the room. "There isn't much chance of that."

AFTER SPENDING THEIR afternoon mostly standing in line for carnival rides, Susanna and her sister found their folks waiting at the Sky Lift exit and went with them to the dairy barn. The dairy barn's cool features consisted of the ice cream and the butter sculptures, which included life-sized sculptures of President Clinton and of a farmer milking a cow.

Once they'd all finished their ice cream cones, Susanna's dad unfolded his map. "Let's go see the exhibits in the Natural Resources Park."

Susanna dragged her aching feet after her family. Visions of the benches in the nature area of the fairgrounds floated before her.

As they passed by a fifteen-foot, animatronic Smokey the Bear, her mom asked her, "Are you okay, dear? You look peaked."

"I'm a little tired."

"Too much excitement," her dad said, grinning wide. "Wait here with ol' Smokey and rest up."

She nodded and her family headed into the main building to view the indoor exhibits. Leaning into the railing, she relieved one foot at a time of its heavy burden. She smiled at the little kids all shouting and waving at an unresponsive Smokey the Bear. She did the same thing at their age. Smokey always remembered her, too, though how he always knew her name was still a mystery. Her parents must have told him, but how had they done it?

"Hello, Sue-Ann, and how are you today?" said a gruff Smokey-the-Bear voice. Must be Jordy. Not only did Smokey sound like Jordy, the real Smokey had always called her Susanna.

The little girls giggled, probably assuming Jordy was her boyfriend.

Susanna smiled up at the towering, animatronic bear. "Why, Smokey, I know it can't be you, you're on break."

The real Smokey replied, "You got it, young lady. It was your boyfriend, who's standing behind you, by the way."

She laughed. It was an honest mistake. "Guess again." She turned to face Jordy and put her hand on her hip in feigned anger. "And what do you have to say for yourself, young man?"

"Isabel was too skinny for her own good and too ugly between her ears. I can't blame my mom for being glad to hear I have been dumped for Brandt."

Susanna raised an eyebrow. Jordy's light tone failed to hide the pain behind his words. "You got a hold of her?"

"Last night. She screamed, 'Stop calling, stop writing, stop breathing for all I care. Just leave Brandt and me alone!'"

Susanna winced. "Ouch, some people are nasty." She added with a note of apology, "You don't deserve dumped like that."

"Thanks." His forced smile clearly didn't believe her.

She eyed their audience. The kids couldn't seem to decide who was more interesting—them or Smokey. She had a feeling their audience included the fair employee running the fake bear also. "Jordy, what are you up to?"

"Right now, I need to crash. My feet are killing me."

"Been there. Been here before, too. The benches are on the way to the restrooms. They're not far. Here, I'll show you."

"Thanks, my feet and I appreciate it."

Susanna showed Jordy over to the park benches. He collapsed on one without shame. She started to leave, but he called out, "Wait!"

She turned back. "What?"

A hint of pink crept into his cheeks. "You don't have to go. I mean, uh, you look tired, too, so why don't you stay? Us Chicago guys get lonely fast. You'd take almost any company over being by yourself."

You're lying. You don't mind solo. And you definitely prefer to interact with me one-on-one. She squinted at him. *What's your game?* "Insulting me won't encourage me to stick around, no matter what your ego says. Besides, I'm supposed to stay near Smokey, they won't be able to find me if I don't."

"That's their problem, isn't it?" He patted the bench.

Her aching feet begged to take him up on the invitation, so she sat on the bench beside him but at a safe distance. "It is, indeed."

For some time, they sat, both facing forward, in a soothing, comfortable silence, listening to the birds chirping above the distant din of the state fair.

Jordy twisted toward her, and his racoon eyes stared, soaking her in.

"What is it?" she asked, shivering.

He shook his head. "There's something different about you today, but I can't put my finger on it."

Susanna wrapped a lock of her hair around her index finger. Oh, wait, of course. "Most of the time, I pull my hair up into a ponytail, but I left it down today, plus it behaved this morning for once. You're not used to seeing me properly groomed, with how laid back things are at Glenshire."

"I've noticed you sometimes wear the same outfit all weekend."

Her cheeks burned. *Note to self: stop that.* "It never made sense. I only got dirty again, and Mom gets mad if I change clothes more than once."

Cara marched up. "There you are! Sis, I've been looking all over for you. Mom told you not to go wandering off by yourself."

Susanna looked down at her shoes. "I wasn't by myself."

Cara glanced at Jordy. "Oh." She did a double take. "Oh! I see. He's here. Boy, Dad was wrong. Not once, not twice, but three times you run into him? Though, in this crowd, it is unlikely to run into anybody you know, let alone Jordy. Anyway, somebody move over already."

Instead of doing the reasonable thing and sitting between them, Cara tried to squeeze onto the two inches of bench beside Susanna, forcing her to move next to Jordy. Susanna turned her back to him, but not before her eyes betrayed her. Darn it, Amy was right.

Cara whispered in Susanna's ear, "What'd I tell you?"

She hissed back, "This changes nothing."

Cara whispered, "Even if he is totally gorgeous?"

Susanna's cheeks flamed. Why did Cara take joy in embarrassing her?

Jordy started, "Karen—"

"It's Cara. You remember my sister's name, why not mine?"

"Why were you giving her such a hard time? Sue-Ann's sixteen. She can take care of herself. She doesn't need her baby sister following her around."

Cara seethed. "For your information, she's fourteen."

"What?" Jordy asked, shock in his voice.

"I'll be fifteen next month," Susanna said quietly. So no one thought to mention she started school a year early because of when her birthday fell.

"Fifteen, sixteen, whatever. She can still take care of herself."

"How?" Cara snapped. "Without glasses, Sue-Ann's as blind as a bat."

Susanna sank low on the bench. How could Cara do that to her?

Jordy growled. "Sue-Ann, what's the little monster talking about?"

Susanna glared at her sister. "I'm nearsighted, okay? Everything more than five inches away is a big blur of color, without all of the fine details."

After an awkward moment, Jordy said, "No wonder you lost so badly at pool. How did you expect to win without being able to see the table? Now that explains a lot. Squinting isn't attractive, you know. Even if your parents won't let you get contacts, glasses are better than that."

"It also gives me terrible headaches. I had glasses, but someone . . ." She poked Cara. ". . . broke them the Saturday before last."

"You can't see me, can you?" Jordy asked.

Where had that come from? Susanna shook her head no.

Jordy sighed and gently turned her to face him, but she shut her eyes. He groaned. "Sue-Ann."

Fine. Susanna opened her eyes. She sucked in a breath as Jordy came into focus. Why oh why did he have to have eyes as blue as the summer sky?

"Can't you see me now?" Something vulnerable shone in his kind eyes.

"There you kids are!" her dad called.

Her folks caught up and her mother asked, "Are we interrupting?"

Susanna shook her head. It was too late. Somehow, it felt as if she had lost something before she even had the chance to find it.

Chapter 7

SUSANNA'S PARENTS FLOPPED on a bench across from her own bench on the tree-lined walkway in the nature exhibits area of the fairgrounds.

"I'll be!" her dad said, cursing. "It's the Durant boy again."

"Jordy, sir," he said through gritted teeth, his voice strained.

In between him and her sister, Susanna stared. He was upset about the interruption, too?

"Right, Jordy," said her dad. "So, what brings you back here?"

"Just looking for a place to rest my aching feet a while. I'm supposed to go to the concert at 8:30 with my mom."

Susanna's mom said, "Why, Wynona Judd is my favorite country singer. We're going, too."

"Why am I not surprised?" Jordy said. "What time is it?"

Susanna checked her watch. "Seven o'clock."

"I've got an hour and a half to kill, then."

"Speaking of the time," her dad said, "what do you kids want to do?"

"We haven't ridden the bumper cars yet," Cara said.

"I know what we're going to do," her mom said. "You kids are going to go have fun while Elliot and I sit here. Later, we'll go over to the flea market. If you don't catch up with us there, meet us at the WNCI booth outside of the concert. Jordy, why don't you go with the girls? You shouldn't be here alone."

He hesitated. "Sure, I don't have anything better to do."

Cara hopped to her feet. "Okay, then, let's go already!"

At the bumper cars, Jordy chose the car behind Susanna's. When the whistle blew, he rammed into her.

That did it. They spent the rest of the ride chasing each other.

On their way out the exit with Cara, Jordy nudged Susanna's shoulder with his elbow. "Okay, say it! Jordy is The King of Bumper Cars!"

She thrust out her lip. "It's not fair. You've got your driver's license."

"So? What's that got to do with anything?"

Cara frowned. "I see you had a blast. Without me!"

Susanna waved. "Oh, Sis, don't be a baby. I had to get Jordy back. I saw you and you were having a blast."

"Sure I didn't."

"Well," Jordy said, "I'm going to the midway to win my fortune."

Cara wrinkled her nose. "Don't bother, it's rigged."

"Oh, it's all in fun," Susanna said. "Maybe we'll get lucky this time."

Jordy said, "Yeah, now that your lucky charm's here."

And the male ego returns. Susanna rolled her eyes. "If I wanted a lucky charm, I'd go down to a grocery store and buy a whole box full of them."

Jordy took two steps closer to her, revealing the twinkle in his eyes. "You could, but I'd last longer."

A tiny smile twitched the corners of her mouth. Were his smart remarks all friendly banter? "Perhaps, but Lucky Charms would taste better."

Jordy grinned. "How would you know?" He tapped his lips. "Try me."

Heat flashed over her face. She stepped back. "Jordy, no!"

"It was a joke!" He stepped still further away. "Oh, duh, I'm an idiot," he groaned. Flushed, he raised his hands and edged back in. "I was only playing, but that's your problem with it. I totally respect that. It slipped out without thinking, I'm sorry. You have a right to your limits. I'll remember that one."

Biting her lip, she stared at the pavement and took deep breaths.

Cara growled. "Cut it out, you two, before I gag! Figure yourselves out, I sure can't. I don't even know my own sister as well as some guy from Chicago does, clearly!" Cara stormed off down the midway.

Our bad, we forgot life is all about her. Susanna sighed and followed after her sister. "Cara! Okay, you've gotten left out a little. Don't leave."

Jordy ran ahead and caught up to Cara. "Hey, we didn't mean to hurt your feelings, kid."

Cara spun around. "I'm not a kid. I'm only a year younger than Sis. And for the last time, my name is Cara!"

Jordy threw his hands up. "I'm sorry I have trouble remembering your name. I don't know why. What do you want? To arrest me? Go ahead, there's a cop right over there. Go have him lock ol' Jordy up and throw away the key, if it'll make Queen Cara happy."

Susanna laughed. "The Governor will pardon you. And if he doesn't, I'll run for Governor and pardon you myself."

"Whatever." Cara jerked her head sideways at the midway games. "Prove you're both sorry and come on. My money's burning a hole in my pocket."

They played a couple games and won nothing worth keeping. While her sister waited for her turn at a squirt gun race booth, Susanna wandered by a darts game booth with balloons tied to the back wall. Teddy bears hung from the rafters, one of which was a lovely shade of lavender.

"Burst the balloon and win a teddy for your lady!" The carnie called.

Jordy had followed Susanna. He pointed up. "Think it's cute, huh?"

She shifted. "Just admiring it. I could never win a bear that size."

"I'll give it a shot." Jordy gave the man a dollar, accepted five darts, and burst five balloons.

The carnie looked at the tickets and whistled. "Must be your lucky day. That's five medium prizes or one large."

"What's that one?" Jordy pointed at the bear that caught Susanna's eye.

"Purple one's a large."

"I'll take her."

The carnie cut the lavender bear down and tossed it to Jordy.

Jordy handed it to Sue-Ann. "See? It just takes practice."

"Thank you." A fuzzy warmth enveloped her. No. Avoiding his gaze, she pulled a dollar out of her pocket and thrust it at him. "Here."

He pushed it away. "Don't worry about it."

Ignoring his insulted tone, she continued to hold it out.

"Sue-Ann . . ."

She raised her eyes to his and thrust the dollar out farther. She couldn't accept this gift. That would mean accepting the warmth enveloping her.

He blew out a loud breath and took the dollar.

She sighed. Darn. Paying for the bear hadn't changed how she felt about him winning it for her one bit.

She glanced away to Cara, who'd finished her own game and now stood staring at them with her lips parted. Oh gosh. She'd never seen her sister so green with envy. "Sorry, Sis. I'll buy you a snow cone."

Once Queen Cara had her snow cone in her royal hand, she tagged along at her arm's length. Susanna and Jordy strolled together down the midway, five inches apart. Past the games, a clown juggling bowling pins rode in their direction on a unicycle. They stopped to watch until the clown passed.

The scent of Elephant ears, funnel cake, corn on the cob, caramel apples and cotton candy tickled Susanna's nose, but the smell of pizza made her stomach growl. That reminded her; they hadn't eaten since lunch.

She turned to her sister. "Want pizza?"

Cara nodded. "Sure."

Jordy dug into his jeans pocket, marched on up to the pizza stand, and slapped a bill on the counter. "A slice of pepperoni and a coke." He glanced back at the sisters. "What do you girls want?"

The eldest girl gaped, her stomach fluttering weirdly. Her heart raced.

Cara elbowed her side. "We'll take the same, please, thank you."

Susanna glanced at her sister from the corner of her eye. How could she answer such a question as if this were an everyday occurrence? A second ago, she couldn't remember her own name.

The pizza guy rang up the order and then slid them the food and drinks.

Cara took hers over to the side of the adjacent pretzel booth and plopped down on the ground.

Jordy stacked the two remaining plates and took them plus his coke. He sent her an apologetic half-smile. "Since your hands are too full."

Act normal. Sue-Ann took her drink and settled against the side of the pizza booth, seated across from her sister.

Jordy put his coke down near Sue-Ann's knee and sat beside her, leaving less than a hand's breadth between them. He turned toward her at an angle that likely put her sister in the corner of his vision and held a plate out to her.

Sue-Ann hesitated. What should she do with the stuffed bear? It didn't seem right to set it on the ground, but she could hardly hold onto it and eat also. She set her coke down next to Jordy's and tucked the bear under her left arm. There.

With both hands now free, she took the offered slice of pizza. "Thanks."

"No problem." Jordy took a bite of his pizza.

She focused on her food. Thank God for silence; it gave her racing heart a chance to slow down. Where had the arrogant young aristocrat gone? Why did Jordy keep being so nice to her today? Though, dinner could be payback for insulting him over the bear. At least he included her sister this time.

She peered at her sister's forced smile and sucked in a breath. Her sister would be smoldering inside, if she knew that look, and she should. She had worn it herself, the time her parents dropped her off at the movies with her sister, and the friend her sister was meeting there had proved to be a date. Cara was taking this all wrong, surely, but no matter how Susanna looked at this, Jordy Durant didn't fit in the hole she pegged him in at all.

Susanna chanced a glance up at Jordy. He caught her eye and sent her a reassuring smile. A small smile made its way onto her own lips.

Jordy swallowed the last bite of his pizza and licked his fingers. "Food's the same at all fairs, ain't it? Sticky and delicious."

Susanna patted her belly. "And fattening. Like I need the extra pounds."

"I'm not falling for that trap." Jordy rolled his eyes. "You're fine. There's girls three times your size."

"Yeah, but I bet the girls you've actually kissed are half my size."

Jordy hesitated, tapping his fingers. "Isabel is a mistake I've made more than once, but I honestly don't stay attracted for long to the half-starved girls with ugly going on in between their ears. And there was one not in that mold. Her name had this funny sound at the end, so I shortened it to Vera. She was overweight and she told me by how much. She knew who she was; that was all that mattered. You can't help but like a girl like Vera."

Cara asked, "What happened to her?"

Jordy's expression darkened. "Her dad transferred to LA."

Susanna winced. "Don't you hate it when friends move away?"

"I bounce back fast." Jordy shrugged.

Cara giggled and loudly sung the chorus of "Hakuna Matata."

Susanna groaned. Really, sometimes, her sister could be such a child.

Jordy laughed. "Please, I've had enough of that silly song. Brandt and I were forced to watch *The Lion King* with his little sisters like a dozen times. Whenever he'd get stuck at home, babysitting, he'd con me into coming over and helping." Jordy cleared his throat. "What time is it?"

Good question. Susanna peered at her watch. "Quarter after eight. Cara and I have to meet our parents."

Jordy stood and brushed himself off. Susanna and Cara stood, too.

He stepped close to Susanna and held her gaze. "I have to find my mom, but maybe I'll see you around sometime." He turned and headed toward the amphitheater, but glanced over his shoulder as if he didn't want to go.

"Bye." Susanna swallowed a strange catch in her throat.

Cara cooed, "Miss him already?"

"No." Susanna simply couldn't break her eyes from Jordy's slow retreat.

Cara folded her arms. "Mm-hmm."

JORDY HEADED TOWARD the amphitheater, forcing his feet to keep going in the right direction. Why did he promise his mom to go to this stupid concert? He glanced over his shoulder, but ripped himself back around toward the amphitheater. *Man, just forget about it.*

Would it really hurt his mom to wait another five minutes?

Oh, heck. He spun around and let his feet go where they wanted.

Sue-Ann met him halfway, clutching the violet teddy bear close to her chest. "Did you forget something?"

"Uh . . . yeah, there was something I wanted to say, but for the life of me, I can't remember what." His cheeks flamed. Man, that had to be the lamest thing he had ever said.

Her sister snorted. "Cut it out you two before I gag. Why don't we just walk over together?"

Sue-Ann sent her a blank stare. "I don't know. I guess we could."

"Sure, if we're all going there anyway." Jordy tried to ignore the rising hope his mom and Sue-Ann's folks would be late or indisposed.

Her sister tapped her foot. "Then let's go already. I like Wynona, too."

"Actually," Jordy admitted, "I haven't the faintest idea who she is, except that she's some country singer my mom likes."

"That's something, isn't it?" Sue-Ann asked.

"I guess so." Jordy caught her gaze. Why couldn't he tear himself away from the evergreen fire in her eyes?

Her sister pointed toward the amphitheater. "There's our mom and dad! We gotta go!" She grabbed Sue-Ann by the arm and dragged her away.

Sue-Ann sent one last glance back. She looked torn between not letting her sister boss her around and not admitting she didn't want to leave him.

The crowd absorbed her into itself.

Odd, why did he feel lonely? He shook his head. What was happening?

Yesterday, Sue-Ann couldn't stand him. And today?

His mom ran up. "There you are! Well, let's go to the concert."

He nodded and followed her to the line outside the amphitheater. One thing was certain. A whole lot more was different about Sue-Ann today than just her grooming. She'd cleaned up as well as he'd suspected she would and then some, but could it really have that big an impact on her behavior?

Part of it surely had a lot to do with the discovery the girl was running around half-blind. That made her impervious to winning at pool and to his charm. After he'd learned to stand where she could see him, they had fewer misunderstandings and seemed to enjoy each other's company.

Jordy's mom handed him a concert ticket. "Come on."

He followed his mom to their seats and blinked as a woman's beautiful alto singing voice filled his ears. Not bad, for country. Though he'd rather not listen to any more of a song about how her ex-husband had broken her heart. He'd almost prefer more of Mufasa nagging him to "remember who you are."

He scanned the crowd for Sue-Ann but sighed. Wasn't running into her four times enough? He'd been shocked enough in the parking lot just by the transformation of her frizzy, ratty ponytail into gorgeous loose curls that fell halfway down her back.

But, the real change didn't come until he teased coaster girl for freaking out on the pirate ship, not to mention how she ran away at lunch. That still made no sense. She didn't mind him cornering her by Smokey. It didn't take much embarrassing arm-twisting to get her to stay, albeit she did sit as far away as she could without sitting on another bench.

A little girl wearing glasses and doing the 'I have to pee' dance squeezed past his knees.

He sat up straighter and almost laughed out loud. Women. So that's why Sue-Ann sat so far away, that odd phobia of looking at him. Now, that was a new one. Maybe it really was fear behind Sue-Ann's ill treatment of him.

Still, it was strange and overwhelming, the desire to really be seen by her in the moment he made her face him—a moment her parents had ruined, by accident. Mrs. McCoy struck him as a good woman under significant stress due to whatever was off with Mr. McCoy. It'd been a relief when Sue-Ann's cool mom had noticed they'd interrupted and sent her daughter off with him, though it would've been nice to have ditched the pesky kid sister.

Shame Christine wasn't there. She would have grabbed Sue-Ann's sister and split, sending a knowing wink at him. Jordy sucked in a breath to hold back the tears threatening. Enough self-torture. Christine wasn't there and she couldn't ever be there.

Jordy's mom put a hand on his shoulder. "Son? Are you okay?"

He glanced at her. "Uh . . . yeah. I'm fine."

"Then why do you look ready to cry?"

He swallowed and listened to a few strains of the current number. This tear-jerker was evocative of Christine. "It's just this song."

His mom side-hugged him. "I cried the first time I heard it, too."

The emotionally manipulative concert faded out of focus as Sue-Ann's smiling cat-green eyes rose. Funny. When she wasn't biting his head off, she was rather nice. She was at least half what Gramps said of her. In fact, the old goat had her pinned down. Once she understood he wished her no ill will, her attitude toward him had instantly improved.

Despite his missteps, he did get through to her today. She could see him now, like she couldn't see before. Still, he hoped she didn't look too close—or she'd send him right back to square one.

Chapter 8

JORDY RUBBED SLEEP sand from his eyes after he'd wandered down into Gramps' country kitchen. A rooster wall-clock said it was already past one in the afternoon. His father sat at the table, hunched over the local newspaper.

Jordan looked up. "Look who finally dragged himself out of bed today! Have a nice night?"

Sure, until it took him forever to get to sleep after getting home from the Ohio State Fair. Jordy grunted and dropped into a chair at the table. "Give me a cup of coffee. Black, two sugar servings."

"I figured you'd want something when you woke." His father grabbed an insulated coffee mug off the counter and slid it to him.

Braced for a bitter drink, Jordy sipped it, grimaced at the sweetness, and glared at his father. "This is a cold mocha without any coffee in it!"

His father chuckled. "You think I'd give a sixteen-year-old coffee?"

And who gave Jordan the right to decide whether he was old enough for coffee or not? "Sixteen-year-olds drink coffee in Chicago all the time."

"We're not in Chicago. This is Ohio. And in Ohio youse littl'uns don't a drink cough-ee."

Jordy laughed despite himself. "If that is supposed to be an Ohio accent, that's how Pa Ingles would talk, if he'd been from Chicago." Jordy mocked how his dad had always said "Chicago," with slight exaggeration.

Jordan asked, "Is that what I sound like to you?"

"That's how everybody over thirty sounded, on our side of Chicago."

"Oh, and you don't?"

"Nah, this is the MTV age. Most kids just sound fast and sloppy, like we don't have time to enunciate."

Jordan pursed his lips. "Son, you are aware we're not from Chicagoland? My old job took us there, albeit before you were born."

"Oh, right. You and Mom grew up around here. I forgot."

"So, then, smarty pants, what do central Ohioans sound like?"

"Fast and sloppy."

His father raised an eyebrow. "Oh really? Out here in the cornfields?"

Mostly cornfields, woods, and quaint little towns lay between here and the Columbus beltway. Jordy ducked his head. "Yeah, Sue-Ann got me good. She knew what I'd expect a country kid to sound like, so she gave it to me. Probably intended it as a not-so-funny joke."

His father shook his head. "Do you know where she lives?"

"South from here, about half an hour away."

His father snorted. "Geography wasn't your best subject, I take it? Were you asleep on our drive up here from the airport?"

"No, what's your point?"

His father stood. "I've got to get back to work. Your mom left food in the microwave."

"Where is Mom, anyway?"

"Columbus, you know, the state capital twenty miles south of us."

Hey. Jordy glowered. "I'm not stupid. I'm sure more than Columbus is to the south and thirty minutes away from here. If not, it's only the state capitol. It's not like she's from Cleveland."

"Oh, is that how it is? Ohio is just like Illinois? The capitol is a mid-sized city, and the major urban center is on the lake?" His father chuckled and left.

Jordy rolled his eyes. "Whatever, Jordan."

SUSANNA GRIMACED, SQUIRMING in the black torture seat by all the medical devices for testing her eyesight. On the peachy linoleum counter, Dr. Martin wrote out Sue-Ann's death sentence. Her eye doctor handed her prescription to her mother. "I included instructions for the technicians to put a rush on the order so her glasses will be in before school starts."

Dr. Martin turned and shook a finger at her. "In the meantime, no more reading and watching TV without your glasses, young lady. And take it easy on the aspirin, kiddo. Addictions to sleep aren't nearly as painful."

Susanna followed her mother out of the exam room. Her shuffling steps slowed the closer she got to the optical center.

Her mom glanced back and frowned. "Hurry it up, Susanna. You know how your dad is. Fool around and he'll come in and pick a frame out for you."

Susanna shuddered. Her dad always chose the clownish plastic frames. She'd better risk asking an attendant for help finding stylish wire frames that would suit her face. She all but ran the rest of the way.

AT THE BUZZING OVEN timer, Susanna set her book down on the lime green kitchen counter beside her slate blue oven mitts. She pushed herself up from the wooden chair she'd dragged in from the adjacent dining room. She put on her oven mitts, opened the steaming oven, and removed the last batch of the chocolate chip cookies to the turned-off gas burners on the stovetop.

"What smells good, dear?" Her dad padded in via their dining room and blinked at her. "Oh, it's you, Susie Q. I thought it was your mother."

Susanna took the last batch out and set the cookie pan on the stove top.

Her dad stole a cookie from the basket on the counter and took a trial bite. "Not too bad. Clean this mess up." He grabbed three more cookies and took them with him back to the living room.

After doing dishes and wiping down the counters and the stove, Susanna added the last batch to the cookies' straw basket and poured milk into a blue mug. She selected three cookies from their basket and carried them and her milk down the hall on the right. She stopped on the floor's furnace vent just outside of her room, facing it. Her parents' room was on her right. The spiral phone cord stretched across the hall from the rotary dial phone on the wall behind her and by the bathroom. The stretched cord led into her bedroom.

Cara sat upon the bottom half of their bunk bed, her left ear glued to the phone receiver at the end of its long cord. "Whatever! Can you believe they'd, like, so totally ignore me?" Cara fell silent for a moment. "I know! How could she hog all of his attention like that? Like she has anything I don't! As if!"

Spoken by a girl who once ditched me at the movies for a guy. Susanna ducked under the cord, set her cookies and milk down upon her own dresser, and threw off it Cara's lacy white bra. Her sister's clothes and trash lay tossed all around. The baby blue walls bore tacked-up souvenir pendants and askew white sheets. The latter poorly covered the holes in the old plaster. Cara had finally outgrown starting such roughhousing, only to take up doodling on the walls, the door, and the furniture with loud nail polish.

Why can't I have anything of my own? Susanna cleared her throat.

Cara looked up. "Oh, thanks. No, not you, Yoli, my sister. Can you bring them over here, Sis?"

"That is *my* bed," Susanna said through clenched teeth. She glowered.

Cara rolled her eyes. "Duh, like the phone cord will reach all the way to the top bunk."

"Still, you could've asked me first."

"You weren't around. Can I have my cookies or what?"

"These are mine. Go get your own."

"Fine, be that way." Cara turned back to the phone. "My sister is being selfish, so I'll talk to you later, Yoli. Bye." Cara got up and left the room.

Breathe. Susanna sucked in dusty air, moved her mug and the cookies over to their night stand, and climbed into her bed on the bottom bunk.

After finishing her cookies, she rested her aching eyes. Images from the fair swirled before her, with guess-who hogging most of the shots. Err. Why did Jordy have to go and change on her? Still, she couldn't dare risk going bonkers over City Boy. His rejection would hurt too much.

ON THE WAY UP TO GLENSHIRE the next morning, Susanna sat back in the red captain's chair behind her mom's front passenger seat, beside her sister's seat behind their dad's driver's seat. Ginger leaned against Susanna's left leg as the dog lay unrestrained in the aisle. Missy's soft fur brushed Susanna's head as the cat held on for dear life to Susanna's headrest.

Susanna's sister leaned toward their Mom. "Will we go to the barbecue?"

"What barbecue?" Susanna asked.

Cara groaned. "That's right. You were asleep when Marissa asked us."

Susanna shot her sister an annoyed look. "Who?"

"The woman who bought the house across the alley. I met her yesterday. Her family is moving here next week, and she's getting the place ready. She invited us and our other neighbors over for a barbecue in her backyard next Wednesday after school."

"Is it a potluck?"

Cara shook her head. "No. She's making everything."

"It's a house warming," their mom said. "We'd have to bring a gift."

"So?" Cara folded her arms. "It's not like we're poor."

"We're not made of money, either," their dad said. "Not like the Durants. They've got plenty, why do they keep raising the prices every year?"

At school, Susanna would ask what the Durants had to do with anything. At home, conversations lacking logical flow were normal and questioning the shift was rude. Susanna shrugged. "Inflation affects everyone. When Phill's prices go up, so do ours. I doubt he consults his whole family on that. It's just Phill compensating for his increasing expenses."

"We can't afford a lot of extras, Susie Q."

Her mom shook her head. "Oh, we can afford a little something, Elliot. Can't we at least try to be a little social every once in a while?"

Dad just grunted.

Susanna put her seat all the way back and turned over on her side. She was being contrary, definitely not defending Jordy. Though, she still had no idea what the new neighbors had to do with the Durants.

SUSANNA EXITED HER trailer and headed for the van still half-packed. Her sister was inside it, dallying.

Her dad turned in his wooden deck chair and pointed up to the loop of Road C with his beverage's foam OSU can holder. "Isn't that the boy from the fair in Phill's truck?"

Through the trees, Susanna spied the fuzzy, red and white pick-up. That did look like Phill's 1979 F150, but the blurry driver could be anyone.

Cara pulled a bag of clothes out of the van and turned to glance toward the approaching truck. "Yep. It's Jordy."

The privileged prince was back. Susanna wrinkled her nose. "Doesn't he know you have to be eighteen before Phill will let you drive in here?"

"You wanna tell him that?" Her dad sipped his drink. "Be my guest."

Her stomach fluttered. She took a deep breath. No point in hiding from Jordy now. Sue-Ann jogged out to meet the truck. "Hey, City Boy!"

The truck stopped. The driver twisted toward his open window. Jordy called back, "Yeah, Miss Country?"

This would go easier if she could see him. She leaned into his window and rested her right hand on the sill. "Do you know that His Royal Highness, King Phill, has banned minors from driving in the Kingdom of Glenshire?"

Jordy laughed. "Yeah, so? What's Gramps going to do? Kick me out?"

Cute. Not. What was with this guy? "How'd you get past him?"

Jordy donned a tough-guy face that didn't reach his amused eyes. "You know inner city kids. Hot-wiring cars is second nature."

Play along. She faked a gasp. "Jordy!"

He grinned with an unfamiliar twinkle in his eyes. "Yeah, well, seriously, Gramps can refuse to ever trust me with his keys again for this. But I'm not above stealing car keys, if I get bored enough, and I'm keeping my gate pass. So maybe I'll take you for a joy ride some time."

That sounded as dangerous as the way he was looking at her felt in her gut. She raised her eyebrows, doing her best to hold back the smile twitching at the corner of her mouth. "What makes you think I would go?"

His smile managed to broaden. "What makes you think you won't?"

If weren't impossible, the intensity of his eyes on hers would make her think he was serious. She replied in an overly sweet tone, "Jordy, you could walk through fire for me, and I still wouldn't get in any car with you, let alone a stolen one." Oops. Her own impish smile had slipped out.

"We'll see." Jordy chuckled and took her hand from the truck's window. He hesitated, squeezed her hand once, pushed her back, and drove away.

Susanna stared after him until the trunk disappeared over a hill. Huh. She returned to the porch. Thankfully, her dad had gone inside their trailer.

Cara sat on the bench, staring. "Well, I'll never." Her eyes widened. "Oh! Of course! Why didn't I see it?"

Uh-oh. Susanna narrowed her eyes and joined her sister. "See what?"

"I never thought I'd see you do *that* with a *guy*!"

"Whatever. He's not supposed to drive here. That's all."

"Not. You guys were flirting!"

"Excuse me? You thought . . . ."

Cara furrowed her brows. "You truly had no idea? How could you have missed that he was flirting? You flirted back."

"I did not!" Susanna's cheeks flamed. Her heartbeat sped up. "That's not possible. Guys like Jordy don't—they don't flirt with girls like me."

Cara rolled her eyes. "Susanna! He has been trying to flirt with you since day one. Obviously, guys like him do. But, maybe you could miss it. Jordy is a rather visual flirt. He relies on what Ricky calls charm. A toss of the head, a smile, a movement of the hand all have hidden meaning, but those visual cues can go right past you because of your eyes."

Susanna hesitated. If she hadn't been able to see Jordy, she would have chewed him to pieces for what he said and stormed off in a rage. Instead, the exchange remained pleasant.

"Okay, so, um, fair warning. Jordy was feeling out whether he'd still get shot down, if he asked you out." Her sister's smirk had a cruel feel to it. "And you've cluelessly signaled you're not ready to say yes, but that you'd like him to continue his efforts to hotwire *you* and start *your* cold engine."

No way. Susanna stomped off. Grr. Her sister's allegations were only a vengeful attempt to humiliate her, but what if she had been misinterpreting Jordy's behavior? What if he hadn't changed, what if she'd misread him from the beginning? But why would he ever flirt with her?

What game was he playing here?

JORDY'S STOMACH RUMBLED as he stepped into his grandfather's house. He sniffed at the aroma coming from the kitchen. Pepperoni pizza. Maybe he'd get lucky and everyone else would have eaten.

In the kitchen, his father sat at the table with a clear glass of lemon-lime soda planted on the lid of the opened pizza box. The man held out his half-eaten pizza slice like an olive branch. "Want some?"

Oh well. Jordy sat down at the table and took two slices. "Sure, Jordan. I guess I'm hungry." He wolfed down his first slice. "Where's Mom?"

His father hesitated. "In Columbus. She'll be here in the morning."

"Oh, I guess that's okay."

"So, I heard you ran an errand for Dad in town today."

"Yeah, Gramps finally let me take the truck." And the keycard to get in the front gate had also worked on the gate he'd not been given permission to open and drive past. Jordy flinched. Must he be reminded about the incident with Sue-Ann earlier? He'd tried to forget how badly he'd behaved.

But why the guilt? Isabel was history and, really, what was the harm?

He grimaced. So he would've done that if Isabel were still in the picture. And, if he kept this up, and this went anywhere, he'd choke, like always, and Sue-Ann would end up like all the others. *Thanks, conscience. You're a pal.*

Jordan took a drink from his soda and set the cup down. "What else did you do today? Did you see that girl?"

Why can't you leave me alone tonight? Jordy glowered. "That girl. It's always 'that girl' with you guys. Like they're all the same, one girl just as good as another to me." Wasn't that the point? "Okay, before, it never mattered. Never mind how many times I played the same shell game. A few charming words, and I'd have conned yet another into believing she was special. Then I'd turn around and say the same thing to another, and another, and another, and me never caring who got hurt. My typical target 'deserved it' for taunting 'dweebs' like the boy scout that I once was. But in the end, it caught up with me, and she played my own game on me, with my best bud!"

His father stood and shook him by the shoulders. "Whoa! Son, you need to remember who you are. Nothing can ever change your true identity."

Not reassuring, dude. Jordy pushed away, his hands out. "No, Jordan. Neither of us are who we used to be. But one of these days, I am gonna prove to the world that the rogue I've become can also change for the better. And I'm gonna prove it to myself."

Jordy ran upstairs to his room. He collapsed on his bed and buried his face in his pillow. Bitter tears of defeat stung his eyes. Who was he kidding? Only the evergreen fire in Sue-Ann's eyes reawakened the boy scout in him at all. And the boy scout he'd once been had a tidy time line for his life where "start dating" had been planned to immediately follow "start college."

Before Jordy's world exploded and left the life he'd planned on in ashes.

No excuses. He griped the edge of the bed and took deep breaths to stop his dweeby tears. Sue-Ann was the last person who deserved a broken heart. If nothing else, he had to stop flirting with the poor girl, before she got hurt.

Still, he hoped he'd never have to face the day he had to confess his sins to Sue-Ann. She'd never, ever forgive him.

Chapter 9

SUSANNA LAY ON HER side in bed, facing in her sister's direction, curled up under her well-worn blanket. Two warm lumps lay at her feet. One was the size of her dog. The other felt like her sister's upright back. She peaked an eye open at her watch, but let her eyes droop closed again before she could focus on the digital numbers. What did it matter, on a Friday during her vacation? Why not sleep a little longer?

Her dad asked from her parents' end of the trailer, "So, who wants to go out to breakfast?"

"Sounds good to me, Elliot," her mom replied. "Let's go to Shoneys."

Susanna groaned and turned over as her parents drew their curtain.

"But I want to go swimming!" Cara said.

Susanna sat up. "Why make Mom cook? Let's go."

Cara sighed. "Fine, we can go swimming afterwards."

Susanna glanced at the stonewashed flare jeans and blue T-shirt she'd changed back into after her shower last night. She needed to get dressed but had to wait until her parents got done in the back. To kill time, she scooted up and retrieved her wet comb from the counter next to the kitchen sink. She turned to face the mirror on the bathroom door and pulled her ponytail over her shoulder. Ponytail? Mustang-tail was more like it. This was futile.

Still, she had to try to tame the wild beast. She yanked her scrunchie out and brushed her hair with the wet comb.

Cara tapped Susanna's shoulder. "Sis, it's not like we're going to a party. We're not trying to impress anybody."

"Oh, you never know. Romeo might show up."

"Your Romeo's going to be at the pool. It's already muggy out."

Susanna turned back to the sink and ran the water. She sprinkled it on stubborn frizz for lack of anything else to soothe it. Yeah, still no desire to go swimming. The pool was right outside of the game room that Jordy haunted. Him, seeing her in a bathing suit? She'd surely faint in the pool and drown.

Besides, with her luck, her soul mate, so to speak, was on the other side of the planet. In her imagination, he'd always had light brown hair and eyes bluer than the summer sky. But most importantly, to him, she'd be beautiful. Even when she became old and gray and as heavy as her mother, in his eyes, she'd be beautiful—though no one else would ever think so.

"Sue-Ann?" Cara asked, waving a hand in front of her face.

Susanna shook away the silly fantasy and shut off the water. "I must've dozed again. Romeo's not at the pool, just Jordy and his new buddies. It's sad to see the heir of Phill's heir turning into just another of Boo's cronies."

"Of course, you'll never own this place. I seem to recall that being on your to-do list."

That fantasy was even sillier than her hopes God had someone out there who'd love her. Why did she ever tell Cara anything? She shrugged it off and said playfully, "Oh, I'll think of something."

"Yeah, you and Jordy could—"

"Say it and I'll kill you."

Cara smiled innocently. "Arm wrestle for it."

JORDY FOUND HIS MOM frying pancakes at his grandfather's stove. No one around to see him act dweeby. He grinned and hugged her. "Mom, when did you get in?"

"'Bout an hour ago," his mom replied, letting him go.

He settled in at the kitchen table.

She scooped the last pancake out of the skillet, joined him at the table, and served them both. She bowed her head. "Father, we thank you for this meal. And we thank you for your promises, for we know your Word will not return to you void. We ask you to bless this food and to continue drawing Jordy back to you, Lord. In Jesus' precious name we pray. Amen."

Jordy gritted his teeth and waited until his mom finished her morning guilt trip before he dug into his pancakes. He had to give Jordan some credit, at least he could say grace without harassing him.

His mom studied him a moment. Concern filled her eyes under her knit brows. "What's wrong, son? Does your pallid look have anything to do with your outburst last night?"

Jordy hung his head. "Jordan told you?"

"Yes. I explained what he said wrong. He didn't know. I was afraid to tell him. I knew that he'd take it hard, what our family's grief has done to you. I should've warned him, but I didn't realize you're going through . . . changes. If you'd like to talk—"

"I don't!" Jordy took a breath. "Sorry, I haven't slept well in two days."

"Don't be afraid to change your mind."

"Okay." He resumed eating his breakfast. His mother had to be the last person he'd ever discuss girl trouble with. Three years ago, he'd have gone to his dad. Venting to Jordan had still been an instinctive way to cope with his painful emotions boiling over. So stupid. His dad would be ashamed of him, if his dad hadn't shamed himself. Jordan was a stranger with Dad's face, one who wouldn't care enough to do anything about Jordy's "acting out."

He'd better not try, either.

Between bites of pancake, his mom said, "Anyway, I would appreciate it if you'd stop calling your dad by his first name. It's time to gather together what we have left and be a family again. I know you blame him for our losses. Please understand—he blames himself, too. That's why he fell apart. At first, your dad threw himself into his work, trying to escape from the pain. Then, he would blow most of his salary drinking and gambling."

Gambling? Jordy's eyes widened. The dad he knew and loved refused to ever touch anything used for gambling, even when bets weren't on the table. Just as his dad would've never drank so much as a drop of alcohol.

A faraway look entered his mom's eyes. "We couldn't pay the mortgage, so I sold the house and went to work myself. And we all needed counseling, his behavior was deteriorating, and I got so mad, I threw your dad out—"

"You what!" His Southern Baptist, submissive stay-at-home-mother had kicked to the curb the head of the house?

His mom hung her head briefly before raising her chin. "My counselor said I had to stop enabling him, if I wanted any hope I wouldn't forever lose him and you also. And his drunken behavior *was* so bad that he got himself fired by his secular employer."

"I remember. That was right before our family moved, and Jordan and his stuff never made it to our apartment."

She bit her lip. "Your dad's sin cost him everything he had left all on the same day, yes, son. You don't know how fortunate we are. Your grandfather tracked your dad down and brought him home, cleaned him up, and restored the inheritance he'd spurned. Phill also required your dad to get the help he needed to recover and to process our original loss. And that has led to him reconciling with me. If it weren't for Phill, we'd still be stuck in that dinky apartment, all by ourselves. And thank him for your school clothes, and the therapy, and plenty of our other bills that he's paid over the last three years."

Tears threatened. Jordy winced. Therapy was the unpleasant hour of the week where his psychologist had called him out for his "masks" and tried to get him to talk to her as the grieving former boy scout she said he truly was.

The evergreen fire in Sue-Ann's eyes somehow still saw the boy scout.

"Son, stop fighting," Mom crooned tenderly. She rose, met him where he was, and knelt on the floor beside him. "Please. Come back to us."

Him giving in to his grief supposedly would save him, not just humiliate him. His shoulders heaved. "Why, Mom, why? I was so sick—if only Dad had kept his promise—I wasn't there! I should've been there! I heard you, Mom, when you thanked God that I didn't see it. For two years, I have seen it. I still see it in a recurring nightmare."

Jordy surrendered to his total humiliation and let his mother hold her overgrown baby. He sobbed like Christine had died only yesterday, not three years ago. Her golden curls, round face, and cat-green eyes haunted him still.

"I'LL TELL YOU WHAT," Jordy's mom said after the embarrassing tears finally stopped. "Why don't we change into our swimsuits and go for a dip in the pool and cool off a bit?"

Jordy smiled weakly. "Okay, Mom."

He jogged out, heading up to his room. His mom wore shapeless swim-dresses, but it could be far worse. Like bikini-worse. It was so uncomfortable when Brandt's curvy, young mom had worn one of those.

On the way to the pool, Jordy entered the office with his towel draped from his arm. He wore his regular shirt over his knee-length navy swimming trunks. Slightly ahead of him, his mom's towel swung over the tank-top-style sleeve of her very-mother-like blue floral swim dress.

Gramps stood behind the counter and lifted his hand in greeting. "Goin' for a swim?"

Jordy's mom nodded. "Yes."

"How's the house coming?"

"It's finished. It was fun. I liked interior decorating. Now that Jordan's back and Jordy's older, I'm considering going back and finishing my degree."

Jordy raised his eyebrows. "You went to college, Mom?"

She glanced back at him. "Yes, for three years. Your dad finished school and had an offer for his dream job in Chicago. So, I did the only reasonable thing for a girl to do in the seventies. I quit school and followed him."

Jordy shifted. Why did it feel like his fault?

His mom smiled. "I wasn't worried about any yet-to-be children when I moved to Chicago with my husband."

Gramps cleared his throat and addressed Mom. "Sweetie, I'm so grateful that you, Jordan, and JJ have all come home now, though I do wish it wasn't under tragic circumstances. I would have liked to—" Gramps caught Jordy's glaring eye and halted. "Well, she must have been something."

More like everything; her death shattered everything. Jordy's hand flew to the sapphire ring dangling over his heart. This better not be all he had left of her. "Mom, what happened to . . . ." If the guys walked in and overheard him asking about Christine's things, they'd so get the wrong idea. "You didn't leave anything of mine in Chicago, did you?" Oh man, that was still lame.

Mom smiled. "Sweetheart, the rest of your belongings are all at the new house, including the items you're too embarrassed to ask about. I can't wait until you see what I've done to your room. You're gonna love it."

He'd love it if she'd put everything where it went. "I'm sure it'll be fine."

"Thanks. Let's hit the water." She ran out the swimming pool exit.

Jordy waited a moment. He pulled the chain hiding under his shirt over his head and laid it on the counter before Gramps. "Could you hold onto this for me? I don't want to risk it getting damaged or lost in the pool."

"I will guard it with my life." Gramps caressed the chain's girly sapphire ring, set with diamond chips, like he understood Jordy's secret. "I'm sorry."

"Me too. Thank you." Jordy headed out of the pool exit. Nearby it on the concrete, he dropped his towel and his gym shoes beside his mother's stuff.

He removed his shirt and joined his mom in the otherwise deserted pool, where they mostly swam laps at an arm's length from each other. He won.

From above, Boo called, "Whad'ya know, Jordy's a momma's boy!"

Ha, ha. Jordy glared up at three of the guys. Boo, Ty, and Greg were all diving into the pool's deep end. Jordy smirked. He'd show them a momma's boy. He sneaked back behind his mom and dunked her.

She came up with a gasp. "Dunk your poor, old Mom, huh?"

Laughing it off, she shoved him under by the shoulders right back.

Holding his breath, he circled around underwater and came up for air a little ways off. He smirked at his mom. "Thanks for returning my favor."

"Dude, we were just fooling." Boo threw a football, saying, "Catch!".

The football hurled toward Jordy's face. He caught it first and threw it to Ty. From the office's window, Jordan caught Jordy's eye and shook his head, sending him the look that his dad used to always give him for disrespecting his mom in any manner. Jordy scowled and turned away.

"I think I'll get out and work on my tan," Jordy's mom said.

Jordy gritted his teeth. What a joke. His mother wore enough sun block for two people. She was putting dentures into Jordan's toothless bark. "You don't have to do that, Mom."

"Play with your friends, Jordy." She headed for the steps.

Jordy shrugged. Giving herself a time-out was how she typically handled his disrespectful mouth, but perhaps this time it was also her being kind. He would rather go play with the guys, teasing and all.

He swam after them, stopped to catch the football Ty threw at him, and tossed it back.

An hour later, the other guys dried off and headed in the office via the game room in search of food. Jordy practiced his backstroke in the deep end.

"Hey, Jordy!" Greg had stuck his head back out of the door to the game room. "Aren't you coming?"

Jordy swam to the edge. "Nah, I'll catch you later. I'm not hungry."

From behind Greg, Ty shouted, "If you feel like creaming us again later, we'll be shooting pool."

"Yeah, note to self:" Greg wrote across an imaginary blackboard. "Never make pool bets against guys from Chicago."

Boo peered back out also and snickered. "I know why he's staying. His girlfriend's coming in the pool's back gate."

Sue-Ann? Jordy resisted the urge to look toward the gate by the pool's outbuilding at the far end of the lawn. That would only encourage him. "You must have me confused with someone else. I don't have a girlfriend."

He took a deep breath, faced the put-put course, and dove underwater. He twisted to his left, swam down to the deepest part of the pool to touch the bottom, and swam out to the rope. It divided the deep end from the shallow end. He came up for air and found his footing on the edge of the five-foot level. The guys had stopped crowding the game room's door.

Sue-Ann and her sister wore gym shorts over their one-piece swimsuits. They were putting down their towels in the middle of the strip of lawn along the side of the pool facing the empty steel playground.

Jordy glanced at his mom, up nearby the door to the office's store. She looked asleep, but he couldn't be certain of it with her back turned to them.

He twisted back toward the McCoy sisters as Sue-Ann slid her shorts off. Her bright green, skirted swimsuit flattered her curves. And from this angle the view was, er, most interesting. His face warmed. Uh-huh. His weird body would find her proportions so appealing at any pants size.

He swallowed. *Dude, stop it. This so isn't cool.*

She took off her scrunchie and her watch and stuffed both items into her gym shoes along with her socks. She hesitated as if forgetting something then glanced in his direction and froze solid.

Why couldn't he look away when he knew he should? He bit his lip. Her true beauty made the state of neglect he'd found her in tragic. Though, since the fair, she'd traded in the disheveled look and had discovered where she put the rest of her wardrobe. She still mostly lived in the ponytail she'd taken down, but she could pull off a grandma bun, with her gorgeous mane.

Her sister jumped feet first into the deep end. The splash hit Jordy like a much-needed cold shower. Her sister surfaced fifteen feet away and started treading water.

Sue-Ann headed for the steps.

Her sister called, "Oh, Sis, just jump in."

"Is it cold?" Sue-Ann asked suspiciously.

"Nope."

Should he tell Sue-Ann she had a liar for a sister?

Sue-Ann shrugged and jumped in. She came up squealing. "Cold! You little twit!" She dunked her sister.

"Hey!" Her sister squealed and splashed her.

The girls engaged in a splash war. Jordy resisted the temptation to join them and instead resumed practicing his backstroke.

Sometime later, Sue-Ann's sister said, "Let's race."

"Why?" Sue-Ann said. "I *always* win."

In the water was implied. Jordy stopped mid-stroke and stood. Always wins, huh? Maybe he'd change that. And have a little fun in the process.

Her sister lifted her chin. "Maybe today will be different."

Sue-Ann shrugged. "If you insist." The girls lined up. Sue-Ann pressed her left foot against the wall, favoring her right foot. "Okay. Ready, set—"

She pushed off and propelled away from the wall.

"Go!" her sister shouted at the same time and took off.

So her sister knew about that trick. Jordy sucked in a breath then dived underwater and swam out to the middle of the deep end.

As Sue-Ann swam over him, he grabbed her right ankle and pulled her under. He dashed to the rope and surfaced. She burst up gasping, her twisted face red with fury. She spotted him and her eyes narrowed. Unable to resist, he sent her his guilty-as-charged smile and waved.

Sue-Ann took off after him like a shark out for blood.

Uh-oh. Jordy shot off at full speed but couldn't shake her hard pursuit of him. His lungs burned. He stopped in the deep end to catch his breath and instead got a mouthful of chlorinated water before it registered that dainty hands had grabbed his shoulders and shoved his head underwater. He burst back up through the surface gagging.

Sue-Ann stood above him next to the wall, grinning triumphantly. He crossed the few feet separating them, found his footing on the ledge, and put her back where she belonged—shorter than him.

"No one dunks me and gets away with it." She folded her arms. "That wasn't cool, City Boy. We don't play that way here."

"Noted, thanks. If it makes you feel any better, no one's ever gotten me before." No one who wasn't related to him, anyway.

Her arms slipped out of the folded position and into the water. "That was mean, but it was clever."

The anger had melted from her voice as well as her posture. Jordy let out a relieved breath. "Where did you learn to push off the wall like that? I've never seen it done that way before."

She shrugged. "I don't remember. Cara does it, too, so who knows?"

"Not left-footed, she didn't."

"Oh. That." Sue-Ann twirled the water. "I broke my right ankle in June while roller skating. I just recently got out of a cast and off of crutches."

Whoa. Jordy's eyes widened. He'd hurt her. "I'm so sorry. I had no idea."

"It's okay."

No, it wasn't. Ignorance didn't make his low blow okay. But he'd been a hypocritical dweeb enough. "Um, so where did you learn to swim? At the Y?"

"My mom taught us. She also taught my dad. He'd almost drowned as a kid. Mom couldn't believe he didn't know how to swim."

"That's interesting."

She blushed. "Right, I'm rambling, sorry."

Huh? He was the dweeb asking lame questions. "You're fine."

"Not. I must sound so pathetic."

"Really, you're fine when you're not biting my head off."

She winced. "Oh, that. Sorry, sometimes I have trouble trusting people. Besides, I have a feeling we've misunderstood each other."

"It'd explain a lot." He hesitated. Why did he feel this strange yearning to spill his guts? She'd just end up telling her sister, who'd tell everyone.

The urging insisted even louder, *Tell her!*

"Maybe you do have trouble trusting people," he said slowly, "but you're smart not to trust me. I am a bit of a flirt."

That inner voice nagged him. *A bit?*

He groaned. "All right, so I'm a huge flirt. Conscience, please shut up."

"And—and now?" she stammered. "What about now?"

His gut said that she truly wanted to ask whether his interest in her was genuine. Dweeby butterflies fluttered in his stomach. He focused on the lock of wet hair dangling in her beautiful green eyes, begging him to brush it aside and—no. He wet his lips and shrugged. "So, um, yeah, you are getting called my girlfriend here over my bad of engaging in the behavior that got me far more accurately called Sir Flirtalot in Chicago."

A smile tugged at Sue-Ann's lips. "Are you any relation to Sir Lancelot?"

"I sure hope not. He was plain stupid. There was an entire kingdom of women, why did he choose the queen?"

"Does one really choose who they love?"

Must she tempt him to repeat his dad's long, complex answer word-for-word, like he would've at thirteen? He studied the hair dangling in her eyes. The urge to brush it aside talked loudly.

What had the question been, again?

Sue-Ann's gaze strayed downward. She sucked in a breath, looked away, and then stirred the water. A flush creeped over her.

Jordy held back his grin. So she *did* notice how puberty had so kindly helped this recovering dweeb pull off his shell game as Sir Flirtalot.

Sighing, she looked back up but not quite at him. "Cara tried to tell me you were, you know, but I didn't want to hear it. Guys like you don't, you know, don't do that sort of thing with girls like me."

What did that mean? Jordy eyed that hair in her eyes. Was he suppose to snob her? Why? All her teasing—for whatever reason, she truly saw him as someone above her socially. "From two different worlds."

"Yeah," Sue-Ann said weakly.

Jordy gave in and brushed the hair from her face. His stomach tightened as his lips neared hers. At the last second, he forced himself to turn aside and whispered in her ear, "Things aren't always what they seem."

He pulled back. Her wide eyes captured him with a gaze that could stop time. His heart thundered in his ears and his stomach tied itself in knots as he resisted the temptation to try again. No, he'd promised.

Dude, the shock on her face also knew what he'd almost done.

"I have to go," she squeaked out before she spun and fled.

Jordy dropped below the surface of the pool and tapped his head against the cool metallic surface. *What did you think you were doing?*

Chapter 10

JORDY WORE HIS CHAIN hidden under his shirt as he leaned over the pool table, about to win another game for his team. "Eight ball, side pocket."

Gramps came in. "Jordy, your mom called. She has dinner ready."

Jordy sighed and handed his pool stick to Boo. "Here, take my shot. I have to go."

Boo nodded. "Sure. See you around, Chicago."

Jordy let the rib pass and headed out. He stopped short in the store. Gramps had gone back to the cash register. "Aren't you coming?"

Gramps shook his head. "I'll just eat here. Go on."

At Gramps', Jordy halted in the dining room doorway. His jaw dropped. What? Both of his parents? Worse, his mom looked like she'd prefer sitting in Jordan's lap. "He's eating with us?"

His mom frowned. "Of course."

"You've managed okay so far, son," his father said quietly. "It shouldn't be any different with your mom here."

Jordy jerked his chair out and flopped in it. He went to serve himself.

His mom held out her hand. "You're forgetting something, Jordy."

Was she daft? He narrowed his eyes at her. "Don't even think about it."

She took his father's hand and then grabbed his. "We're a family and we're going to do this as a family. Now grow up and take . . ."

"Marissa . . ." Jordan started.

Jordy jerked his hand out of his mom's grasp. "No."

His mom scowled. "We talked about this, Jordy."

Jordy stood. How could she be so cruel? "You want to be a family, Mom? Have a nice, old-fashioned family dinner? Fine. Let Christine hold his hand."

He fled up to his room then flung himself face down on the bed. For the second time that day, tears stung his humiliated cheeks. He brushed at them, but they wouldn't stop this time. What was she thinking? How could his own mother do that to him? How could she possibly not understand?

Later, his father came in and put his hands behind his back. "Jordy—"

"Go away, Jordan. I don't need you."

His father held up his pleading hand. "I know, I know. You hate my guts, and I might as well be dead, too, but I need to talk to you. You don't have to say anything, just listen."

Jordy sighed then reluctantly sat up.

His father swallowed. "I'm sorry that your sister died. I'm sorry I haven't been there for you. And I'm sorry I didn't anticipate and prevent that scene downstairs. Your mom didn't mean to hurt you, son. She just wants things to be the way they used to be again so bad, she pushed you too hard. I'm sorry. I've talked to her, and it won't happen again."

"Are you done?" Jordy asked coldly.

His father flinched. "Yes."

Jordy stood. "Then let me say something. Mom said she told you about me, and you're sorry, all right. You can just keep on being sorry. You killed Christine, and you killed her brother, too. He's as dead as his precious daddy. Take a good look at me, Jordan. Take a good look, 'cause I am just like you. Not a faithful bone between us."

His father crossed the room and stared Jordy in the eye. "No one knows better than me just how hard Jordan Durant fell. I fell, and I fell harder than you will ever know. But there is one important difference between you and I, son. I got back up."

Jordy shoved past his father, ran down the stairs and out the front door. He slammed it behind him.

He had a date with a cue ball with Jordan's face on it.

SUSANNA STRADDLED THE fallen oak tree down in the ravine.

Cara walked up the oak to where branches split off of the trunk, turned around, and headed back down toward the roots. "Sue-Ann, what's up with you and Jordy? Don't lie. I know something's going on. If I thought you were acting weird before, you two are really acting bizarre now."

Jordy's last stunt in the pool flooded back in a flush. Breath catching, she leaned forward as she pressed her hands hard into the tree's bark. He'd left her feeling like Medusa, turned to stone by the sight of her own reflection in his sapphire eyes. She bit her lip. What had Cara seen? "I've just realized he's a real person with feelings and problems and all that."

Cara sat side-saddle, facing Susanna. "You guys look weird because I've never seen you so friendly with a guy. Or anyone, you're usually so reserved. Or do you become a whole different person at school?"

Susanna shook her head. "Nah, the guys at school are all too immature. I'd never dream of crushing on someone I had to go to class with everyday. I've always had this picture of Mr. Perfect in my head, and none of the guys I knew even got in the ballpark."

"And Jordy? How does he fit in?"

Good question. Susanna slapped her hands up. "Oh, I don't know! I used to. I used to be so sure. He was just another jerk who'd only hang around if he had to. So I kept him out at arm's length. If anybody got hurt, it wouldn't be me. This is my turf. He was one of them. He had no right to be here."

Cara rolled her eyes. "Hello! His grandpa owns this land. His rights here will stand long after ours expire."

"It wasn't about that. To me, he represented the world back home. I'll never have any place in that world. I'll always be just a passerby, there today, gone tomorrow, never mattering." Susanna pressed her hands back into the bark of the fallen oak as she straddled it. "I couldn't let him take this world from me, too. So I reinvented Sue-Ann. Only Jordy didn't belong here, but he doesn't come from my world at all. His world was separate from mine. Until now. Now, it's like we're entangling, and I'm struggling to untangle us."

Cara put out her hands. "Slow down, you've got me confused. I thought you said he represented the city?"

Susanna closed her eyes and drew in a long breath of fresh, woodsy air. She released her breath slowly, focusing upon the texture of the fallen oak's bark to calm the storm within her. She opened her eyes again to meet Cara's gaze. "I was wrong about Jordy, but I still don't want him to meet Susanna. I don't want to be this way with him. At the fair, I don't know what happened."

Not true, she knew. She just didn't know why the hopeless flirt showed her the boy scout, or why that threw her off, too. She sighed. "At the fair, we slipped up and let our guards down. And everything all tumbled together."

Cara rested her hand upon Susanna's shoulder. "Sis, you can't separate yourself from yourself. 'Sue-Ann' is all too willing to take 'Susanna's' hurts out on Jordy, who really didn't do anything to you."

"I know that now. He's human. He's never meant me any harm. Since we've, um, started talking, well—yeah, he's not like the others." She stroked the fallen oak's bark, like she would pet her cat only with both hands, leaning forward as she still straddled the oak refusing to die. "I mean, he and I could almost be fr-friends." She forced the word out.

"Friends, almost?" Cara rolled her eyes. "Oh yeah, 'almost friends' keep getting so focused on each other, you both totally forget I'm even there!"

The hairs on the back of Susanna's neck stood up on end, and the air felt strange. Her stomach knotted. Something was wrong.

"What is it?"

Susanna shushed Cara, switched to sitting side-saddle on the fallen oak, and peered up the trail that headed out of the woods.

A low voice cried, "Hey! Watch the tail, Chicago! That's skin up there."

Sue-Ann yelled, "Jordy, Boo, come on out. Who else is back there?"

Jordy, Boo, Nate, Ricky, Greg and Ty strode down the trail.

The whole gang. Peachy. Five dopes clearly saw her as hilariously weird. Jordy's grin called her "da bomb," as city boys put awesome.

Cara stared openmouthed at Sue-Ann. "How did you know?"

Sue-Ann beamed. "My eyes may not work right, but my ears do."

"How long were you guys up there?" Cara asked the boys warily.

Boo stood in the path as if guarding the exit to a secret tomb. Nate, Greg, and Ty stopped on the bank of the creek, by the boards across it. They shifted impatiently. Thirteen-year-old Ricky climbed up on the tree next to Cara.

Lips pursed, Jordy leaned against the vertical tree roots a few feet from Sue-Ann. "We were there long enough."

Greg snickered.

"Try a minute tops," Ricky murmured into Cara's ear, just loud enough for Sue-Ann to hear him also.

Nate glowered at his younger brother. "Keep yo' mouth shut, kid."

"Yeah," Ty said, "you're spoilin' our fun."

Ricky glowered back at his older brother. "Dude, the McCoy sisters are our oldest friends here. It was wrong to be spying on them to start with!"

"Hey." Greg flicked at him. "Kid, if you're gonna be such a baby, you can go play dollies and tea time with your little girlfriend here and her sister."

Ricky stuck out his tongue. "I'd so take that dare, if Nate goes with, but his for-reals girlfriend would have a huge problem with him and me playing house up here with the McCoy sisters at our ages."

"Enough." Jordy put his hands out. "Settle down, everyone. As a Durant, I believe I have the authority to mediate this dispute."

Sue-Ann snorted and rolled her eyes. Could he get more full of himself?

Jordy swept within a shameless five inches of her face and flashed her a killer grin. "Got a problem with me stepping in?"

Boys. The jerk face's so-not-cool behavior passed for cool with the dopes he was stupidly trying to impress.

Well, two could play at this game. "You don't own this place yet, Jordy, so don't count your chickens. Or do they use that phrase in Chicago?"

Jordy stepped back and glanced over everyone. "Anyway, this *is* a public place. We have as much right to be here as the girls do, and if we were to overhear part of a private conversation, then they shouldn't have a private conversation here in the first place."

"Look," Ricky said, "maybe I am somehow the only guy here who knows the unwritten rules, but around here, folk don't expect other people to spy on us. I always thought this place was safe, myself."

Cara asked, "What were you guys up to, anyway?"

"Not that it's any of your business," Boo said, "but . . . ."

Nate rolled his eyes. "But it *is* the girls' business, if Ricky and I choose to make it so. Cara, we're headed back to our place with the guys so they can try out our new trampoline."

Cara squealed, "Ooh, a trampoline!"

Boo started, "We'd love to invite you girls, but—"

"—But it *is* Nate's trampoline." Jordy folded his arms. "I have decades left before I'll have to decide if I'll truly want to inherit my grandfather's so-called crown." He glanced sideways at Susanna before glaring at Boo. "But it's a good bet you never have, and never will, own this place. So stop acting like you do because it's getting on my nerves. I have news for you, dude. The world's an ocean, and you're a largemouth bass in a goldfish pond."

Boo's fists clenched at his sides. "What did you say?"

"Baby!" At the top of the ravine's steep hillside trail to the campsites in the woods appeared a flaxen-haired teenage girl. She wore a frilled lace slip blouse with a knee-length teal skirt, high heels of all things, and had on so much makeup that she might've still resembled a racoon if Susanna had her glasses. The silly city girl began inching down. "Nate, there you are! I missed you so much, Baby!"

Nate leaped over the creek as he rushed up to her. "You must've missed me, to come. I didn't think you would. Here, let me help you." He put his arm around the girl's tiny waist and escorted her down the hill.

She stopped cold at the creek like a shying unicorn.

Nate crossed the planks over the creek as if showing her it was safe then all but pulled her over to their side of the creek.

The silly city girl eyed her ridiculous shoes and made a noise of disgust at the mud on her heels. Her efforts to get the mud off only made her dirtier.

Puh-leaze. Susanna covered her mouth. Laughing at her was so temping.

Ty whistled. "Dude, do you know how to pick 'em." He punched Nate's shoulder. "Baby." Ty chortled at Nate, and so did Boo, Greg, Ricky, and Cara.

Nate's cheeks flushed crimson. He waved between his girlfriend and the other guys. "Christine, these jokers are . . . ."

At a sharp intake of breath on Sue-Ann's left, she spun to Jordy. He met her gaze half a second with raw pain etched on his face. He pushed past Boo and disappeared up the ravine's trail, headed out of the woods.

Boo stared after Jordy. "That's one weird dude."

A chill crept over Susanna. She'd seen that look on Jordy's face before, when he'd plowed into her and knocked both of them down. He didn't need cruel "normal people" criticizing him for the sensitive soul he sought to hide.

He needed help.

She ran up the trail to the gravel road right behind Crystal's campsite, just outside of the woods, but found it deserted.

No matter. She had a hunch where he was going.

Chapter 11

SUSANNA ROUNDED THE thicket of trees that hugged the lake's bank where its green waters kissed its blue depths. She stopped halfway, at the top of the path down to the rocky beach. Jordy was down there, sure enough. With his knees bent and pulled in toward his abs, he sat upon the grassy mound that once held a mother goose's nest, hiding his face in his hands.

Jordy sobbed.

She continued down to him and accidentally kicked gravel at him.

He stiffened. "Go away, Sue-Ann."

"I'm afraid I can't do that. We really need to talk." Susanna knelt beside him and squeezed his shoulder. "You're good at it, but I have seen past your theater mask, and I know what it's used for, boy scout."

At her admiring tone, through his tears, he flashed her a killer grin. "It's funny how many guys used to hurl that one at me as an insult, intending it to be a synonym for dweeb. See, I am a former boy scout, which in reality puts me among the teenager nearest equivalents of ex-military. If I'm ever not a total dweeb, I have the scouts, in part, to thank for that."

"I believe it." *But I also believe the pain still in your eyes. I'm not letting it go.* "If you're okay now and just need to be alone, I get that. I do think it is okay to protect our hearts and all, but we have to let someone in. And I keep secrets way better than who I stupidly keep trusting."

"Your sister." Another sob shook his strong frame. He hesitated another moment, then buried his head on her shoulder. "I miss mine so much."

"Come. I know a better place for this." She spun and led him halfway up the main path alongside the thicket of trees then took a side path to a fishing spot in the trees. Searching, she found her secret passage to the cozy clearing in the center of the thicket. This spot wasn't suitable for fishing, and this trail was technically nonexistent, so no one would find them here together.

No one ever found her in this secret hiding place.

Jordy followed close. He touched her back. "Are you sure about this?"

Susanna hesitated just outside her secret place, with only one oak tree branch still in their way. Her gut agreed with his inference; her taking him somewhere this special was crossing a major line. And there'd be no return. If they continued, she'd never get untangled from him. She wanted to resist the entanglement but couldn't remember why.

"Yes." She lifted the tree branch out of their way then stepped into the clearing. They sat close beside each other, with her on his left, facing the lake on a rotting tree lying flat on the alive soil slowly growing out of its death.

Jordy covered his tear-stained face. "I'm pathetic. It's been three years and look at me—still blubbering like a baby."

The boy kept fighting his tears. She pulled his hands from his face. "It's okay to cry, Jordy. It'll just keep eating at you inside if you don't."

Leaning in almost too close to her, he asked her lowly, "Are you my new therapist?" He sighed. His tears flowed free. "My sister's name was Christine. And she was a sensible girl who'd have never been so ridiculous."

No wonder. Susanna clicked her tongue. "Older or younger?"

"Younger, by six minutes; we're twins. Fraternal, obviously, though folks did think that we looked alike as tiny tots. We got way too much of 'are you sure your identical twin brother is your fraternal twin sister? Here, I'll pull Chris's pants down, trying to prove you're lying about her not being a boy. Why is she crying like that? She's too little to be that upset over having her privates exposed in front of everyone.' That lead to our fun childhood hobby of going to family therapy." The tears flowed heavier. He sniffled and bit his trembling lip. "I failed her. If it wasn't for me, she would still be alive."

Susanna shook her head. "No, Jordy."

"No, it's true. The day we lost her, I'd been out sick all week with the flu. She had stayed after school to get *my* homework. If I'd gone to school, she wouldn't have stayed after. It was the last day of school before spring break. If she didn't get my work, I'd have to wait a week before I could. I should've gone and got my own work. She was my twin. I should've known."

He swallowed and stared at the ground. "All too frequently, I see it in my dreams. Christine comes out of the school building, carrying our books. She stops to help a teacher with her things. The teacher thanks her and offers her a ride. I beg her to say yes. She says, no thank you, it won't kill her to walk. The teacher says, all right, if she's sure, and heads to go back into the school.

Christine heads for the crosswalk and begins crossing the street. The truck's engine roars as it speeds up. I shout a warning but it's already at the corner and barreling into the intersection, right at her. She freezes from, um, shock. Before she can recover, the truck mows her down—on purpose. The teacher turns back, and we run out to Christine. And . . . I wake up screaming."

Susanna wiped at her misting eyes. *God, I need your help. What's the appropriate response?* She waited, listening to the silence.

On impulse, she took Jordy's left hand and squeezed it gently.

He continued staring at the ground. "The never-identified driver who murdered my sister fled before anyone got a good description of the vehicle or the license plate number. What did get reported was that a muscle truck had sped up to hit her on purpose and that it had a horrifying bumper sticker advertising that either the driver or their kid went to school with us."

"When was this?" she asked.

"The end of seventh grade, seven weeks before our thirteenth birthday. And, yes, our school had students who drove." Jordy grinned crookedly. "We grew up in a town so small, we attended a combined junior and senior high. If you'd asked us where we were from then, we'd have told you we were from Chicago rather than have to explain where exactly we lived in Illinois."

Oh. Face warm, she side-hugged him. "Sorry. I can't imagine—someone killed your sister deliberately, right at your school?"

"Yeah, it shook everyone up that a member of our own community had so violently killed any child in a school zone, let alone the twin battling a list of trauma-induced brain wiring issues that made my much-shorter list look like nothing in comparison. Almost made me glad when we had to move."

Jordy broke down into heaving sobs.

Heart shattering along with his, Susanna drew her arms around him and held him close. He held her tight, too, resting his head on her shoulder as he curled up to her crossways and facing her, the way a young child would cling to his mother. Tears ran in rivers down her cheeks as she rocked him.

After an eternity, Jordy quieted and seemed asleep in the strange peace that so often came over her whenever she had wept here in the silence, alone with God. A sweet surprise, this mystery hugging both of them together. In her imagination, the light of the same eternal fire blazed within both of their hearts and shone all around them.

Jordy pulled away, straightened up, and smiled. He slipped his left arm back around her and cupped her cheek in his right hand, tilting her head.

Danger shone in his sapphire eyes. Her awareness shifted keenly to the short and shrinking distance between their lips. This time, he wasn't going to stop himself, and at the moment she didn't want him to, either.

The fear his tears had held at bay broke loose, and she pulled out of his embrace. "It's getting late. I should go. My mom will worry."

Disappointment filled Jordy's face. "I guess you're right."

She stood and turned to take the path leading toward the shallow end of the lake. How could she just leave him here? He'd be hard pressed to find the trail back when it didn't exist. She glanced back.

Jordy had stood, too, and had turned toward the way they came in, his shoulders slumped.

Why did she bring him here? She sighed. "Come with me. It's easier to get out from this way."

He spun and crossed to her like he would've run to her, if permitted by his dignity or the terrain.

She headed down the narrow path, brushing branches aside. Once in the open, she stopped, glanced to the gravel road at the top of the grassy slope, and glanced to the tunnel-like, foliage-enclosed passageway to the other side of the lake. She gulped. She couldn't believe she was even considering this.

Jordy came up beside her. "You don't really have to go yet, do you?"

She bit her lip then squeaked out, "Not for another hour."

"Well, that leaves only one question." He nodded to the cavernous green tunnel. "Are you afraid of the dark?"

Despite herself, she laughed at his playfully serious tone. She sucked in a breath and headed into the tunnel. Something about Jordy's ability to set her at ease frightened her almost as much as the torrent he'd stirred within her. What was it about Jordy that made . . . the dark less scary?

A rose by any other name would smell as sweet.

The tunnel's shadows gave way to the gray of twilight. Susanna glanced at the young man beside her and quickened her pace. He matched her pace, which elicited a mixture of dismay and gladness. She bit her lip and forced her thoughts off Jordy before things got even more dangerous.

After a while, they reached the tree stretching a low branch out over the lake. Jordy stepped up on the branch and walked several paces out, holding onto the overhead branch that was much closer to his own head. He twisted his back to the lake and faced the sunset.

She joined him on the branch and turned to watch the rosy display over the distant tree tops, all too aware of his presence behind her.

After several minutes, Jordy broke the silence. "It's pretty, isn't it?"

Susanna took a slow breath before facing him. "The sunsets are so pretty here. Glenshire's beautiful, at least it is to me."

"It's not the . . ." He turned away and looked out over the lake.

"Not the only pretty thing here?" She swallowed a lump in her throat.

"Beautiful," he said sheepishly. "Like Glenshire, you're rough around the edges, yet still somehow refined."

Two days ago, she would've taken that as an insult. Today, that seemed to mean what "da bomb" seemed to mean at school. "Flatterer."

He glanced at her, his cheeks a deep shade of red. "Told you. See? I can't help it. Maybe you were right about fate. Maybe, once you go past a certain point, you are what you are now, and nothing can change that."

"No, Jordy. Anybody can change, if you want to."

"Can we now? I've been sick of Sir Flirtalot and feeling strangled by that mask for a while now. I want to change. I've told myself I will a million times. But nothing ever changes. I make the same mistakes, over and over."

"Change doesn't happen overnight. I never meant to ask that of you."

"What do you want from me?"

Susanna steeled herself. Did she dare want anything from him? "What do you want to give? A girl needs her pride."

Jordy stepped closer and traced her jaw line. "Pride can be deadly."

"Love can be deadlier. Ask Romeo and Juliet." Her cheeks flamed. Of all the times to have Shakespeare stuck on the brain, why now?

He studied her a moment. "Christine was too good to me. Or too good for me. This world didn't deserve her. And she didn't deserve to die." His jaw tightened. "A clueless jerk once thought the best way to comfort me and my parents was to claim it's good that someone murdered my sister, since now she is in Heaven and happy to be healed of all her pain in this life."

Wow, what do I say? "Um, what faith are you? Just curious."

He chuckled. "Oh, as far as my parents know, I've converted to atheism, but in truth God and I are simply no longer on speaking terms. Church is on the list of things I haven't done since she died."

"Like the Boy Scouts. Phill had already spilled that, by the way."

"Ugh. So when was Gramps talking about me behind my back?"

"When he twisted my arm into giving you a tour. And gave me less than twenty-four hours' notice. Either he happened to think of it as I walked in, or he didn't want to give me time to back out. My feelings about rich city kids aren't positive. I've been snubbed by the type more than once, an' I'm pretty doggone tired of it." She slipped into her hillbilly routine.

Jordy laughed. "Gramps *is* loaded, but my broken family is climbing out of a financial disaster, so we both should've listened to him trying to warn us about our inaccurate assumptions. On the tour, it was meant to help me out, I see that now. He must have figured it'd work best with a young person and didn't trust the others. Seems you've done something to impress him."

"Yeah, I grew up. We've been going up here since I was three years old. Phill has always treated me and Cara as if we were his own granddaughters."

"Anyway, what about you? On the faith question."

Susanna shrugged. "I haven't been to church in a while, either, only my entire family suddenly quit going one day, and I'm not sure why." Or why her chest ached so much, thinking about it. "I haven't lost faith. I guess, I've just tired of organized religion. I have to take my own path."

"Would that mean that is how your parents now feel about religion, and you are not allowed to have an opinion of your own, as well as not allowed to go to church or otherwise continue to actually practice your faith?"

Awkward. Per her dad's thinking, she'd tricked Jordy into attending her church tonight. Susanna cleared her throat. "It'll be dark in the woods now."

"I'd walk you, if you wanted."

Was he offering? "Certain people would get ideas about us that wouldn't be good for your reputation."

"I don't care about my reputation."

He could've fooled her. "My mom really will be upset. She forgets it stays light out longer out here and worries about us running around in the dark."

"It's not safe to run around in the dark."

Oh, small-town-boy *had* spent the last three years in the city. "This isn't Chicago. There's no child molesters waiting in the shadows to grab me. Do you honestly think Phill would let a person like that in the park?"

"Do you honestly want to go? I'm in no hurry."

That tied her stomach in knots. "The longer we stall, the harder it will be to say goodbye." She bit her lips. "The only male-female relationship the guys up here seem to grasp anymore is boyfriend-girlfriend. They'll crack gross suggestive jokes, and you'll wind up acting macho and doing stupid stuff to impress them, blah, blah, blah."

Jordy winced. "Okay, I've been a jerk. What can I say? I'm sorry. What's it matter, anyway? They already call you my girlfriend, and that's on me."

"No, those guys will jump to any conclusion profitable for them. They're only doing that because it drives you crazy."

"True, the more I discouraged them, the more they did it."

"You were awful quick to deny liking me. It wasn't just them, either, you told Cara about four times."

Jordy's face turned three shades redder. "Things were different then."

"Are they?" She imitated his favorite grin. "As in, now we might have to convince the guys we detest each other before they have us off and married in the grapevine?" She laughed with him. "That wouldn't work on Cara. She and her friends have this silly rule that, if they say they don't like you four times, that means they do. I think she provoked you to cause trouble."

"Somehow, I don't doubt it."

"Do you really like those guys?"

"They're okay, but I'm not sure if they like me or the fact my grandfather owns this place. You're not the only one to hassle me for being from Chicago, or to mistake me for Mr. Moneybags, for that matter."

"Do you and Boo always get along so well?"

Jordy shrugged. "Let's say we have more in common than he realizes, and sometimes it gets to be too much for comfort."

Susanna laughed. "At this rate, we'll end up camping out here."

Jordy chuckled. "All right, I can take a hint."

They hopped down from the branch and headed back to the other side of the lake. Jordy asked, "Are you sure you don't want me to walk you?"

She hesitated. "Just to the road. I don't want you to go out of your way."

They walked in silence. He reached for her hand but she pulled away.

At the road, Jordy faced her. He caressed her cheek. "Are you sure?"

Her skin tingled where he'd touched her. She sucked in a breath and nodded. "Yes." She made herself turn away but couldn't resist a glance back.

A shiver ran down her spine as her eyes met Jordy's.

Things would never be the same again.

Chapter 12

JORDY STRODE WITH SUE-Ann away from the lake, nearing the gravel road at the top of the grassy slope. His stomach fluttered oddly. He couldn't recall the last time he'd dealt with anxiety in combination with his body's hopes for a certain yes. He'd get slapped, if his impulse control failed further, and he needed his own walk home alone to recharge his drained batteries.

Why would he rather walk Sue-Ann home first? Oh, fine. He stopped on the crossroad, faced her, and caressed her cheek. "Are you sure?"

She nodded, her quiet reply inaudible, then turned away.

Go home, dude. Instead of listening to him, his body stood there like a dork, staring after her, urging him to ignore her intended no and follow her.

She turned back and met his gaze.

Yay! Why am I being such a dork tonight?

She swallowed. "To the edge of the woods. If you walk me any farther, Nate, Ricky, Boo, or Amy might see us together."

So? Jordy fell in step beside her as they headed toward the woods. "Why does that matter? What's the harm in walking a friend home in the dark?"

"They wouldn't see it that way and you know it."

"Of course, but what matters is how *we* see it. And this . . ." He pointed at her heart and at his own. "Whatever this is, this needs a name. And, if I'm reading you correctly, friends is all you're ready for us being."

"Friends is good, yes," she said to the gravel. "Sorry, I don't feel up to us running into anyone we know tonight, not together."

"It's okay." Privately processing what he had allowed tonight did appeal when their new emotional bond suffered the complication getting his friend called his girlfriend. He let his hand reach for her hand. Their fingers clasped on the sides of each other's hands at the same time.

Blissful silence fell except for chirping crickets and humming cicadas.

Several sweet minutes passed before his dear friend released his hand. He resisted the temptation to take her hand back. It was getting way too hard to recall why this behavior was a bad idea. Still drained, he gave in and put her hand back where it belonged, safely enfolded in his, preschool-style.

So weird. Not long ago, Sir Flirtalot would've been bored stiff. Tonight, Jordy might as well be Ricky's age, never kissed, and out with his first crush.

The closer the woods came, the more Jordy and Sue-Ann slowed down, stretching out their walk's last five feet. He halted. "What are we doing?"

Sue-Ann smiled wanly. "I was hoping you knew."

Stop it, dude. He forced himself to let go of her hand. "I'm sorry about, well, you know." He waved ahead, to the woods. "I guess this is it."

"Thank you," she whispered.

The words "my pleasure" leaped into Jordy's throat, but he swallowed them. "It's the least I could do. I have to go." *Before I break my word.* He walked away at a near sprint, lest he turn back again.

What happened tonight? How could a girl go so quickly from biting his head off to rushing to comfort him? Only one explanation. Christine—or the spiritual power she had brought into his family's lives, challenging them to reconsider their old notions of what God was still doing in this day as God's power was made perfect in her weakness.

Jordy trembled. Why Sue-Ann? Why would God show up like that now? Where was he three years ago, when he could've done something?

Too drained for this. Jordy forced his mind to go blank as he headed up the gravel road going along the edge of the woods. He focused on the songs of the crickets and the cicadas and various toads. A hooting owl joined in the chorus of the night. Colorful party lights glinted from multiple RV sites. He breathed in the faint, savory traces of campfire smoke.

Once safely past the turns back to her, near to the turn toward home, he stopped on the roadside, next to a thick maple tree, and he pressed his hand to the rough bark, grounding himself still further by feeling the texture.

The subtle knots of tension left his body, and his brain drain eased.

Smiling, he closed his eyes and enjoyed the lingering, ghostly sensation of his friend's warm embrace. Funny, in one day, he had shared more of his heart with Sue-Ann and had become far more emotionally intimate with her than he had ever been with any of the girls he'd once been on kissing terms with. Truth be told, Christine had been the last girl who had meant so much to him, and his body was so not-cool with him likening Sue-Ann to his sister.

Still, him, in love? Yeah, right, that would be a real first. Every girl who'd ever tried to wiggle into his heart had gotten the boot, and Sir Flirtalot had a strict rule against female friends. Acquaintance, sure, true friend, no.

Yes, that was why everything felt so strange. He'd never attempted to be close friends with a girl who wasn't his sister, especially not one so kissable. Well, their agreed-upon attachment he'd live with, but he so needed to learn to quit flirting with Sue-Ann or sooner or later, she'd get hurt, and he wasn't about to hurt her. No matter what, he would not hurt Sue-Ann.

IN THE DARKNESS CLOSING in, a floodlight showed Susanna the way home through the woods. Multi-colored "fairies" glowed on both sides of the gravel road, but the party lights at her campsite were white.

Fire crackled and glowed orange in their fire ring. Her mother's comfy, apple-shaped figure hunched beside it on one of the campfire benches made from logs with thick boards slapped over them. Susanna cut through their site's small cluster of young trees. A branch stretched out toward the sparks flying away from the fire, dying out just short of hitting the branch's leaves.

Her mother waved her over. Susanna hesitated. She'd planned on going to bed and pretending she wasn't still too wound up to fall asleep, to avoid her sister. But perhaps a few minutes by the fire wouldn't hurt.

Susanna tumbled onto the bench and risked a hug. "I love you, Mom."

"Love you, too, sweetheart." Mom patted her back and pulled away, her eyes back on the dancing flames glowing inside the fire ring. "Where did you and the Durant boy go tonight?"

Her stomach sank and her heart fluttered oddly. She bit her lip. "Does that mean you've seen Cara? What's her mouth saying about us?"

"Please don't start any fussing." Mom wrung her hands. "Your sister just said she's out with Ricky, something about a new trampoline."

Ah, so what Cara wanted, Cara got. That figured. Wait a minute. "If Cara didn't tell you where I have been, then how do you know who I was with?"

Mom smiled at her sadly. "Let's see, you weren't out here at the fire with me or inside reading a library book. And my baby's eyes are smiling like they haven't smiled since you were six years old. Except when *he* was around."

Tears threatened. Susanna blinked them away. It was okay to cry down at the lake, safe in her hiding place. Here, she needed to be happy and to help her mother keep everyone else happy, too. She took deep breaths and risked saying, "Please don't tell Cara, or I'm afraid she will mess this up for me, but I think maybe I've finally made a real friend, all of my very own."

"Oh honey." Mixed emotions crossed her mother's face, including the usual silent accusation that her husband and daughters were failing in their job of being the perfect, happy family that she'd dreamed of as a little girl.

Susanna closed her eyes. That was all in her imagination. She was being too sensitive as usual. Why couldn't she simply be the normal, always happy daughter that her mother deserved?

What is wrong with me?

Tears escaped her careful control.

"Oh, honey, please don't cry." Her mother hugged her, crying herself.

"Sorry, Mom." Susanna wiped her face and studied the soothing, warm, flickering light of the fire crackling on the split logs slowly turning black.

After several more minutes, her mother said, "You know I can't promise anything, but I will talk to your sister and ask her to back off and let you and the Durant boy sort yourselves out."

"Thanks." Susanna beamed. *Please make Cara listen to Mom, God.* "Oh, by the way, his name is Jordy, and he is a nice guy, just clearly accustomed to having to hide that to avoid getting jumped. I'm sure he could handle himself in a fair fight, but in Chicago he would've been way out-numbered."

Her mother patted her arm and kept watching the fire burn.

Oh, she needed to figure things out all on her own, like Mom had to do, since Mom's mother had died when Mom was six. Right. For the best. She should be glad to have a cool mom who was happy if her kids were happy.

What is wrong with me?

Twin white beams flashed in the darkness. The crunch of a car's wheels on gravel followed. Strange, not many folks came or went anywhere this late, at least not in a motor vehicle bigger than a GoCart.

A 1986 Ford Taurus approached at fifteen miles an hour, the speed limit here, and parked at the empty campsite beside theirs, ahead of her. The very slow-moving joyrider got out, his hands in his pockets.

Her heart thudded fast. Jordy stepped out of the darkness and into the light. Her face warmed. She focused on the fire again.

Jordy headed to her mother's side. "Ma'am, sorry to bother you so late, but may I have a semi-private word with your daughter? It's important."

Wow. All of Cara's friends would've approached Cara.

Her blinking mother glanced between them and mustered a smile. As she stood with a groan like getting up hurt, Jordy reached for her arm as if to help her up. Her mother brushed him away, amusement on her face.

Mom hugged Susanna and whispered in her ear, "He *is* a charmer. Have fun, honey." She headed over to the porch, sat on the bench, and shamelessly turned her head to watch them and the fire from there.

"Sorry," Susanna mumbled to the boy settling beside her at the fire. She gripped the edges of the board their weight pinned to the logs it rested on.

"We're fine," he said, and mirrored her posture, placing one hand beside hers skin-to skin.

After watching the fire together for a while, she relaxed and found her gaze pulled away from the mesmerizing fireplace as their eyes met. She took a breath and found her voice. "Jordy, does your mom know where you are?"

His lips curled. "No, dear, but I sweet talked her into giving me the keys. So she does know I'm out clearing my head, hoping I'll sleep better tonight. If I do, thank you." He glanced down and swallowed. "I'm sorry."

"For what?"

"Tonight was amazing for me but so selfish. I—" He growled, shaking his head, as if with frustration. "I need to check something." He twisted to face her, their knees brushing. "Usually, I'm more subtle about this, but I *do* care about you, so I'll be clear. This is only a test. Please hold your hand like this."

He raised his hand with his fingers spread.

What was this about? She mirrored his gesture.

He placed his palm against hers, with their fingers in the gaps. In this odd position, her fingers naturally curled around his, into a hand-hold that she'd never witnessed, let alone done. It felt so sweet. His eyes held hers.

Danger crackled in the air around them, like an electrical storm.

Jordy smoothed his hair and rested his hands on his upper thighs, while still twisted around facing her. He smiled grimly. "Yep."

Susanna reflexively copied his posture and raised her brows. "What was that? What did it mean?"

"That I'm despicable," he muttered to the fire. "That was Sir Flirtalot's more mature, more reliable version of your sister's juvenile test." He met her gaze and leaned in slightly. "I've been careless with your heart. I'm sorry."

Not Cara's childish test that falsely claimed "I hate you, I hate you, I hate you, I hate you" meant "I love you, please marry me!" She laughed nervously and found her hand clutching her ponytail. She forced it down. "Worry about my sister and Amy, not me."

"Amy is a child barely out of elementary school, if she is out. Your sister is a pest on my ignore list. You're the one I've put in danger, Sue-Ann."

"Not likely. I locked the door to my heart and threw away the key." She wet her lips and glanced to the fire. "I dream of being a bride someday, and I guess I figure the guy that God meant for me will find the key. But he will not be able to unlock my heart and keep his own heart." She met his gaze, raising one eyebrow in challenge. "So worry about yourself."

"Test me then." He held out his hand with the palm up, and his fingers all curled already, eager to resume the test's handhold. "This is a reversal for me, so my bad habits shouldn't throw off the results any."

The vulnerable look in his eyes, like he was holding out his own heart to her, asking her to accept it. No. She knocked his hand aside. "No."

"Okay." He watched the fire. "But we do need to talk, if you're willing to hear what I have to say from the likes of me."

"You're my friend, Jordy. Please just talk to me as my friend."

"Okay." He waved to the fire. "Did this just happen to us? Just one day, we sat down here, and, poof, a fire appeared here all by itself?"

"Of course not, my mother built it."

He grinned at her. "Right, I didn't work for this one. I simply had to go before your mother with respect and accept the gift of her fire with gladness. That is how parental love is supposed to be. But you've been taught romantic love is the result of a lightning strike beyond anyone's control, right?"

"That sounds fair enough."

He gestured around both of them. "Well, we do have lighting in the air, and two young logs with plenty of kindling, and definite sparks, according to my selfish little test, but fire isn't inevitable. A threat, yes, inevitable, no."

What? He did not mean—oh he did. Susanna's face burned. She stared at the fire. His beloved Sue-Ann wasn't real. "I'm sorry, I didn't think—what have I done to you? I'm so sorry."

"This isn't your fault. This is my responsibility, since I have been taught better. And those boundaries of yours? Awesome. You're awesome for me. But I am terrible for you. And I need to grow-up and start putting you first. Because the kindling we're trying to ignore? It's already on fire, Sue-Ann. I need to act, and quickly, to protect you."

"No." She closed her eyes, chest heaving, but sighed. "What do we do?"

He waved at the fire. "How would you put this out quickly? If your water rations were too low to spend them on that."

"I'd get a long stick and separate the logs from each other. That alone is usually enough but you can also smother them with ashes. So? Why?"

He stared at her. "My family will be leaving here sometime before school starts, and that's this coming Wednesday. Our hours are already numbered, and every fiber of me hates this. But to protect you, I have to separate us."

Why can't I ever keep a friend? She sucked in a pained breath. "Thanks for coming back and explaining rather than just suddenly avoiding me."

"Thank you for understanding, my friend." He hugged her from side.

"So I guess this is goodbye?"

"Sir Flirtalot's policy was 'don't call me, I'll call you,' so let's reverse that. Once I get my contact information myself, I'll have it left at the office here for you. My dad will like you enough to do me that favor just for me swallowing my bitterness for five seconds and calling Jordan that."

Susanna nodded and stared into the fire, forcing herself to breathe.

"Please really do call me, my friend," he said in her ear.

As he walked away, Susanna's ear worm began crooning the chorus from Neil Diamond's "Don't Turn Around."

JORDY LEANED AGAINST the wall near the cue stick rack, watching Ty take his shot at pool on Sunday afternoon.

Jordy's mother appeared in the game room doorway. "Son, say good-bye to your friends, I need to talk to you."

Jordy put his cue stick up. "See you guys."

Boo glanced at his watch. "I should get going myself."

"I might as well go too," Ty said, "We'll be breaking camp soon enough."
Ty and Boo started knocking in the balls left on the pool table.

Jordy followed his mom out through the store. "What's up?"

She led him out of the main doors and sat outside on the steps down to the hillside walkway. She patted the spot beside me. "Sit a minute, Jordy."

He shut the door behind him and complied. "What's going on?"

"I should've said something sooner, but it seemed like pulling teeth just getting through the weekend together, so I'm afraid we put this off."

Oh no. His mom starting an announcement backwards was never a good sign. "Put what off?" Duh. He narrowed his eyes. "Are we heading out to the new place? With Jordan? Right now?"

She nodded. "You don't have to like this. All I ask is you treat your dad with respect and try to forgive him. No rush, take as long as you need to, but please, Jordy. Please."

Tears shone in her eyes.

His gut tightened painfully. He'd anticipated this, already said goodbye to Sue-Ann and gave himself some hope of her ever speaking to him again. So why did leaving her, to never return here to her, still hurt so much? Why did he feel like a fool who'd wasted their last two days together?

What else could he have done? He didn't want to keep yanking on Boo's ponytail to escape awkward spots, such as Jordy having known why Sue-Ann was petting a tree. To the guys, it'd looked dirty, and it wasn't yet his place to intervene for her directly when their friendship was still so new.

On top of that, he couldn't trust himself around her one-on-one, either. Making himself stay away from her for the last two days had been painfully difficult already. The more he gave in, the harder it'd be to protect her from himself. It was in her best interests if they never saw each other again.

Pain ripped through his chest. Man, compared to the idea of him losing Sue-Ann, Isabel had just injured his pride. Even fouling things up with Vera hadn't ever stung this badly. Couldn't give in, though. What he'd become as Sir Flirtalot violated every principle he'd held dear. Sue-Ann deserved better.

"Jordy." His mom squeezed his shoulder. "Please, I'm begging you."

He blinked. "Sorry, my mind wandered. What was the question?"

"Get more sleep." His mother hugged him. "I love you, honey. It's time to go home. Everything's packed. Are you ready?"

No. Heh. Two weeks ago, he never would've ever believed he'd feel like this today. "Is there any way we could come back here on the weekends?"

His mom mustered a tiny smile. "Your grandfather said we're welcome to stay with him anytime. I'll have to talk to your dad, but I don't see why not. The weekends are the busiest work days, and since your dad's days off are going to be Fridays and Sundays, it might work out for the best." She stood. "Come on, your dad's waiting for us."

He followed her. "Can I drive?"

She laughed and handed him her keys. "Here. I'd rather ride with your dad anyway."

Half an hour later, Jordy pulled up behind his father's car in front of a slate blue house with white shutters. Real curtains billowed in the windows. His parents got out of his father's car. Jordy rushed out of his mom's car and ran up to her. "What did he say?" He added, "About Glenshire?"

His father smiled at him. "It's fine with me, son."

Jordy ignored the urge to hug his father. "Thanks, sir." He turned to his mom. "Did you pack my suitcases?"

She waved at her car. "They're in the trunk. Also, I have an extra house key on my keyring for you, make sure to take that."

He retrieved his suitcases from the trunk, located the house keys, and switched one to his keyring. He tossed his mom her keys and followed his parents inside. Their cottage-style furnishings fit far better in the new living room. Their TV was a boxy, thirty-six-inch analog set sitting upon a low oak entertainment center. Its shelves bore his old Super Nintendo game system, a VCR, and VHS tapes. This did beat the cramped apartment.

His mom grabbed one of his suitcases. "Let me show you your room."

Downstairs, they set his suitcases on the floor between the dresser and a wardrobe his mom must've bought to replace the missing closet. He glanced around and recognized almost everything else, including the double dresser. In the corner by a high-set window sat a new-smelling cedar desk and an HP, Windows 95 desktop computer. His mom grinned ear to ear. "Surprise!"

"Does it have internet access?"

She faltered. "We will look at getting AOL's dial-up service next month, probably just on our shared desktop upstairs."

That was a no. He grunted, grabbed one of his suitcases, and unzipped it on his blue twin poster bed.

His mom asked, "Aren't you even going to say thank you?"

For what, the homework machine? Oops. He looked up. "Thanks, Mom. I'm sorry, I'm just not used to getting excited over doing my homework."

She slapped him playfully. "It has a few games, too, smart-aleck."

Once his mom left, Jordy abandoned the suitcase. Where had his mom put Christine's stuff? He drew his chain from his shirt and fingered her ring. He'd start by looking for her jewelry box. That belonged on their dresser, but instead their silver boombox sat alone.

He opened the wardrobe. The gold jewelry box sat on the top shelf with the rest of her stuff. He sighed with relief. He'd been scared to death her stuff would get lost. Or worse, that his mom would cart it all to a thrift store.

Now, Jordy eased Christine's jewelry box off the shelf and gently put it back where it belonged on her side of their dresser. Much better.

He eyed the wardrobe. At the bottom sat his comic book collection and his dusty basketball. It never left his closet anymore. Playing without her had hurt too much. He rarely played video games at home, too. They had always done such things together. He glanced around the room. Another basketball hoop hamper and more Chicago Bulls posters hung up on the walls.

Somehow, it felt like there were gaps left, asking him if he'd ever replace the churchy posters that he'd torn down and ripped up three years ago.

Maybe someday. Hard to forgive God when he was wrong to be mad at God, and talking to God like he talked to his dad would only make his corner of Hell hotter. Best to just avoid God and hope he ever got his faith back.

He sighed. He'd badly neglected everything since Christine died. Three years ago, he had given up all of his old passions, hobbies, and interests. All were tied to Christine. In Chicago, he had taken up avoiding getting jumped, playing pool, and playing the mean city girls for fools. He'd been infatuated with Vera for real, but he'd fouled up that thing before it got truly serious.

This thing with Sue-Ann felt like a far worse mistake. Him, of all people, falling in love? The kind that drove a man so crazy, he got married? How? He still had a heart left to lose while stealing her heart?

What had he been thinking, trying to pick the lock on Sue-Ann's heart? It'd never been justifiable with her. Why hadn't he been able to stop himself from doing something this despicable? And now she was his friend, and the closest friend he had left, too. What a mess he'd made. How could he move forward now, without hurting her? He couldn't do that to Sue-Ann. She meant too much to him to play his games with her.

Please don't let it already be too late. Please.

Chapter 13

THE TUESDAY AFTERNOON before school started, Susanna leaned forward in the van. Her stomach tightened. The day that she picked up her new glasses had never before felt like doomsday.

She asked, "Are you sure I can't get contacts?"

"Positive," her dad barked from behind the wheel, in front of her.

Beside her, Cara smirked at Susanna with an air of superiority. "What's wrong, Sue-Ann? Too vain to let Jordy see you in glasses?"

Susanna glowered at Cara. Why did Cara have to know her so well?

This earned Susanna a lecture from her mom on just being herself that was confusing when, if she stopped playing the good daughter at home, she'd get in bigger trouble for being a brutally honest daughter.

She said, "yes, ma'am" at appropriate intervals and tuned out. Her mom didn't get her. Jordy acted like he'd simply be relieved when she could see again, but how could it truly not matter? His beloved Sue-Ann did not need glasses. Susanna the Nerd did. And Jordy would hate her for deceiving him.

At least she didn't have to go to school with him. It'd been difficult at times to fight past her nerves on the stage of Glenshire, where she functioned at her best. It'd be impossible to keep this up at Easthaven High.

Ever since sixth grade, she'd proved her mother right to fight for her and had done well in classrooms for gifted students, but the common areas' noise and chaos still hurt her ears and made her brain feel weird, and that still led to her acting weird outside of class, and so her peers had still rejected her.

While seated beside her mom in the glasses shop area of the eye doctor's office, she asked, "Why can't I get contacts?"

Her mom glared, her teeth clenched. "Susanna, we've already discussed that. Now grow up and act like the young lady you are."

"Sorry," she muttered, shoulders slumped. It was vain to hope contacts would've magically made Sue-Ann real and kept Jordy in her life. It was her brain that needed something to magically make it stop feeling so impossible for her to go beg his dad for his phone number, let alone to then call Jordy.

Never mind her friend's too-obvious crush on a girl who didn't exist. Her brain would still react like she would die unless she put down the phone.

The lady came back with her new glasses. "Okay, try these on and we'll see how they fit."

She complied.

The lady studied her and smiled. "Looks like a perfect fit. Do they feel okay?" She nodded. The lady said, "Here's the mirror. How do you look?"

"Fine," she lied. The lonely girl in the mirror was a homely, overweight teenage girl wearing blue wire-frame glasses. No awesome country girls here for Jordy to confuse by suddenly confessing he had a crush on Sue-Ann only to abandon her. Just a weird, rejected city girl named Susanna.

What had made her think she could befriend a guy like Jordy?

THE NEXT MORNING, SUSANNA found her homeroom assignment on the list on the display case in the main hall at school—room 209. She had freshman biology there last year. She shifted her backpack as it hung on only her right shoulder then headed upstairs.

In the class room, only three other students had arrived. She sat down at the front and center lab table and faced the black chalkboard. Several more hung on the side and back walls behind shelves full of preserved gross stuff.

Three guys came in and grabbed seats at the back of the room. Next, two girls named Lindsey and Terrilyn came in and sat at the lab table behind her. Lindsey and Susanna remained the only two white students here. If they had the same students as the "nerds" homeroom from last year, there would be a total of eighteen Black students, six Asians, and five Caucasian students. All but Susanna switched fluently between Ebonics and Nerdy English, and she knew Ebonics too. She was just too afraid of using it wrong and offending.

Lindsey had seemed like a good friend prospect—being over six foot tall and female could make high school difficult for her, too. Like the four-foot-eleven Terrilyn, Lindsey seemed nice but last year they had followed along with their peers when two mean white girls had taken a sudden disliking to Susanna and had excluded her as usual.

"What, Susanna?" Terrilyn asked. "Not going to say hi?"

Huh? She turned her chair to face them. "Sorry, I was zoned out."

"Thinking about a cute summer love?" Lindsey asked in a teasing tone.

"Who me?" Susanna sputtered. Why was her face warming? "I spent my summer in a cast, so I've mostly slept. What about you?"

Lindsey laughed. "Girl, I have five younger brothers and sisters. I got to babysit and go to basketball camp, that's it. Oh, sorry about your bummer."

Terrilyn said, "Mom and I spent the summer in South Carolina."

And she'd returned with a true Southern accent, sweet. Susanna smiled.

The bell rang. Susanna glanced around. Yep, the students of last year's Freshman Biology For Nerds were all back together for homeroom, minus two happily absent faces, namely the mean girls who had bullied her. She'd ignored their cruelty and kept to herself. Fighting was against the rules.

Behind her, their home room teacher cleared his throat. He spoke with the voice of Mr. Robinson from Freshman Biology For Nerds, who sounded like a loving sitcom Dad. "Kids, I know you're all excited to share about your summer vacations, but I need everyone to be quiet while we go through the paperwork. Oh, and, Susanna, Marquez, and Kiesha, if you'd please face your own desks, I'd appreciate it. Susanna, I must say I'm surprised at you."

"Sorry." She sheepishly turned her chair around. The skinny, middle-aged blond teacher was indeed Mr. Robinson.

After the bell, Susanna shoved her backpack over her shoulder, gathered up the paperwork she collected in homeroom, and braved the chaotic school hallway. Now for the challenge of locating her assigned locker.

Terrilyn came up behind her. "Hey, which locker did you get?"

Susanna turned just as Lindsey caught up. Susanna glanced down at the thin slip of paper with her locker assignment. "2213."

Terrilyn grinned. "Awesome, that's right between ours."

At the lockers, Lindsey held out her class schedule. "I've got Chem next, what about you guys?"

Chem? Oh, Chemistry, duh, everyone in their homeroom needed to take that Junior-level course this year instead of next year.

Terrilyn took Lindsey's schedule and grabbed Susanna's schedule out of her shaky hands. "Let's see what we got. Chem, English, lunch, History, and Algebra 2. Awesome, we had almost no classes together last year, Susanna.

You guys take Spanish instead of French, but that's one more class together for you." Terrilyn passed their schedules back.

Huh? Are we friends again, just like that? "Uh, yeah, that's great."

AT EASTHAVEN HIGH, Jordy and his mom waited for nearly forty minutes unnoticed in the frenzied main office before a black-haired, white guidance counselor took them into her office. She sat at her desk, but it faced the pale green cement wall, so she turned around to face them. "Have a seat, please. I'm Mrs. Riley. How may I help you?"

Jordy and his mom sat in the office chairs behind her desk.

"I enrolled Jordy in school a few weeks ago," his mom said. "But we just got an answering machine message that said I needed to fill out more forms."

The guidance counselor spun to her desktop computer. "Ma'am, do you know his I.D.?"

"She won't remember it but I do." He gave his school I.D. number from Chicago. *That carried over, right?*

Riley typed on her keyboard. "I don't have it. Let's try your name."

"Durant, Jordan Jr," he said, sighing. *That was bad, and teacher's grade books often made it worse by leaving off the Junior. Regardless, he was in for a full day of having to say, "Jordan is my dad" as well as "where is . . . ?"*

The guidance counselor entered his information, pushed her chair away from the desk, and stood. "Your first problem appears to be that your records didn't make it into the computer. One moment, please."

She returned twenty minutes later and held up his school records from Chicago, paperwork stuffed in a tan file folder. "I finally found him." She laid the file folder by the desktop and handed to his mom an inch-thick stack of forms on a clipboard. "Ma'am, you can fill these out while Jordan and I—"

"It's Jordy. Jordan's my father."

"Sorry, Jordy then. Anyway, we can't find a schedule for you, so let's fill that out while your mom does the paperwork, okay?"

He shrugged. "Sure."

The guidance counselor settled in her desk chair, seated profile to them, and pulled out his transcripts from his file folder. A wide smile crossed her face. "Not bad. You're in luck, Jordy. Besides the alternative schools, we have the best honors program in the district."

I.E. his dweeb classes, post his surprise in ninth grade of the city girls deciding that he'd become too attractive for them to keep calling him a nerd. Jordy glowered at his mother. "I'd rather take the regular courses."

The guidance counselor started typing on her keyboard. "Oh, you don't want to do that. You'd be bored to death."

So? He opened his mouth to protest.

His mother patted his hand. "Jordy brings home suspension notices for fighting when he's bored to death."

Jordy tightened his jaw. Now what? His least wrong strategy for evading violent altercations with bullies was pretending to be stupid, plus pretending Sue-Ann really was his girlfriend, and being honest about him valuing their privacy. He wouldn't brag even if an honest report would impress anyone.

Several minutes followed of him trying to force his mind off of Sue-Ann and his body's wrong idea of melting through her boundaries.

Why was separating the logs taking so horribly long to cool him down?

The guidance counselor stopped typing. "I have all your core courses in, so now for electives. Eighth period is open in your schedule. Available classes include Spanish 1 and Family Connections, a home EC course."

His mom clasped her hands together. "That sounds wonderful!"

It sounds like group therapy, at my school, horrifying. Jordy said, "You know, I always wanted to learn Spanish."

Once his mom finally finished with all the forms, the guidance counselor wrote Jordy a hall pass and handed it to him along with his schedule. "We're in third period now. For you, that's American History, Challenge. Go straight down the hall, past the main corridor. Your next class will be the first door on your right."

"Thanks." He kissed his mother on her forehead then headed to class, glancing down at his schedule. He'd only missed one class, Chemistry. This was definitely the "uncool" course load for college-bound students. He could also see why he wasn't offered a study hall for eighth-period—the Chemistry lab only met in second period on Mondays and Wednesdays, so he had one study hall scheduled for three days already. Ugh. He'd need an exit strategy.

In history class, Jordy surveyed his classmates—eleven black students, six

Asian students, and three white students if he included himself. Heh, his school in Chicago had been nearly 1:1:1 on its students' racial ratios, and the suburbs he'd grown up in were so white, he'd already had a rude awakening on how privileged his life had been before his family had lost everything.

Okay, Sue-Ann definitely won their argument regarding Columbus, Ohio not being a cow town. Wherever did it get that reputation? It was tiny, by Chicago's standards, but still also a major urban center. Thankfully, this new neighborhood's feel provoked far fewer urges to look over his shoulder. He might not even need his dweeby compass to fidget with at school, instead of the knife he'd carried in Chicago, when he wouldn't be in a school zone.

He glanced to the hand hidden in his jeans' pocket, already playing with his compass automatically. *Okay, still carrying a concealed compass that is only not a weapon if I must show it to someone who can arrest or expel me.*

WHILE SUSANNA WAITED for the bell, after her English teacher ended their studies early for the day, she worked up the nerve to ask Lindsey, "How come you're hanging out with me this year?"

Seated over at the school desk between Susanna and the short Terrilyn, Lindsey hesitated. "Sorry about last year. Cassie and Jade suddenly decided to hate you for no reason. They made hanging out with you too awkward."

Meaning they hadn't wanted bullied, too. "Where are they this year?"

"I don't know. Most of the rumors involve them getting expelled, so that part is probably true, but I suspect no one really knows why."

The bell rang.

Susanna headed to her locker, but Terrilyn stopped her and gestured at Susanna's books. "Take 'em with ya. We'll use 'em to mark our table. We'll drop 'em off after lunch."

A silly, inefficient act, their class after lunch was in the complete wrong direction from their lockers. But worth it, to avoid having to sit alone again this year. The school cafeteria was so horrible. In there, if not for these girls' kindness, her weird internal difference would've left her standing frozen, if she couldn't just find an empty table and do her best to shut out the chaos.

Instead, grinning, she just followed her new favorite classmates.

While all three girls stood in the lunch line closest to the cafeteria doors, Lindsey poked Terrilyn. "Hey! Who's that guy?"

Terrilyn asked pointedly, "Which one?"

Lindsey pointed. "That one, in the other line."

Terrilyn whistled. "Hey! I don't know his name, but for a white guy, he's fine! Hey, check out the white guy in the other line, Susanna!"

So not treating anyone like meat, that felt wrong, but she'd humor them a little. Susanna surveyed the lunch line over by the dirty windows, across the too-loud, too-crowded cafeteria. No one stood out that would explain the tone suggesting the person of interest was a novelty. "Who?"

"Him." Lindsey turned Susanna's head to the back of the other line and pointed again, from right behind her.

Jordy? Susanna gasped. *Not him. Not here. Please, not here.*

"What is it?" Terrilyn asked. "Do you know him?"

"No, I don't know him," Susanna lied. *Jesus, save me. I'm toast if Jordy sees me and recognizes me.*

JORDY PAID FOR HIS lunch, faced the packed cafeteria, and shook his head. This energy-draining place was an introvert's worst nightmare. Well, he'd take lunch over study hall but still. Good luck to him, not outing himself as a dweeb without going back to Sir Flirtalot.

He spotted the table he deposited his books on earlier. All but one chair had disappeared from it. Sitting alone was not an option, so what now?

Two guys from his classes came up from behind, also carrying yellow foam trays.

The white one said, "Hey, man, I didn't catch your name."

"Jordan Walker Durant, Jr. Call me Jordy."

"Cool, Jordy. I'm Mike."

The bald guy shook Jordy's hand. "Sean Harris. Glad to meet you. We got a table in back. Join us?"

Jordy shrugged. "Sure."

Mike and Sean talked about everything from basketball to sex. The salt-and-pepper bros were too eager to ensure he knew they were into girls.

Jordy might as well have stayed in Chicago.

After Mike's extremely vulgar request for Jordy to brag about the girls he'd been with, Jordy felt himself blanch like a dweeb. *Dude, you've handled this problem before, you had a plan, why can't you remember what to say?*

Sean laughed. "Leave 'im alone, Mike. He's got virgin written all over his face. Dude, with your looks, that is obviously by choice, so just be straight up about your religious practices. We're cool with religious diversity here."

Jordy's ears burned. "My family is religious, thanks."

The bell rang and Jordy sighed. Hopefully, things would get better here. Where he'd lived in Chicago, in eighth-grade, he'd been ridiculed for being a virgin. Then, he'd planned to not start dating until college. Now, the rumor mill at his last school claimed he'd knocked up half a dozen girls. Most of his shell game's victims had stupidly spread trash talk about themselves for him after they'd suffered the cruel end to his shell game.

Mike scooted back from the table. "I guess we better get to class. Where you headed?"

"Let me check." Jordy grabbed his books from where he'd left them earlier and checked his schedule. "English, room 108."

"So are we," Sean said. "We'll show you where it is, since you're new."

"Sure, thanks." Jordy followed the guys down the school's main hallway. They turned left at the intersecting corridor.

After they had passed their history class, Mike and Sean stopped at two lockers, opened their combination locks, and deposited their books.

Mike waved at his locker. "Jordy, you can leave your stuff in here until they assign you a locker in homeroom tomorrow. You in 118A?"

Jordy dumped his textbooks in the locker. "Thanks, man." He glanced at his schedule. "Actually, I do have 118A for homeroom."

"Great, so do we."

They turned to go. By them strode a petite girl less than five feet tall with two Caucasian girls. The tall one had a basketball player's build. The familiar one had an intriguing, curvy figure and a gorgeous, long, auburn ponytail.

Whoa, his Sue-Ann, here, huh? Jordy stopped the guys and pointed at the red-head who'd be too tempting, if it wasn't her. "Hey, who's that girl?"

"Not sure," Mike said, "looks familiar, though. I think her name's Susan or something like that."

"Sue-Ann?" Jordy asked.

Mike shrugged. "It doesn't matter, she's a sophomore and not worth the effort. She don't play—or ever go along with any crap. I've seen her around, in the halls and stuff. When everyone else is egging it on, she'll walk out."

Jordy half-smiled and half-frowned. *Yeah, that does sound like my girl, who totally is worth all the effort to win her over, jerk.*

Sean elbowed Jordy in the side. "Dude, what's your interest?"

The short girl glanced over her shoulder at Jordy, poked the red-head, and whispered in her ear. She stopped in her tracks before turning around.

It couldn't be her. This girl wore glasses, had terror on her face, and the eyes of a dying deer. It wasn't fair to judge by that. His sister would've been reduced to his clingy shadow, if they'd both been stuck at a school this loud and chaotic. But still, what would Miss Country be doing here?

Jordy turned away. "Never mind. Let's go."

He followed Mike and Sean to class. Sean murmured, just loud enough for Jordy to hear, "Good call. Her name ought to be Rapunzel, because she's in a Strong Tower, and I'd say *his* name is Jesus. Given she should be dead."

"What?" Jordy gaped, his head spinning.

"The Class of 1999 entered high school last year full of punks bragging they were gonna rule the school as freshmen. Sports-wise, they *do* have the best athletes. They also had the worst hoods. Two girls full of darkness, to the religious, and just plain crazy to everybody else. Nobody would stand up to them. Except her. She stood alone, a stonewall who wouldn't move, a light quietly shining in their darkness. And they shoved her down the stairs."

Mike rolled his eyes. "If how you tell that story were true, she'd be either in a wheelchair or six feet under."

"Dude, I saw it. She fell head first, a good twenty feet, tumbled midair, and hit the back of her head on the concrete landing. And she stood up and walked away with hardly a limp. So, Jordy, don't mess with Jesus Girl." Sean pointed up. "Her Daddy in Heaven fights for her with Power."

Grr. Jordy's heart beat fast and his body blazed. *Okay, God, we need to talk, sometime after I pull together my courage and confront Miss Country.*

Chapter 14

AFTER THE BELL RANG, Susanna, Terrilyn, and Lindsey collected their books then ran upstairs and deposited them in their lockers. On the way downstairs to History, Susanna held onto the stair railing tightly.

Lindsey asked, "Susanna, you sure crutches ruined your entire summer? You're glowing like a girl who had a more interesting vacation than that."

Susanna's conscience pulled up a picture of Jordy. Her face warmed.

At the bottom of the staircase, she pulled her ponytail over her shoulder and played with it. "We did go camping frequently. My family has a lot up at this place called Glenshire. It's pretty cool, but no big deal to me. We've been going there since I was three."

Terrilyn whistled. "Dang, that is a long time, girl. My family never does anything together. But, of course, my parents have been divorced for years."

They crossed the main hall and passed three junior guys congregating at the lockers. Susanna said, "I didn't know your parents were divorced."

Terrilyn nodded absentmindedly, her eyes unfocused.

"I'm sorry, are you okay?" Susanna asked.

Terrilyn looked behind her then whipped back around. "Nothing."

Susanna shrugged. "Suit yourself."

Terrilyn glanced back again then elbowed Susanna. "Don't look now, but that guy back there is staring at you."

Susanna stopped in her tracks. "You're joking."

Her friends stopped too. Terrilyn said, "No, I'm serious."

"Who's staring at her?" asked Lindsey.

"Looks like that fine white guy. The one that might be new here?"

Susanna couldn't resist looking.

"I told you not to look!" Terrilyn whispered.

Jordy stood maybe fifteen feet down the hall. He caught Susanna's eye and frowned as if uncertain of her identity. Maybe if she split, he'd decide it wasn't her. She turned back and dashed inside her history class.

Lindsey and Terrilyn followed her.

"Are you sure he doesn't know you?" asked Lindsey.

Susanna answered honestly, her chest aching, "No, he doesn't know me. He doesn't know me at all."

AFTER SCHOOL, JORDY found his mom waiting in the school parking lot in the passenger seat of her car. He slid eagerly into the driver's seat.

His mom said, "I've invited some of the neighbors over for a little get together at four. Don't worry, it's not a pot luck."

"Mom!" He groaned. School was draining enough, now a party? "Why did you do that to me? You know I hate those things."

"Oh, honey, I wanted us to get to know the neighbors, is all. I thought if we made everything, it'd be all right."

"Then why did you wait until the last minute to tell me?"

"It slipped my mind, with everything going on."

Jordy grunted and shifted into drive. *Yeah, well, I'll be in my room, reading my collection of Spidey comics.*

SUSANNA'S SISTER DROPPED into the chair beside her in their living room after school. Susanna turned off the TV. "And how was your first day?"

Cara waved as if bored. "The same old, same old. Tonight's the barbecue at the new neighbors', remember?"

"I remember."

"Do you think they'll have any kids? If we're lucky, maybe a cute boy is moving in! Oh my gosh! What am I going to wear?"

"What's wrong with what you've got on?"

"Duh, I wore it to school."

"They won't know the difference. Besides, the chances of it being a cute boy seriously interested in us is slim to none."

Cara stuck her tongue out. "You're such a pessimist."

"Change then. I won't be the one chewed out for making extra laundry."

Cara crossed her arms and jutted out a pouty lip, but forwent making a fool of herself by dressing up for a barbecue, to Susanna's satisfaction.

At four forty-five, Susanna and Cara met their parents in the kitchen. Cara asked, "Are we still going to the party?"

"Of course," their mom replied. "We already accepted."

"What are we getting them?"

Their dad pulled a card out from his windbreaker's pocket. "This. Your mom stuck twenty bucks inside it and signed our names. Let them buy their own present."

"Can I give it to them?"

Their dad handed the card to Cara.

Outside, they crossed through their overgrown backyard and the alley to reach the backyard directly behind their own, the one with the above-ground pool. The elderly Walshes, the middle-aged McKays, and the elderly LaRosas were congregating in the far left corner, chatting amongst themselves.

On the deck, a middle-aged man with a light brown crew cut grilled hot dogs and hamburgers with his vaguely familiar back to them. The Walshes' grandchildren were playing a game of tag, and the McKays' twenty-year-old daughter played with her one-year-old son in the pool.

A woman with curly dark blonde hair came out the back door carrying a large salad. She set it down upon the folding table between the deck and the pool then smiled at Susanna's family. "Oh, great, we're all here."

Cara ran to the woman and gave her the card. "This is from us, Marissa."

"Oh, thank you. That's sweet of you." Marissa opened the card. Her eyes widened. "Oh, nice. Everyone's being so nice to us here! I'd almost forgotten what good, old-fashioned hospitality was." She glanced back to the man at the grill. "Honey? Where is that boy of yours?"

Cara's face lit up at "boy."

The man at the grill spun around. "Oh, now that he's acting up, he's my son?" He sighed. "I think he's in his room. I'll get him."

Susanna's heart about stopped. The man headed inside. She'd seen him before—at Glenshire. He was Phill's son Jordan—and Jordy's father. Which made Marissa Jordy's mother. And her favorite closet introvert was having to be forced to go to his family's own party.

And he'd already be in a surly mood when her lie got exposed. Susanna moaned inwardly. *Why, why, God, are you doing this to me? Why?*

Mr. Durant returned with his sullen son behind him and headed back to the grill. Marissa ushered her son around the yard, who had his hands in his pants pockets, with one hidden hand playing with a Swiss Army knife, from the looks of things. Marissa was introducing her son to everyone by family. Susanna waited with hers as she watched the surly young man.

She would be dead meat the second they were re-introduced.

All too soon, Marissa dragged him over to them. "I'd like you to meet my family. I'm Marissa Durant. My husband by the grill is Jordan, and this here is our son, Jordan Jr. Jordy, this is the McCoys, Denise and Elliot and their two girls. The youngest is Cara. She's in the eighth grade. Their oldest is only a grade behind you. Her name's Susanna."

Over her real name, Jordy snatched her glasses. "Hello, Sue-Ann."

JORDY STARED AS HIS mom made the final introductions, not listening to a word. He already knew the McCoy family. He met the adults at the fair. Mrs. McCoy frowned like she was trying to figure out where she saw him before, but Mr. McCoy didn't seem to remember him at all. There was no mistaking their youngest daughter, either. She arched her brows up like she recognized him and was surprised to see him here.

Where his Sue-Ann should be indeed stood the auburn-haired Rapunzel from school, looking even greener now than she had before.

It was her. Clark Kent's disguise was a bit better than he'd thought. And Jordy was an idiot who forgot about her glasses. He took them from her.

Evergreen fire flashed in Sue-Ann's naked eyes. She snatched back her new glasses and put them on again.

Seething, Jordy gritted his teeth. "Hello, Sue-Ann."

His mom stared at him. "You two know each other?"

"We've met," Jordy replied.

Mr. McCoy touched his chin. "The kids must've run into each other up at Glenshire. We've camped there for twelve years."

"Why," Jordy's mom said, beaming, "if it isn't a small world. That would be it. Jordan's helping his dad up there, that's why we moved back. Plus, we needed a change of scenery." She glanced sideways at Jordy, not at all subtly enough. "The last three years were bad ones for us, but especially for Jordy."

Hey. Jordy glared. "Mom!" He cleared his throat. "If you'll excuse us, Sue-Ann and I need to have a chat."

He grabbed her hand and dragged her over to the overgrown backyard across the alley, with an unpruned rosebush by a sky blue house in need of repainting. Flies buzzed around all the dog feces contaminating the grass. He slammed the chain-link fence's gate behind them. "What were you thinking? You lied to me, City Girl! What else didn't you tell me?"

Sue-Ann trembled and chewed on her lip. "It wasn't supposed to go this far—it was only one little tour. I didn't think—"

"And that's supposed to make everything okay? You think you can lie to me and yank me around and get away with it? What else didn't you tell me, Sue-Ann? That isn't even your real name!"

"Jordy—"

He waved it off, fury shouting over his conscience's orders to chill out. "I don't want to hear it. I can't believe this. You're sitting there, ribbing me for being from Chicago, and here you're as much a city kid as I am! In fact, if *you* grew up *here*, scratch that, reverse it, *I* grew up in Smallville, City Girl!"

Tears welled up in her eyes. "I'm country at heart."

Must. Chill. He took two deep breaths. "You have two minutes."

"Yeah, it's true." She gestured toward the house with peeling sky blue paint at the rear of this sorely neglected backyard. "This is my home, Jordy. I've lived here for my entire life. But, every weekend of camping season since I was three, we've camped at Glenshire. It's our second home; a little slice of Heaven. We've always been in the same lot with the same trailer, the same swing set, the same everything! The same safe places to hang out and to hide from the world. I grew up there."

Jordy continued to focus on his breathing, truly listening now.

She stared at the grass. "Mom and Dad don't let me run around here like they do at Glenshire. My freedom's up there. I can do what I want, when I want, there. Here, it's different. Here, I answer to other people. My parents, my teachers, my classmates." She hesitated. "My reputation. Here, I'm an outsider, a nobody, one lone speck in a grand desert. But, at Glenshire, when someone's missing, you notice. I fit in there. I never fit in here."

A child of the desert, held especially dear by Daddy God. Like Christine. Jordy closed his eyes. Jordan and Gramps had both tried to warn him of the false impression she'd given him. Really, she didn't lie to him. She'd just kept parts of her life from him. Not like he'd disclosed everything, either.

He opened his eyes.

Tears streamed down her face and welled up in her glasses.

Oh no. He rushed to her side, held her loosely in his left arm, and wiped the tears from her cheeks. "It's okay, Sue-Ann. I overreacted. I'm so, so sorry. Can you forgive me?"

She pulled out of the embrace but she took his hand. "If I'd been totally honest from the start, this wouldn't have happened. But, I didn't think I'd see you again. It was too easy to give you what you expected."

"At the time, I deserved it. I apologize for blowing up at you." He added lightly, "Did I forget to mention I can have a bit of a temper?"

She shook her head then took her glasses off and dried them with a corner of her shirt, exposing an intriguing corner of her lower abdomen.

He mentally cleared his throat and made himself look at her face. "Well, I'm clinical. My therapist insisted that I'm depressed due to losing my sister. Supposedly, I'd stop acting like a jerk, if I'd let myself grieve."

"Please do." Sue-Ann put her glasses back on. "I think she's right. I've seen a big improvement in your attitude, since you've opened up to me."

Whoa. Jordy shook his head. "You're a good friend. Too good. I don't deserve you." His stomach tightened. How could he get so mad at her, when he left out far more critical details? "But, I haven't told you the worst."

"A person's sins always seem worse to them if they're basically good, not sins at all if they're basically bad." She smiled at him shyly, but a spark of the evergreen fire glinted in her eyes.

His gut twisted. Avoiding her wasn't working. Until she understood who Sir Flirtalot was, she'd be in danger. "Look, I shouldn't have gotten so mad. I haven't been totally honest with you, either."

She stiffened. "It can't be as bad as your tone suggests."

His gut tightened more, almost nauseated. She didn't want to hear it. If he was right about why, he had to tell her.

Heart wrenching, he clasped her hand. Soon, she'd strike him across the face, ending a friendship he treasured far too much to not destroy. "Dear, I'm a heartbreaker, a two-timer, a player, whatever you call it. As I ran my shell game, at any given moment, I'd have at least two or three hearts I was toying with, while withholding my own heart. The vast majority got dumped and told what I truly thought of them, at a rather cruel moment."

"In the middle of a make-out fest?" She was turning green again.

The shame flooding him matched her visible pain. "Um, if I had been the girl, I would've been called a tease, except I then added extreme insult to an 'injury' that we have every right to inflict. Whenever I didn't dump girls that cruelly, I rubbed the other girls that I was stringing along in their faces, then I gave them the cold shoulder and refused all contact. It never mattered how many girls I played, another came around to take the last one's place. There was always another fool who still wanted a piece of me."

Sue-Ann became rigid and her grip on his hand tightened.

Why am I hurting her like this? He glanced to her hand clasped in his. He'd thoughtlessly interwoven her fingers with his. Oh, not good. Worse, he couldn't bear to let go, and she'd gripped his hand harder while in this hold.

How would she react, when she realized its true meaning? She was even less ready than himself for a romantic bond meant to be unbreakable.

Yeah, best to keep telling her the awful truth. "My old high school had a set of triplets and a set of twins. My most infamous maneuver was dating all five girls at once. The craziest part is, when the girls found out, one of the twins still wanted to go out with me. Instead of being grateful, I moved on to my next victim. Patti managed to wrangle a commitment out of me and hung in there two whole months. She thought I'd changed. I hadn't. I cheated on her with Oriana an entire month. Patti finally caught me and called it quits. Oriana, however, decided she wanted it all. And all I gave her was the boot.

"In February, I met Vera. She was different, a real sweetheart, my actual type of girl for once, which I'd destroyed my chances with. Girls like you and Vera don't fall for Sir Flirtalot when you can see me working a room."

Sue-Ann's pleading, denying eyes didn't want to hear anymore.

Jordy took deep breaths, far too close to tears. He was still an evil jerk. This shame, the pain of what he'd done, was far too centered on Sue-Ann and how he'd long since thrown away what they could've had, someday.

No. He gulped. "But Vera was new at my old school, so she didn't know what I was when she first asked me out. I was so surprised, I accepted. Her new friends later did warn her, but she didn't listen. Like the others who'd wanted a commitment, she decided to give the bad boy a chance."

Sighing, Sue-Ann shook her head. Likely, she agreed with his therapist that him behaving badly was somehow different than him being a bad boy.

He stared at the dog excrement in the grass. It felt like he'd been rolling in it. "After a while, even I hoped I'd change for the better. But I'd fallen so far, I was *proud* of myself for only cheating on her twice. The second time, she caught me, and even though I'd messed up royally, she gave me another chance. I finally had the decency to feel an ounce of guilt again. I promised myself I wouldn't hurt her again."

Sue-Ann's feet stepped back, and their joined hands finally parted.

"This last May, Vera's dad got offered a big promotion in LA. He talked to her about it, and she didn't want to move still again, so he was trying to arrange for a permanent position in Chicago, but I got scared. That is when Isabel approached me, playing my own game. Pride had me so blinded, I fell for it. I let her kiss me right at school. Vera walked in. She was gone within days. Isabel and I became official a week later. I couldn't justify cheating on Vera to myself, as I always had, so I sought to redeem myself by being better to Isabel. I've managed to go this whole summer without fooling around."

"But this time, she was the one cheating on you?"

"Yes, that humiliating crash and burn was still underway when my mom announced Jordan had returned home to Gramps and I got forced to fly out to Glenshire, kicking and screaming. I didn't care if Jordan had turned his own life around. I knew this 'vacation' would be far too tempting for me. If I wasn't stupidly trying to make up for my sins, Isabel would've gotten the ax back in June. So, yeah, I did leave Chicago wondering what the girls here are like. After all, how could she find out?"

"And me?" Sue-Ann whispered almost too lowly to hear her.

"If I keep acting up, keep striking me out. I can't remember the last time merely holding a girl's hand was so awesome, it's amazing. But, yeah, calling you my girlfriend was really Boo's idea of giving you a friendly warning. He saw what you didn't. At our hello, I was half-heartedly resisting thoughts that were wrong. From the start, you've been Vera all over again, times ten."

She whisper-shouted, through her teeth, "I was a mess."

"Yeah, a hot one." He smiled sheepishly. "As I recall it, I was tempted to mentally hose you down, Sue-Ann. I like curvy, not starved."

"Oh," she said in a doubtful tone.

Yep, he had blown up his credibility. At least she was safe from him. She played with her hair. "So, is that all of it?"

He breathed deep. Huh. His shoulders felt lighter. Why hadn't he gotten slapped like he deserved? "Um, I can't think of anything more."

"Then we better go back. People are staring."

Not what I expected. Jordy bit his lip. Apparently, this would take time to sink in. "Sue-Ann, no one confesses to what I've done unless it's true."

"Oh, I believe you. I just don't care."

Yeah, right. He touched her shoulder and forced himself to look her in her pained eyes. Their chests heaved at the same time as their faces broke. She hugged him, sobbing against his chest.

Huh? He pulled her back but leaned their foreheads together, breathing heavy, just letting himself feel the agony of having done this to her, the self-hate for caring about that and not the victims of his shell game. He should've listened to his therapist and asked why they all did what they did.

Her lips moved in silent prayer.

Another good reason he couldn't have her. Gulping, he backed away.

Evergreen fire sparked as she gazed up at him with the strength of the up-rooted oak tree that should be dead yet somehow still lived.

He took another step back.

She followed and touched his shoulder. "Where did you first hear what you told me at my campfire last weekend?"

Huh? His heart thudded. His shoulders hunched. "At a church youth camp, in seventh grade." *Where Dad was a lay leader.* "The long, preachy version of that talk was followed up by a writing assignment meant to get us thinking about, um, someday and what we want, um, someday. Christine and I broke the rules and read each other's assignments. I kidded her for wanting to marry Jesus. Christine accused me of wanting to marry Christine."

"Or an unrelated girl who fit a description your twin also fit, rather?"

His face burned like he was still twelve. "Before I specified 'red or brown haired and is not my sister,' but so? Why remember the dweeb who went so overboard in planning my future, Sis thought I was in love with a girl I had never met?" His voice began breaking oddly. "I angrily drove a truck over the dweeby boy scout and his dweeby dream."

Sue-Ann smiled. "Boy Scout, by the grace of God, here you stand."

"I wish," he muttered, his fist clenched over his heart, around Christine's ring. *Bro, is this really for me or for your unmet fiancée?* "Sis never let up on my 'engagement' to 'Not Christine.' I wish I never let up on my waiting."

She took his face in her hands. "My friend, you're forgiven for falling into the darkness. You're forgiven for still being in the process of coming out of it when we met. I am certain you're not there anymore. If you were, you would've never given me a second glance. Players don't play with me."

"I know, a Jesus Girl like you is off-limits, that's why I'm kicking myself so hard over our thing. In my mind, it makes me the lowest of the low."

"One, we're still only friends. Two, if you were still in such darkness, you would not confess it. You are free. And I don't hold your *past* against you."

Jordy stared. Whoa, she was right. He'd been there and done that with empty promises, but this confession could've never come from Sir Flirtalot, because he wasn't Sir Flirtalot.

Not anymore.

I see you in her eyes, tempting me to thank you, God. Grinning, Jordy embraced Sue-Ann tight and whispered in her ear, "You're too good to me. Much too good." By the time he got to the last "good," his lips could taste her ear and they begged for more. His hand weakly turned her head to comply.

An "Amen" shouted from across the alley knocked some sense into him.

Okay, thanks. He released Sue-Ann and smiled sheepishly. "I'm afraid that's Durant for, 'Come and get it.'"

She just nodded, eyes wide as saucers.

Right, time for some space. Jordy returned to the barbecue and helped himself to a couple burgers and a salad, then found a quiet corner by a bush.

A big, furry, four-footed, black beggar planted itself across the fence. He shooed the Labrador Retriever twice before he gave up and ignored the dog.

This freedom, he could never repay Sue-Ann or God for, and it gave him serious hope of him ever actually hashing things out with God. Still, once the truth sunk in for her, she'd realize her ever trusting him again would still be stupid, and he would be freed from Sue-Ann's friendship as well.

Sobbing threatened, and for once it had nothing to do with Christine.

Chapter 15

HEART FLUTTERING, SUSANNA entered the gate to the Durants' yard. Oh, City Boy had become Neighbor Boy. Could Jordy truly now have a crush on the girl next door? Well, across the alley but still.

Glaring, Cara grabbed Susanna's arm. "What was that?"

Susanna closed the gate. "What was what?"

Cara motioned toward their yard. "That! You and Jordy!"

"Jordy started it, not me."

Cara clenched her teeth. "And what did he want?"

Good, then her sister had missed that Jordy had almost gone right back to—why, why? He couldn't truly have any desire to kiss a girl so homely, only Jesus could love her, so why keep trying it, and why have a rule against it?

Mary Anne Walsh padded over in Durants' well-kept lawn. "Sweetheart, what did the fellow want? He seemed upset."

Susanna shrugged. "We're okay now. He just wasn't expecting me here, and we had some private matters to hash out."

"Oh, I see." Mary Anne patted her forearm. "Hang on to him, Susie Q. He strikes me as a good boy."

"You wouldn't think so, if you'd overheard," Susanna said ruefully.

"Oh, I did." Mary Anne chuckled. "Have you noticed that he likes you?"

Face warming, Susanna said lowly, "Jordy and I are only friends."

"Even so, the pup's got it bad for you, Susie Q." She bobbed Susanna's chin, then got in line behind Mrs. McKay.

Once Mary Anne was out of earshot, Susanna muttered, "Not a chance."

"Sue-Ann," Cara said, "it seems to me he does—"

"—how can he truly, when he doesn't even know me? I didn't have magic slippers, just broken glasses and a roaring headache." She pushed her glasses up her nose. "Now, Cinderella's got a new pair of glasses, and it's game over."

Cara wiggled her eyebrows. "Jordy is the perfect Prince Charming."

Susanna frowned. If her sister got wind of what he'd told her, everyone in a thirty-mile radius would hear. "Were you eavesdropping on us, too?"

Cara snorted. "I wish. Mom wouldn't let me."

Susanna sighed with relief. "Remind me to thank her."

"What were you guys talking about, anyway?"

Susanna shook her head. "It's too personal."

Cara glanced at the line to the buffet. "Okay, I'll let it go for now, but you owe me a full report. Remember, I told you about his folks."

"This is different." In that she wouldn't spill even if Cara tickled her.

Her sister rolled her eyes. "Sure, it isn't. Let's get in line, I'm hungry."

After the girls ate, Cara played with the baby for his young mother, who was now out of the pool and eating dinner with her own parents.

Maybe she was wrong about why Jordy didn't want to come. This adult party was as boring as her peers' parties were too loud; she'd stopped getting invited to those in elementary school. Should she go home? No, that would be rude. Where was Jordy hiding?

She spotted him sitting behind a bush, teasing Shadow with the burger he had almost gone.

She crossed over to the boy, got a tail thump from the dog, and smiled at the boy. "Why are you over here with Shadow, Neighbor Boy?"

Jordy startled and glanced up. "I'd figured, after my blabbermouth, you wouldn't want anything to do with me. Girls with a brain tend to avoid me."

Susanna settled in between him and the bush. "I'm not going anywhere. I may be a nerd, but I don't abandon a friend."

He finished his burger. "What's your real name, again?"

Face warming, she shook his hand. "Susanna Quinn McCoy."

"Well, Susanna, I don't yet know you as well I'd like to, but please don't negatively label yourself. Now, I do that to myself, I feel I deserve it, but you don't. Mom's had me stuck in the brainy classes since fourth grade. I used to always carry a 4.0 GPA, and I still make the honor roll when I actually study and cooperate with my therapists. Does that make me a nerd?"

She stared. His tone was mildly argumentative, but his face truly wanted to know. Jordy made seeing a therapist sound like seeing a dentist, and he had any doubt on how cool he was? "You're way too—you could never have been either a nerd or a dweeb. But a lot of people would disagree about me."

"Then a lot of people are not only wrong, they know you even less than I do. The Sue-Ann I knew wasn't a nerd."

"She doesn't exist." A stray tear trickled down Susanna's cheek. Jordy stole the tear. "I know she was real because she was you."

She shook her head. "You don't understand."

He met her gaze. "What makes you imaginary? Because you've only just now trusted me with your full legal name, you faked an accent that is long gone, you misled me about where you live, and you were half-blind? I'm used to you without glasses, but I fail to see how all that makes you non-existent. It's great if you're not the girl who had me wondering why I kept running a gauntlet trying to reach you. But your sister didn't find that nonexistent. She said you were acting out of fear. Unless the Sue-Ann I supposedly don't know is fearless, I'd say she's the exact same girl I do know."

She bit her lip. "I wish to God I was."

Jordy took her hand. "Let me tell you a secret, Sue-Ann. I know evil has tried to break you. Yet here you are, alive, and with a fire in you that I haven't seen in a long, long time. You have a choice whether to let jerks like me keep you down or to face your fear. If anything, this summer, you did the latter."

Her lip quivered. "Jordy, I hate it when you're right."

A sweet tenderness spread over his face. He scooted closer and slipped his left arm around her. "Shh, no one's watching."

"Since when have I cared what others think? Never."

Jordy squeezed her hand. "If you say so." His face crept closer to hers.

A warning flooded her stomach. This again, why? She pulled away and pushed herself backwards with both hands. The bush pricked her.

He cringed. "What did I do? Have I made you uncomfortable?"

Aw, even such a cool guy sometimes felt as vulnerable and uncertain as she did. She patted his arm. "There's no place I'd rather be. We were simply sitting too close together, too publicly. Someone might get the wrong idea."

Jordy laughed. "I thought you didn't care what people think?"

Her face warmed. "I don't, but we do need to be careful, for your own sake. You don't need the pressure. What about your reputation?"

"What about it? I've done worse to it than hang around you."

Curiosity thy name is Susanna. She leaned back in. "Like what?"

"Besides having run a shell game that had my last therapist worried I'd land my behind in jail before the age of twenty-one? Try the time I threw a chair across the school cafeteria. I'm lucky I didn't hit anyone."

"You what!"

He shushed her. "This one is so private, when I told my mom, I got sent to therapy as the patient, and all the gritty details are only for my therapist's ears. So, in my freshman year, some girl at lunch was complaining about her siblings. I'm so not wanting to hear this, so I stand to leave, but she turns to me and says, 'So, Corey, you don't have any siblings, do you?'

"Now I'm getting mad, but I grit my teeth and say, 'I had a twin sister.'

"She says, all perky, 'Really? Then, where is she?'

"I grip the back of my chair, well knowing I'm about to explode. Instead of hitting a girl, I hurl the chair across the room and yell, 'She's dead, you moron!' After I then ran out, I locked myself in a stall in the men's room and spent the next few hours in there blubbering and missing my sister."

Instinctively, Susanna held Jordy's hand. "What happened?"

"I laid low, hoping that the dweeb from the suburbs exploding would be forgettable, but it wasn't. I'm sure they're so glad I'm not back this year."

Susanna swallowed. "I'm sorry."

Jordy shook his head. "That wasn't the worst part. Then, Brandt stayed loyal to me even though he'd already started running with the crowd that had hated us. Brandt wanted to smooth things over for me with our old crowd by explaining about Christine, but I decided I'd rather deal with the cold stares. What shocked and confused me, and turned me into Sir Flirtalot, was which kids had stopped giving me cold stares. Aggressive girls who had mocked me were suddenly all over me. It was scary. So I took control." Regret shone in Jordy's eyes. "It was never like this. I never knew this. Thank you for this."

Aw, he truly was free—from a horror *forced* on him. Susanna said a brief prayer and hugged him. "Jordy, I'm so, so sorry. You had every right to be angry some witch had 'run a truck over you' in such a horrifying manner. Is that what's truly caused your recurring nightmare? Does the truck come back around and run you down, too, with that witch driving it?"

"Yeah, thanks." He hugged her tight and released her. "You're the first person besides my mom and my therapists who didn't find something wrong with me saying no rather than with a girl refusing to respect my no like that."

"I'm so sorry, that's horrible. I wish I could do more for you."

He held her hand in their own special "best friends forever" way. "Dear, you've already done more than I expected from anyone, let alone a girl. No girl's meant as much to me since Christine died, and that's saying something. If I could've traded places with her, I would've."

"Boy Scout, I'm glad that you weren't ever literally dead, because then I would've never met you. Whatever 'our thing' is, I hope it lasts a lifetime."

He smiled shyly and squeezed her hand. "Me, too, Sue-Ann."

Warmth buzzed about her crown. Okay, he truly did care about her, but his wording—on one hand, it sounded like the adorable boy once had 'Marry Not Christine' penciled in for some time after college. On the other hand, she had still been just compared to his sister.

What was she dealing with here? Did it matter? Could it last, with Jordy attending her school? What if social pressures tore them apart?

"ME, TOO, SUE-ANN." Jordy's heart fluttered. His entire body felt wired. His sweet, innocent new best friend for life hadn't meant to propose. Nor was she hinting for him to, at least not any time soon, but what that idea did to him—time to go. He stood. "I'd better go see what's left of desert."

He grabbed the last slice of his mom's raspberry pie off the table, then took a seat with his parents. He ignored their chatting with an elderly couple whose names he couldn't remember and could barely taste the pie.

Why had Sue-Ann sought him out? The one time he recalled her doing that, she'd used the pretense of scolding him for violating Gramps' rules. This time, no pretenses. The last thing he'd expected his confession to do was to bring them even more closer together.

"Jordy?" his mom said. "Mrs. Walsh asked you a question."

"Oh, sorry. I—I have to go in a sec. I'll see you later." He got up, dropped his plate in the trash, and raced inside the house. He shut the door behind him and leaned his forehead against the cool wood, his breathing ragged.

Not losing Sue-Ann initially elated him, but dread and self-disgust now smothered most of that. If he hadn't excused himself, he'd be presently busy kissing her in the bushes. Why did his feelings for her keep sending all sense flying from his head? He knew better than to make the same mistake again, and when his girl was officially just his closest friend at that.

How could it work out like this? He told her the truth to protect her, so she'd know her first instincts about him were right. Instead, she tried to help him and continued with him on the same dangerous course. And what did he do? Went along with her, dug them both in deeper, and then confessed how much he loved her, which earned him an actual verbal admission the feeling was mutual. His foolish heart had soared to cloud nine, but that was in truth terrible news. She deserved a guy who loved God like she did.

He sucked in slow, deep breaths. Their bond had to be why the truth didn't phase her. Perhaps it was good he knew where he actually stood with her, that an exciting and terrifying idea was brewing in both of their hearts. He'd have to be far more careful, lest Sir Flirtalot rise from the dead to claim yet another victim and cost him such a precious friend-for-now-anyway.

His mom jiggled the door. He jumped back. She got the door open and knit her brows. Her eyes shown with concern. "Son, what are you doing? Are you okay? Was it that girl? Did something happen?"

"No, Sue-Ann's awesome, and I'm cool now. Did you need something?"

"Oh-kay. If you're sure, would you go get me your CD player, please?"

"Sure." He jogged downstairs and grabbed his boombox off the dresser. Once back outside, he handed it to his mom. "Here."

She plugged the boombox into a socket near the door and turned the radio on. Oldies music poured out of the speakers. He groaned. "Peachy."

"Would you prefer I tuned it to the Christian station?"

Once, he'd have said yes. Jordy winced. "Oldies will be fine."

The old lady that his folks had been talking to earlier approached. "May I have this dance?"

He hesitated. "Yeah, sure, I guess."

She took him to the far corner of his backyard, away from the others, on the opposite side from the bushes where he had been hiding out earlier. The old lady leaned against the fence. "I bet you don't remember my name."

Evidently by dance, she meant talk. "I'm bad at names, I'm afraid."

"It's Mary Anne. I sat for the girls when they were little. Sue-Ann was a live one. Such a chatter box, so much energy! Then, grammar school rolled around. Her crying momma told me the happy, bouncy baby she'd known had been replaced by a listless shadow. Yet, when I sat, sometimes she would be the same feisty Sue-Ann I had always known." She studied him. "But now, you see it too, don't you?"

"I have seen the fire in her eyes. I took it for granted until I ran into her at school. I hardly recognized her, but I think I'd scared her out of her wits, and the glasses didn't help, either."

The lady chuckled. "I see. Something at school did try to put her fire out, but underneath her cold, dead ashes, live embers still burn. You can see hints of her old spirit in her eyes at times. She must've felt a lot of strong emotions around you. Once, I'd hoped, if something buried it, surely we can unbury it, but our bumbling only makes more trouble for her. So I've stopped searching for the fountain of youth and accepted her as she is today. The world's had enough Ponce de Leons, if you know what I mean."

"Yeah, I do." Too well. She was advising him to join her in seeing signs his girl was suffering from a disease that just so happened to be affecting her brain and doing nothing. He bit his lip. So things were that bad. He'd learned of the socioeconomic reasons that Sue-Ann had endured a prolonged lack of mental health care, but it still felt like her community had seen her teeth fall out and 'accepted' her as toothless instead of taking her to the dentist.

Maybe he wasn't the only one who saw her need and still wanted to help.

Maybe there was a reason beyond random chance that her "live embers" and his own "live embers" had kept getting thrown together.

Maybe a certain Daddy in Heaven was relighting the fire in their souls.

It'd explain why he clearly had been depressed, now that it was gone.

DUSK FELL AND THE DURANTS turned on party lights and the radio. Susanna sat up on the edge of the deck and watched her sister dance in turn with their dad, Mr. McKay, Jordy's dad, Mr. Walsh, and Mr. LaRosa. Cara even dared to dance with Jordy. From the radiance on her face, if anyone had a crush on Jordy, Cara did.

And I'm not jealous. Nope, nope, nope. Not jealous. Not jealous at all.

The opening strains of "Susie Q" poured out of the radio's speakers. Face warming, Susanna sucked in a breath. *God, please have mercy on me. Just this once, could Dad not announce they're playing my song?*

Jordy came over and offered Susanna his hand. The twinkle in his eyes matched his playful grin.

She forced her traitorous hand to stay put. *Don't even think about it.* It was bad enough he asked. Her parents wouldn't know Jordy didn't know the significance of this song—and Cara was liable to conveniently forget.

Jordy dropped his hand. "What? You don't like to dance?"

"It's not that, it's just . . . I'm Susanna Quinn, remember? I.E. Susie Q."

After another second, a light donned his eyes. "Oh. So? It's not like I'm asking you to marry me." Jordy laughed. He spread his hands. "All I will ask, all I want, is to spend the rest of tonight with you, out where our parents are watching us and we'll both feel safe. It's not a date. To be blunt, I'm also not thrilled with myself for continually making eyes at a fourteen-year-old."

"Technical much, my friend? I'll be fifteen this September sixth."

Jordy pulled the chain around his neck out of his shirt. From it dangled a girl's sapphire ring with diamond accents. "The month of the sapphire."

"Yeah, that is my birthstone. What's the significance?"

Jordy fingered the ring. "Christine loved sapphires. I bought her this for her last Christmas. It was her favorite present, she wore it constantly. Mom gave it back to me when she died. As Sir Flirtalot, I hid it under my shirt, but I never stopped wearing it as the memorial my sister would wish for it to be."

Susanna touched the ring. "It's beautiful."

Jordy left it out on display. "Just like Christine."

"I wish I could've met her."

"If she were here, she'd have roped me into making friendship bracelets with you two, then roped you into playing the games that I liked with us, and generally helped me keep my hands off you. She was always the good twin."

"No, because that'd make you the evil twin."

"Guess you don't know me all that well, then."

She put her right index finger to his lips. "Trust me, Jordy, you're a child of the light, just as I am."

He kissed her finger and hopped up beside her on the deck's edge. "You know, I actually understood what you meant."

She didn't fully understand, so how could he? "And what did I mean?"

"You don't know." He stared ahead. "We're a real pair, you and I. You have the heart for God but little head knowledge. I have the head knowledge, but I have lost the heart for God, if I ever truly had it. Yet, the more time we spend together, the more I remember, the less I feel like a hypocrite, and the more I feel the light burning inside of us."

"Yes, that's it exactly." Her voice trembled and her crown glowed.

He twisted to face her. His knee brushed hers as he offered his hand to her. She gave her hand to him in return and intertwined their fingers. Their eyes met. Her heart thundered as she got lost in his sapphire depths, but she kept their hands clasped so wonderfully until their dads approached them.

She stared in the darkness, lit by a porch floodlight. Where had everyone else gone? Clearly these blissful last few minutes had been more like hours.

Her dad asked, "Having fun?"

Susanna glanced at Jordy and got lost yet again in his eyes. "That's one way to put it."

Her dad said, "Say good-bye. It's late and you have school tomorrow."

"She's not the only one." Mr. Durant smiled at his son and at Susanna before he turned to her dad. "It was good talking to you, Elliot." Mr. Durant shook her dad's hand then went inside.

Susanna hopped down from the deck, but Jordy reached for her hand and she let him hold it in a playful, Victorian manner. His eyes sparkled like sapphires. "Alas, must thou depart, fair Juliet? Adieu! Adieu, dear maiden, and good night." He leaned down and kissed the back of her hand.

Susanna's cheeks grew warm and her heart raced. Oh, he was a student of the theater, too. "Ah, you flatter me, my prince. 'Tis that not the lark? Oh, but 'twas the nightingale, I fear. So, good night, sweet prince—"

"And flights of angels sing me to my rest? Dare I dream to have expired and gone to Heaven this good night?"

"Oh, no! I meant 'twas the nightingale, and all fair children must depart to the world of dreams to meet again only by day's sweet breath."

Jordy hesitated then slapped his leg and stood. "Ah, my dear, you have surely bested me, so alas I must depart until morning's light."

He started for his door, but Susanna called, "Hey, Jordy?"

Jordy turned back. "Yeah?"

"I'll see you tomorrow. Wanna wager on when we find each other?"

Jordy grinned. "Sometime before lunch, no doubt."

Susanna's dad tapped her shoulder. "Enough stalling. Let's go."

She said, "I shall resist thou not, Father."

He glowered. "Would you stop that? You're freaking me out."

Sigh. "I'm coming. And where is my so-called sister?"

"Your mom took her home over an hour ago. Come on."

At home, Susanna collapsed on her bed.

From the overhead bunk, Cara asked sleepily, "Sue-Ann?"

"It's me, Sis."

"Oh, good." Cara's head and shoulders appeared upside-down over the edge of the bunk bed. "And how was your evening, Susie Q?"

Susanna ignored her sister's snide tone and held back a laugh. Now that she didn't want Cara calling her that, she would. "You mean before or after you went to bed?"

"Cut it out. I want the dirt. How was Jordy?"

"Oh, so it's Jordy you want to know about. I thought so. Don't deny it, little sister. I saw how you were hanging all over him."

"Why, I . . ." Cara swore. "Sue-Ann, did you or did you not have a good time with Jordy!"

Susanna glowered. "I've enjoyed a private but interesting evening with a good guy who happens to be a good . . ." Her sister had this coming. "Friend."

Disappointed incredulity crossed Cara's face. "Friend?"

Susanna pretended not to notice. "Got a problem with me having a new best friend who so isn't kissing me? If there is, I can always break it off."

"Nah." Cara paused. "If you don't want him, can I have him?"

Susanna threw her extra pillow at her sister. *As only a friend, I'll love you 'til death, Jordy, but I won't let myself or Cara be the next fool you date.*

Chapter 16

SUSANNA RAN INTO TERRILYN and Lindsey at their lockers before homeroom Thursday morning. Terrilyn said, "Hey, Susanna, what's up?"

Last night's barbecue dangled in her mind as a coy smile wiggled out and her cheeks warmed. "Oh, not much."

She got her locker open, shoved her backpack inside of it, grabbed her morning books, and then slammed the door shut, adding her contribution to all the noise that oddly felt less painful today.

On the girls' way to homeroom, Lindsey asked, "Hey, did you guys see Jason Weaver on *Sister, Sister* last night?"

Terrilyn had grinned. "Aw, yeah! It was da bomb!"

Susanna bit her lip. "I love that show! It was on last night?"

Terrilyn frowned. "How'd you miss it? The WB advertised it all week!"

They reached homeroom and took their seats. Susanna turned to face Lindsey and Terrilyn's table. Best to tell half of the truth. "Oh, I had to go to this party at our new neighbors. It was so freaky." Magical more like it.

Lindsey scrutinized her and smiled. "Hey, what about that freaky guy?"

"Oh, yeah! Did you ever find out who your stalker is?" Terrilyn asked.

Hey. Susanna glowered. "He is not stalking me, but he is why the party was so freaky. It was his family moving in!"

Lindsey gasped. "No way. You're joking!"

Susanna shook her head. "Wish I was."

"Way cool," Terrilyn said, "that is totally freaky!"

"You want to know what's really freaky?"

Terrilyn leaned forward. "What?"

"Well, his mom's introducing him to all the neighbors, but when she gets to us and introduces us, he snatches my glasses and says, 'Hello, Sue-Ann.'"

Lindsey frowned. "Sue-Ann? Where did he get that from?"

Terrilyn waved. "He probably overheard one of us calling her by name in the hall and misheard us."

"Actually, my sister and my mom called me that when I was little."

"It does sound like baby talk," Lindsey said. "No heck. My parents used to call me Sweet'n'low."

"I see why that one didn't stick." Terrilyn rolled her eyes. "Is it possible he remembers you from nursery school, Susanna?"

Susanna shook her head. "His family just moved here from Chicago."

Lindsey shrugged. "I guess it's the king of all coincidences."

After homeroom, Susanna headed downstairs to Chemistry with Lindsey and Terrilyn. They gathered at three stations at the front of the room, with Lindsey behind Susanna and with Terrilyn across the aisle from Lindsey. Tall, long lab tables ran beside their desks. Susanna's was on her right, as she faced the blackboard, and behind her once she twisted toward the others.

A moment later, Lindsey bit her lip. Terrilyn frowned and stopped mid-sentence to clear her throat. Susanna glanced behind her and caught Jordy leaning over the lab table in between their desks, about to tap her shoulder. They both started talking at once. "What are you doing here? Stop that!"

Jordy covered her mouth. "You're not my twin sister, so cut it out."

Me? Susanna removed his hand. "Do that again and I'll bite you."

Jordy laughed. "I'd better bite my tongue for once. Oh, by the way, good morning, Sue-Ann. Is this a new record for us?"

Terrilyn demanded from behind Susanna, "Who the heck are you? Why were you staring at my friend in the hall yesterday?"

Jordy kept his amused eyes trained on Susanna as he answered. "Jordan Walker Durant, Jr., call me Jordy, and that's between me and Sue-Ann."

Susanna released her breath. Thankfully, her new best friend didn't feel like going into it, either. He'd embarrassed her enough by making it obvious they knew each other. How would her classmates react?

"Oh, her name's not Sue-Ann, it's Susanna." Lindsey looked at Susanna like she just did her a big favor.

Susanna winced pathetically at Jordy. *Don't make this worse.*

He grinned sheepishly. "Susanna's taking a lot longer to stick, Sue-Ann."

Oh, lovely, she'd always be Sue-Ann to him. At least somebody believed in her. "I always hated that nickname."

"Then I'll work on it, but it'll take a while, I'm usually bad at names. So, dare I repeat the question regarding what we're both doing here?"

Susanna shrugged. "Due to a clerical error, the juniors and sophomores pursing a college-prep diploma all have to take Chem this year to meet our graduation requirements. If you registered late, the other class is likely full."

Dr. Vinoski cleared his throat. "Excuse me, but the bell has rung."

"It did?" Susanna twisted back to face the front. "Sorry, sir."

Forty minutes later, the bell rang. Susanna headed to study hall. Jordy fell in step with her. "Hey, Sue-Ann, study hall's where, again?"

Huh? "Oh, that's right, you're new here. Auditorium, main hall on the left and across from the gym. Come with us, we're all headed there."

In study hall, Susanna sat one row behind Lindsey and Terrilyn. Jordy settled next to Susanna, glancing around like a twitchy soldier in a war zone, his right hand fidgeting in his pocket. Why? Oh—a sexual assault, at school? Whoa. She squeezed his elbow and whispered in his ear, "We're safe in here, I promise. Our study hall monitors are strict. We're not allowed to raise our voices, let alone get raunchy. Oh, you'll get expelled, if that's a knife."

"It's a compass," her best friend murmured back, loosening up a bit. He glowered at her acquaintances. "What?"

Lindsey and Terrilyn had twisted around in their seats to face Jordy and Susanna and were sizing them up with a mixture of curiosity and suspicion. Lindsey asked, "Exactly how do you two know each other? I mean, you're not exactly, well . . ."

"Get to the point, girl." Terrilyn rolled her eyes. "It's not like Susanna to hang around your type."

Jordy winced. "Shows, huh?"

Lindsey glanced between Susanna and Jordy. "Let's change the subject until Susanna feels ready to share how they met, and hence what she actually did this summer, which clearly involves the new guy somehow, Susanna."

Terrilyn pointed at Jordy. "It's Jordy, right?"

"Right."

"So, do you have a girlfriend?"

Jordy squirmed and glanced at Susanna.

Gasping, Lindsey and Terrilyn gawked, wide-eyed.

They think we're dating and find it scandalous! Susanna's face burned, her heart raced, and it felt like green spots would burst soon. Jordy held her hand and squeezed reassuringly. His gentle eyes captured her gaze. He took deep breaths with her, bringing her back to Earth.

He murmured into her ear, "Sorry for that. I just need a little help here."

Oh. She glanced down to the ring he was playing with on his chain, left out of his shirt. This was probably also the first time he'd worn it exposed in public in two years. "My friend here from Chicago is just off a bad break up, and he's left a bad crowd, not just a girl, so he'll be staying single here while he continues to get his head back on straight."

Lindsey wetted her lips. "Oh, I see. That makes sense."

Terrilyn asked, "So, Jordy, what year are you?"

"Junior."

Lindsey winced.

Terrilyn grinned. "Cool! How old are you? Do you drive? Do you have a car? What kind?"

"Sixteen, yes, no."

Terrilyn frowned. "What's the point of a license if you don't have a car?"

"Mom's letting me use her car. She said she'll share with Jordan."

Terrilyn frowned. "With Jordan? Are you talking about your dad?"

Jordy's cheeks colored. "He's recently reunited with Mom and me after a long separation. I'm still getting used to him again."

"I get that, my parents separated. At least after the divorce I knew where we stood. I never knew what would happen during the separation. I mean, were they going to get back together or not?"

"Yeah. When Jordan dragged me 'on vacation' with him, I thought they were getting divorced, but he knew the truth and wanted us to reconnect and regroup. I was still climbing out of a bad headspace, and my mom decided to 'help' by hiding that we were moving here, giving me no notice and no choice on leaving and cutting all ties. It's still sinking in that I'm free."

"Free? Like from the kind of gang that assaults its own peeps on the way in and on the way out? To get you out, your parents didn't tell even you, they picked up everything, moved out of state, and patched themselves up, all just to get you out? Well, congrats, that's dope."

"Thanks, I was a player, not a gangbanger, but my successful reform did require my family to take such radical steps. I'm just thankful it's working."

While Jordy and Terrilyn had chatted, Susanna found herself twisting in toward Jordy, glowering, with her stomach gnawing. Why was she acting like this? What was wrong with her?

Lindsey leaned over the back of her theater seat and nudged Susanna's closest shoulder. "Ooh! Is somebody jealous?"

Susanna's cheeks flamed. "I am not!"

Lindsey winked. "We believe you, huh, Terrilyn?"

"Of course we do," Terrilyn said, tongue-in-cheek.

Jordy laughed. "Rapunzel isn't used to sharing her prince."

Not okay. Susanna said sweetly, "She doesn't mind sharing her prince. She understands he's an important aristocrat with a lot of important people to see. She just never thought she'd have to share her dog."

Lindsey gasped.

Terrilyn stared. "Susanna, I can't believe you said that."

"I can." Jordy flashed Susanna a grin and held her hand. "Are we okay?"

"Zingers at my expense aren't okay." She dropped his hand and lowered her eyes, her stomach twisting. "Especially not at school."

"Sorry." Jordy lifted her chin. "I'll never hurt you on purpose. You're the closest friend still in my life. My loyalties here will always be to you first. If anyone disses you, if it gets back to me, I'll get suspended for fighting."

She smiled shyly. Why was Jordy showing up at school a fate worse than death, again? He did understand—and still wanted to be her friend.

JORDY SAT IN HIS FOURTH period class, his eyes on the clock. This class he could sleep through and still ace it. His mind drifted to his new favorite face and her cat-green eyes, magically locking with his gaze, as if their very souls had intertwined for hours, the gentle glow of her hand in his hand.

Okay, you know where this train goes, dude, so let's get off it here.

So better idea: practicing her name. Sue-Ann. No, Susanna.

Ugh, why did she hide that little trick so long and how? Her family may call her Sue-Ann a lot, but Susanna ought to come out at least once or twice. She might have let her sister in on her prank, but—wait. Usually, when her folks were around, she'd either fled or otherwise acted agitated and nervous.

At Glenshire, most of the guys there had known her mainly by sight and the rest wouldn't mention Sue-Ann was a nickname. But, why didn't Gramps say anything? He had to know her real name. That must've been what tipped him off she was up to something.

Now, it made sense her friends didn't know her by a nickname that she evidently never used at school, but he'd gotten the impression Sue-Ann tried to hide that they knew each other. Why? Was he an embarrassing mistake already? But she continued to signal a close attachment to him. In fact, her unconscious signals were too positive, for their official relationship status.

Maybe it was only her social anxiety. Her friends about had heart attacks at the thought of him dating Sue-Ann, and that was before he'd confessed to being a former player—oh that *former* felt good. But, if the negative reaction hadn't been due to his past, then it was weird to go from her being called his girlfriend at Glenshire to the very idea being so shocking here.

Then again, girls with the kind of brain wiring differences he suspected she had would function better out in nature, while the school cafeteria may be hazardous for her, not just draining. Hard for a girl to play in appropriate ways, either, if too much sensory input overloaded her brain.

Hey, were her mental health challenges what her school friends had in mind when they'd said he wasn't her type? Her friends likely expected him to head straight for the in-crowd and were searching for a polite way to ask why he hung around Sue-Ann, er, Susanna. This also explained her sister's claim she was afraid of him. Her social anxiety likely included being boy shy.

The bell rang, jarring Jordy into looking around.

Mike asked, "Hey, man, you going to join us for lunch?"

"Yeah, sure, thanks."

In the lunch room, Sue-Ann and her friends got in the line behind them. Jordy grinned and waved to her. "Hey, meet Sean and Mike. They're in some of my classes."

Mike raised an eyebrow. "So you do know this girl?"

"Yeah, we had a serious communication breakdown yesterday, but we've worked it out and we're friends again. She and I met over the summer, due to a mutual interest from outside of school. Her name's Sue-Ann."

Glowering, Sue-Ann pursed her lips. "It's Susanna, actually."

Man, she really did hate being called Sue-Ann. Okay, Susanna, Susanna, Susanna, Susanna . . . his rose by another name. He tapped her shoulder and caught her gaze. "Your real first name is so beautiful and sweet, it far better suits you, so I'm working on learning it, Susie Q."

"Thank you," she murmured as she smiled, blushing adorably.

Sean elbowed Jordy and sent him a look considering body blocking him to separate him from Susanna, either to protect Jordy from the wrath of God, or to protect the religious sophomore. He grinned back. Yesterday, his shame over the involuntary loss of his innocence, and over the sins he'd committed while taking his revenge for it, had given an impression that his virginity was far less compromised than it was. In truth, his virginity was nonexistent by medical standards, and only technically existed by the standard of *Clueless*.

And Sean was silently ordering Jordy to back off from the marrying kind of girl. Feeling busted, Jordy mouthed an apology to Susanna, sighed, and moved forward with the line while beside Sean and behind Mike. Jordy slid his sister's ring along on his chain. Someday.

Sean cleared his throat and jerked his thumb toward the sapphire ring hanging from around Jordy's male neck. "Is it okay if I ask about that?"

"If it wasn't, I'd have it hidden in my shirt." Jordy stole a glance back at Susanna. His stomach fluttered oddly like a twelve-year-old boy with his first major crush on a girl and who'd only ever gone as far as holding hands.

What she did to him was so amazing.

She sent him a smile that believed in him and in God's work in his life. *Thank you for bringing this girl into my life. I'll never deserve her.* He kept his focus on her and the grace she'd shown him.

Sean stepped back, making good on the silent threat to body block him.

A real bro. Jordy smiled sheepishly, maintaining his eye contact with his girl, and stoked his pretty jewelry. "Sean, this belongs to my future wife. It's her inheritance from my late sister. Fears of dying long plagued my sister, so she left behind a will, and I've also honored her request for me to wear it like this daily, until I'm sure I've found the girl I'm going to marry someday."

Susanna was beaming a silent "I'm so proud of you for reclaiming that." She also looked like she'd hug him, if Sean wasn't still body blocking.

Jordy glanced into their peers' faces, which were all turned toward him. The other two sophomore girls looked inclined to find the ring bittersweet, not dweeby.

Grinning, Sean returned to Jordy's side and slugged his shoulder. "You are a dude I definitely want to get to know, bro."

Glowering, Mike snorted. "I see your problem with the ladies, Jordy."

If only. "I'm no longer as innocent as my girl." He controlled his tone so he conveyed she was a close friend, not his girlfriend. "I'm just not proud of what I did, with this ring still hanging from my neck as a memorial to my lost virtue as well as to my sister." He glanced into the blushing Susanna's pained eyes. Such costly grace. "I can't change my past, but I can reclaim my future."

"Yeah, yeah." Mike waved dismissively and spun. "The line's moving."

Jordy sighed and caught up in line with Mike and Sean. Behind him, the tall girl said too loudly, "Did you know your friend who is a very cute boy is a Prince Charming with a glass slipper hanging from his neck?"

Sputtering, Susanna answered too lowly for him to make out her reply.

Face warm, Jordy grinned. *It really was a lie that I'm a dweeb. Cool.*

Once through the line, Jordy followed the guys back to their table, then glanced up and caught Sue-Ann's eye as she sat with her school friends three tables away. He surveyed the crowded, noisy cafeteria. His stomach knotted. Even if Sir Flirtalot stayed dead, Jordy was still a grade a head of her. Aside from the jocks and the cheerleaders, who were all Black here, at every table, their peers appeared to be self-segregated by their grade levels.

And the silent tension between their school friends in the line, the tones of the guys' voices when they'd spoken of the sophomore class—the "punks" *had* "ruled the school" last year, perhaps by beating all three classes above them in an athletic competition, given the grudging admission the school's best athletes were all now sophomores.

I'm a Class of 1998, she's a Class of 1999—and we're bitter rivals here.

No, they'd work this out. They had to. Or go around it. Given he used to spend his lunch period flirting, staying with his own classmates was smarter than sneaking off to somewhere quiet, alone with his girl.

AFTER SCHOOL, JORDY drove past Sue-Ann as she was headed home on the sidewalk in Easthaven's quiet, clean, middle-class residential neighborhood. They lived across a major intersection, in a working-class area which was in turn not far from low-income housing just one step up from the Bottoms.

Jordy pulled his mom's Taurus over and rolled down the passenger-side window. Sue-Ann, uh, Susanna walked on by, as if lost in thought.

He called, "Hey, could you come here, Susanna?"

She halted then reluctantly spun and trotted back but stopped several feet away and kept her gaze on the ground. "Yes?"

No wonder her friends about died. His chest ached almost like she'd put a knife in him. It had to be her social anxiety, but what had he done to set it off? "Sue-Ann, please don't be shy with me. Have I ever bitten you before?"

"Last night, my ear did get nibbled," she mumbled to the sidewalk.

Oh, that tasty oops. He held back a dopey smile. "If I promise I'll behave, can I at least get another yes to eye contact? We were cool earlier, so why am I suddenly back at square one this afternoon?"

She ceased staring down at the sidewalk but she still didn't quite meet his eyes. "Things are different here."

"Yes, here I have my mom's car and full driving privileges and hence the means to save a friend a long walk home."

The look on her face was a serious no to getting in the car with him. She took a deep breath. "You didn't hotwire this one, did you?"

He turned the engine off and waved the car key. "My mom's letting me take her car to school, remember? So how about the ride home?"

She backed away with fear shining in her eyes.

What am I missing? How am I still too short on her trust for this?

Her face crumbled. "You think I'm weird like everyone else now."

Ouch. Wincing, he climbed out of the car and came around to her on the sidewalk, his hands spread. "I'm still recovering from a mental health crisis myself, remember? I'm familiar with a lengthy list of brain wiring differences thanks to my sister, and she battled worse than what I've seen you battling. I always stood by her. I'll always stand by you."

"Really?" She sniffled, her lower lip wobbling.

Best to show her. He reached her side. "May I give you a hug?"

Susanna glanced around and nodded.

By an unfamiliar instinct, he hugged her from behind her, with his arms holding her waist. Wow. He lowered his head but forced himself to stop well short of her so-tempting ear and said lowly and softly, "What I'm giving you, I've never given anyone else. I'm giving this to you because I'm dead serious about us. I'm not playing games with you now, if I ever was. It's simply hard for me to behave appropriately for our official relationship, between my bad habits and what you truly mean to me."

She'd slowly relaxed, twisted in his arms to face him, and wrapped her own arms tightly around him. Her eyes met his in the magical way. "Jordy, please don't say it. What I told my school friends about you needing to stay single—it was true. You know it is."

This did feel too good. He sighed, backed off, and held her hand instead of herself. "Intellectually, I agree it isn't wise for me to be dating anyone at present. Sorry, I will try to be a better friend who is only a male best friend that your school friends think is very cute."

"If only they weren't right about that." She blushed.

He grinned stupidly. "Okay then, so, would you like to get in the car, get driven home, and get dropped off in the alley? With my hands on the wheel the whole time instead of on you. Or would you like me to walk back here to get my mom's car after I've walked you home?"

Susanna got in the car.

Chapter 17

SUSANNA SWALLOWED THE last bite of scrambled eggs inside their trailer at Glenshire on Saturday morning.

Beside her, Cara tugged on her arm. "Let's go swimming, Sissy."

That sounded far more fun than homework. "I would, but I've got a huge chemistry assignment. Why don't you go ahead? I'll catch up later."

"You do have all day Monday, remember? Monday's Labor Day."

Like I could've missed the signs posted all over Glenshire, advertising the annual Labor Day Weekend Dance is tomorrow night. "If I don't get started on my homework, I'll never do it. Chem's not an easy course. I can tell I'm going to have trouble in it."

"Yeah, right. To you, trouble is a B minus."

"Hey! A girl's gotta have her standards."

"You set your standards so high, you might as well join a convent and marry God."

"Don't worry, I'll settle one of these days."

"God help her if she does."

Susanna ignored that barb and threw her empty plate in the trash. She grabbed her backpack from the loft and took her homework out to the picnic table on their deck. She glanced at her Chemistry assignment then moved it to the bottom of her mental to-do list.

About ninety minutes later, she growled and slapped her pen down on the worksheet laying over her open Chem book. "I'll never get this!"

Over in the deck chair, her dad looked up from his newspaper. "Having trouble? Whatcha working on?"

"Chemistry."

"Wish I could help, but science never was my best subject. Are you sure you can't get it done on your own?"

Maybe she didn't have to. She opened her Chem folder and fingered the triangular-folded note her best friend had passed her during class the other day. The note held all of his contact information and his weekend plans. "I know where I can go. You mind if I take my work somewhere else?"

Her dad shrugged. "Don't see why not."

Susanna shoved her chemistry stuff back into her backpack and took off toward the ravine. Jordy wouldn't simply give her the answers anymore than she ever did anything of the sort. Still, two brains beat one. If she knew Jordy at all, he had Chemistry left on his plate, too.

When she reached the gate dividing the permanent campers' area from overnight area, her fears started talking, twisting her guts.

She drew in deep breaths and pressed on. If Jordy wasn't there, who else would be there this time of day? If he was there, the odds of him slamming the door in her face were lower than her chances of winning the lottery. The guy insisting on giving her rides to and from school wouldn't do such a thing.

On Phill's doorstep, her stomach twisted into more knots. Frowning, she forced her shaky arm up, rang the bell, and held her breath.

After a moment, Jordy opened the door. Eyes wide, he grinned. "Hey, Sue-Ann! Uh, Susanna. So you hate phone calls this much, interesting. Let me guess, you're hating chemistry, too, right now. Isn't Vinoski awful?"

Her breath rushed out. "I figured we could use the emotional support."

"Yep. If we're gonna be stuck, we might as well be stuck together." Jordy ushered her into the den then sat in front of the coffee table his work was spread out on. "My mother is here, but she liked you, so she won't disturb us so long as we're quiet and actually studying. Which problem are you on?"

She sat on the floor next to him. "Um, the first one."

"Great! Now we can be stuck on the first one together."

A thrill rushed through her. Her guess about his homework was dead on.

"Seriously," Jordy said, "get your stuff out. Maybe, if we work together, we can somehow make two halves equal a whole."

Two hours later, they'd managed to complete the assignment. Susanna got up and stretched. "Man, all that work made me hungry."

Jordy stood. "Tell me about it. I say we raid the fridge."

"Uh, nope. Not a good idea. I mean, you're talking about the same fridge Phill—your grandfather eats from."

Jordy's forehead wrinkled. "Yeah, so?"

"The same guy who to this day plays games with my change whenever I buy something from his store? The idea is too weird." Susanna snapped her fingers. "Speaking of which . . ." She rummaged through her backpack to see if she had any money left. Bingo. "Ah ha!" She kissed the dollar bills. "God bless George Washington. All eight of him."

Jordy laughed. "I'm not the only one with a dramatic streak."

Susanna waved this off. "I'm merely in a silly mood."

"Ooh, dramatic and modest. Just what I love in a woman."

Her cheeks burned. She smiled shyly and shook her finger at him. "Hey, you. I'm in a good mood now, but don't push me or it's gonna get ugly."

Why did that sound so playful?

Jordy put his hands out. "Hey, dramatic, modest, and bossy! Just keeps getting better and better."

Susanna grabbed her Chemistry book and lifted it over her head. "I have a textbook and I'm not afraid to use it!"

"Use it anymore, and your brain will explode. Seriously, now that we've fed our brains, let's go feed our stomachs."

She laughed. "One of these days, I'm gonna have to kill you."

"As in with kindness or 'let's get ready to rumble'?" He sounded sincere.

Ha, even she recognized that pro-wrestling catchphrase. Grinning, she put her Chem stuff away and shoved her backpack over her shoulder. As they headed out the front door, she finally purred, "Mmm, I'll take the rumble."

Jordy replied, "If I thought you meant that, I'd be a bit worried."

"No worries, you've got plenty of time to change my mind." She winked, now half-aware that she was flirting with her best friend for the fun of it.

They headed to Glenshire on the side of a country road cutting through a thick forest. Walking close together, they exchanged sideways glances. Her head tilted slightly as she sent him a tiny, impish smile.

A dangerous look entered Jordy's eyes and his killer smile played across his features. Stopping, he held her with his arms up around her shoulders, above her backpack. She snuggled into their cozy embrace. The ring dangling over his heart pressed into her collar bone.

He murmured in her ear, "Do you realize the high stakes you're playing for this morning, my dear? If I either took you up on that rumble or changed your mind, you'd win at this game your first time playing, but we'd lose it all to each other—and endanger our someday. And I want our someday."

His breath tickled her ear. Danger crackled over her body like lightning.

She gasped, broke away from him, and jogged off, her heart racing. Her body's confusing reaction felt far more pleasant than her words for it were.

He matched her pace. "So, are we done playing with fire?"

Boys. "I started it, and I'm not mad at you for finishing it, but why did it have to go anywhere serious? Why can't we just have a little innocent fun?"

"While the neighbors aren't watching? Do we even have neighbors?"

A point to consider. Few traveled on this road, except to go to Glenshire and most came and left there from the opposite direction. They weren't close enough for any traffic to or from the campgrounds to see them. Out on such a lonely, forest road, with any other guy, she'd be frightened. At the moment, she only felt the usual, harmless butterflies his nearness stirred.

Jordy sent her another killer smile, bowed, and held his hand out to her like a Victorian gentleman. "May I take the liberty, milady?"

Oh, he was much better at fake accents than herself. She bit her lip. He was right. She shouldn't have tested his resolve with such flirty play.

But this was fun. Sighing, she slipped her hand into his and interwove their fingers. "You may have my hand, good sir."

Jordy stiffened but he held her hand until they passed the party house, then he let go with a reluctance in his manner. She shoved her hands in her jean pockets to keep from giving him her hand back. Best not to risk others seeing such behavior and making assumptions about their relationship. She didn't want to hear what he kept trying to say from anyone else, either.

"SUSANNA! GET UP SO I can set the table. Breakfast is almost ready," her mom called on Sunday morning.

Susanna groaned and pulled herself out of bed.

Her mom cleared her throat. "Aren't you forgetting something?"

Susanna wiped the sleep sand from her eyes. "Oh yeah." She grabbed her glasses off the counter behind the bed and put them on. "I forgot."

After breakfast, Cara tugged on Susanna's arm. "Go swimming with me."

Susanna nodded. "Sure."

The pool was packed because of the holiday, but the girls jumped into the deep end anyway. When Susanna came up, she spotted the fuzzy version of Jordy standing in the game room door. He waved. "Hey, Sue-Ann, now that you can see, wanna shoot pool later?"

"Sure. Gotta earn my pride back. Will two hours from now work?"

"Great. See ya then." Jordy went back inside.

It's not a date. Susanna shook her head and chased after her sister.

While the sisters finished off their lunch at the orange dining booth in the office, Amy and Krystal enter it from the pool and ran over. "Hey, Cara," Krystal said. "Me and Amy were about to do put-put. Join us?"

"Sure!" Cara turned to Susanna. "Wanna play put-put?"

Krystal wrinkled her nose.

Jordy swept from the game room and tossed Susanna a pool stick. "You promised me a rematch."

Susanna stood. "He's right, guys. I gotta go."

Krystal sighed with open relief. Amy glared like she wanted to murder Susanna for "stealing" Jordy. Cara and Krystal herded the delusional preteen over to the counter to pay for their miniature golf game.

Susanna followed Jordy into the game room. They were alone, and he'd closed the door to the swimming pool. "Where'd your friends go?"

"You mean my new pool buddies?" Jordy laughed. He put a quarter into the billiards table and the balls came out. He started racking them. "When I returned here after saying my goodbyes, I got a thump on the back from Boo along with 'Whad'ya know, Susanna's boyfriend sneaked out to see his pool buddies.' He also seriously took this as a date, so before your two hours were up, he snickered at me and said the guys will be chilling at his campsite after they play a round of put-put."

"That explains why Krystal was so eager to play all the sudden. She can be rather boy crazy some—well, all of the time."

"She sadly reminds me of far too many of the girls that I used to dump in Chicago, only younger and not yet in such trouble." He pulled the rack off the balls and hung it on the side of the table. "Here, you break."

She chalked her cue stick. "Planning to give me another pool lesson?"

Jordy's cheeks turned pink. "Don't tempt me."

Susanna laughed. "Fair enough." She leaned down to break the balls and managed to hit the cue ball this time. The balls scattered but none went in.

Jordy chalked up, strode around the pool table, and knocked two striped balls into the corner pocket. "You're solid."

"Right."

He bounced the blue striped ball off the nearest wall. It put three others in motion and rolled to a gradual stop by the far corner pocket. "You're up."

She analyzed the positions of the balls on the pool table and took out the solid purple ball in front of a side pocket. She went after the orange ball with a direct line to the far corner pocket but missed it. "Dang it."

He laughed. "Don't worry about it. You've already gotten one more than you did last time." He took aim and pocketed a ball in the other side pocket.

She stared. "Last time, you knocked in all of the balls then managed to lose on a technicality?"

"That is the one part of this game I don't like." He pocketed two more balls and studied the table for his forth shot in a row.

"Hey, are you going to ever let me play or just show off?"

"Would you prefer I let you win?" His tone oddly suggested this would be a bad thing.

"It would be nice if you kindly went easy on me, yes."

He knit his brows and laughed. "Girls. Sorry, that would require another pool lesson, and we both know how well that would go." He took aim again, but didn't hit any balls. "And no, I didn't do that on purpose."

She smiled smugly and took her shot. "Sure you didn't."

A silence fell while Jordy concentrated on a difficult shot with one of her balls in the way of his ball. He struck the cue ball hard and fast downwards, hammering it from an elevated position. The cue ball shot forward, curved around the obstacle, and knocked his striped ball into his target hole.

He made it. Way cool. Susanna grinned, resisted an urge to hug him, and just cheered instead. "Have you ever thought about going pro?"

Jordy shook his head. "I took up pool as a fun, constructive way to cope with my rather angry clinical depression. My parents are cool with it, so long as I don't play for money." He clenched his jaw and added bitterly, "Not that Jordan would have any room to judge."

Oh she had stumbled onto thin ice. "Do you mind if I ask the real reason you call your father by his first name?"

Jordy focused on the pool table and pocketed the rest of his balls as he spoke. "My dad was a lay leader at our church. He was in charge of the junior high ministry and was on the board of elders. Like clockwork, Mom and Dad would drop us off at the O'Brien's every Tuesday night to go out on visitation with Pastor O'Brien. Dad used to boast that he'd never tasted even a drop of liquor. Back then, Jordy was Christine's butchering of Jordan Jr. I took pride in being a junior, and I took pride in him. I trusted in Dad completely."

Jordy faced Susanna. Pain shone in his eyes. "Then Christine died. I was so sick, the whole thing felt like a bad dream. But, eventually, I woke up and discovered the nightmare was real and my dad . . . ."

He choked up. "Jordan was this drunken total stranger, babbling about killing my sister. Dad had been supposed to get off early and he promised to pick Christine up from school, but he got held up at work and forgot." Jordy slammed his fist against the pool table. "If he'd just kept his promise, I would still have my sister. I would still have Dad. We would not have faced financial ruin and crashed clear to the Bottoms. I wouldn't have lost my entire life as I'd known it. And I would not have lost my innocence on top of it all."

Aw, poor boy. Susanna hugged him. "I'm so sorry, Jordy."

He held her in the embrace. "Thanks." Danger shone in Jordy's eyes.

Susanna pulled away. Her body protested like she'd said no to a sweet when she was craving sugar. Strange. Her heart pounded. "Are you sure the guys aren't coming back any time soon?"

"Yes. And even if their opinions mattered, they know that you're why I'm back. In their own juvenile way, they're for us now." He reached as if to draw her back into his arms, but stopped and dropped his hands to his sides with a jerk. "Perhaps we shouldn't keep digging ourselves in deeper."

She stiffened. "Deeper into what?"

"Our thing; it feels like our long hugs release a bonding hormone called oxytocin. It forms all social bonds and has therapeutic properties, but it can have bad side effects, we have a romantic bond, and we're officially friends, so I'd best keep my hands to myself." He wet his lips. "Are you okay?"

"Yeah, sorry, I took us down a rabbit trail." She pulled her ponytail over her shoulder and played with it. "Like you, I once adored my dad. When I was little, his 'I love you, Susie Q!' wasn't embarrassing. But after he started drinking . . ." She shook her head. "Things haven't gone as sour as they did for you, but my dad wasn't all that religious to begin with."

"Is that why you really quit church?"

She arched her eyebrows.

Jordy added, "If your church was anything like mine, the visitation folks must've been pounding down your door on a weekly basis."

She nodded. "He made us stop going over that and because he thought the church was also taking advantage of Mom."

"I still need to properly hash things out with God myself, but I'd love to help you. If you need anything, I can get it." Jordy stroked the palm of her hand with his fingertips.

"A Bible would be lovely," she said shyly and gave her hand to him.

"My dusty shelf decoration is your longed-for treasure. Oh we are such a pair." He laughed, blushing pink. "Consider it done, my dear." He squeezed her hand. "If this is a good time, you should probably know, a meddling ex-babysitter told me about this feisty little girl named Sue-Ann who went off to school and turned into a shadow named Susanna. Or so I gathered."

She groaned. "Mary Anne! How could she do that to me?"

"If it helps, the story did beg the question what exactly happened."

"No, it doesn't help." She bit her trembling lip and stared at his hand. So hard to believe she was holding it. "The district changed the boundary lines in first grade. The kids at my new school noticed some deficiency the ones at my old school missed and ostracized me. I hated group activities. My teacher always had to force me on a group that didn't want me." Tears formed in her eyes. "Now my brain tells me that not even my family really wants me. I don't know what I would've done, without Jesus holding me so close."

Jordy's shoulders heaved. He lifted Susanna's chin until his moist eyes met hers. "You are precious to me, brain differences and all. I recognize them and strongly suspect you do have a diagnosable mental health condition. But that disability was never any reason for anyone to ever mistreat you, just like it's not okay to mistreat the blind for being blind. And I won't let anyone ever come between us, let alone jerks who mistreat you. To be perfectly blunt, our thing aside, you truly are the best friend that I've had since Christine."

"Oh, Jordy." Tears blurred her vision. She hugged him at chest-height.

He slipped his arms around her, one at her waist and the other around her neck and her shoulder. He asked lowly, "What do you want from me?"

All of you, always. Her heart somersaulted, and she held on so tight, his future bride's ring smacked against her collarbone. Dare she?

Yes. She slid her right hand around his shirt, over to Cinderella's future engagement ring and dared to clasp onto it, smiling coyly. "Someday."

Her lips puckered as she leaned in and tilted her head, a strange hunger driving as it overpowered her. He lowered his mouth to hers. At the faintest brush of their lips, groaning, he halted before the contact became a true kiss, pulled away from her, and slapped his hand over his mouth.

They stared at each other, breathing hard, eyes wide.

She trembled. Kissing Jordy would taste better than Lucky Charms.

After a moment, he said, "Do you have any internal sense of the passage of time or any ability to keep track of it without any external aid?"

"Huh? Of course not. Who can know what time it is or how much time has passed without checking a watch, a clock, or the sun's position?"

"Just like my sister," he said wearily, pain in his eyes. "The brain's sense of time isn't machine-accurate, we all lose track sometimes, but we do have a sense of time, when we aren't time-blind as you are and my sister was."

"What does that mean?"

"It means 'someday' means two different things to us. For you, it's a safe fantasy to indulge in while you're just flirting and remain a firm no to us dating seriously now. But I dream of someday because I'm that madly in love with you today. Sorry but the truth doesn't go away if I don't say it or if you pretend I didn't. Due to a disconnect, you don't know this, but your body language was already saying 'yes—wait, no' before today's definite yes. Only you don't mean it. This time, I'm the fool in love when you're just playing."

The pain etched on his face—she'd hurt him quite badly.

What have I done? Her chest ached. "What do we do now?"

"Go home, rest. You're still on good terms with God, so please ask him to help us figure this thing out. Me, I'll go call Sean and see what God can do via that connection. If I have Sean figured out yet, the guy somehow has the gall to show up at his church after a week of him following Mike into a raunchy sewer. And I need that gall."

"Okay." Fighting tears, Susanna fled out the pool exit, found where she'd left her blue beach towel, and hugged it. Why, why had she come so close to kissing Jordy, likely at length? Why?

Chapter 18

SUSANNA LAY CURLED up with a library book on her parents' bed. Her dog stretched out beside her, probably since she still had her shoes on. Her dad was taking her mom to bingo. She hadn't seen Cara since this afternoon.

Her dad's van rumbled up outside. He slammed the door and tromped into the trailer. "Are you meeting the Durant boy at the dance?"

She looked up. "What?"

"Aren't you going with him?"

Going? Her stomach lurched. "Huh?"

Her dad made a sad puppy face. "Aw, he didn't ask you?"

Oh no. I forgot! Heart sinking, she sat up. "No, I'm not going."

Her dad stared. "What?"

"I'm not going." She leaped over the dog and ran out the back door.

She jogged all the way to the lake until she reached the path to the beach then found the passage in the thicket to her hiding place. She collapsed there on the rotting tree becoming alive soil and sobbed.

When she looked up, the sun hovered over the tree tops across the lake, turning the clouds into cotton candy. She glanced at her bare left wrist. What had she done with her watch? She must've forgotten it after going swimming earlier. Oh, well. The sun was fully down at around nine nowadays, so it was eight something now, but when darkness fell, it would be after nine—and the Labor Day Dance would be in full swing.

And she couldn't go because she so badly wanted to go with Jordy.

The note he'd given her had asked casually if she was going to the dance. Even she saw that as him shyly asking her to go with him, when the youth normally went with their families. Like a silly child, she'd read it and re-read it, face warm, thought about it, tried to not think about it.

Never got up the nerve to give him an answer.

She'd even forgotten, until her dad brought it up so horribly too late. She didn't have time to sort herself out, work up the nerve to call Jordy, give him the apology he deserved, and then sort things out with him somehow, too.

Still, he was right about one thing. To her, it was a safe fantasy, her idea of skipping the long season of heartbreak called dating and just marrying her new best friend someday. The future never felt real until it became now and now became part of the past that vanished until now reminded her of it.

But the topic Jordy kept trying to raise, what he really wanted today—it felt too dangerous, too scary. Like if she dared to believe any boy could love her like that today, she'd wake up and find this was all a dream.

The heartbreak on his face when they had parted, though, that was real. And so was the horrible mistake she'd spent the rest of her day hoping for it to stop having almost happened. But the awful truth was, she could already taste his lips when he'd realized letting her kiss him was a mistake and broke it off before she'd even grasped that it'd begun.

How had she come to that? Why had she suddenly wanted to kiss him so much, she'd impulsively gone for it with no thought of any consequences?

And if Jordy was right, on Saturday, when she had so shamelessly flirted with him, he'd seen her mistake coming then and he'd headed it off. Only for his prediction to still come true today, for him to nearly get caught up in the moment, too, and almost fall back into his old ways. Because of her.

He knew to protect me from what he used to be, but we never guessed until this weekend that I could be such a danger to myself and him both.

She buckled over in a sobbing fit, rocked herself, and softly sang one of the few hymns she could still remember, "Amazing Grace."

Wrapped safe and sound in the Holy Spirit's invisible hug, she took two deep breaths. "Jordy says I'm blind, my brain has a disability and it's causing a disconnect, probably between my head and my heart, though it was cheeky of him to dare to think he knows my heart better than I do!"

What if he did? The boy *did* have mad social skills, while hers were, well, slightly better than nonexistent. She'd always figured it was God looking out for her when she did suddenly see the true heart of someone lying.

Right now, a part of her wished she could command that light to shine and reveal the truth of her own heart. And a part of her was terrified of what she'd see if she asked and God answered.

Kneeling over the death becoming life, she bowed her head so low, her forehead touched the decaying tree. "Jesus, I'm here. I'm blind. You give me peace when I give you my pain. I felt nearly dead and starved, when that boy suddenly walked into my life. We were coming alive, shining again, so happy. Now, I feel darkness closing back in. Show me what you want me to see."

His invisible hug wrapped around her still closer.

Memories whirled. The feel of Jordy's arms around her as he gave her a pool lesson, as he reeled in a fish for her, and on many more occasions not at all ordered by time. Hugging Jordy here, him hugging her back, holding onto each other as they wept together for his sister.

Here, Susanna had held her heartbroken friend, as her friend Jesus had always sat beside her, invisible, and held a heartbroken Susanna as she wept.

All the times of her crying like a baby, and Jesus in effect responding by picking her up and holding her, had a powerful impact. Even as a little girl, she'd loved him with all of her heart, as her new Daddy. For years, her fearful heart had also only trusted Jesus alone to be her true friend—her best friend.

The hugging she and Jordy had indulged in had a powerful impact too. And he wasn't her Savior, a father-figure she trusted completely, or her best friend. Jesus still held all of those titles in her heart.

Letting Jordy into this hiding place had led to her also letting him into the secret place of her heart that she called someday. Her someday had been already in her heart *before* she'd met Jordy. It'd come from beyond her, from eternity. And the true meaning of her someday now bearing his name was far deeper and realer than she had blindly imagined.

It blew her mind so much now, it felt like reality had quaked physically.

Now it all made sense. She'd been attracted to Jordy for nearly as long as he'd said he'd been tempted to mentally undress her. She'd once caught him checking her out, when she'd been in her bathing suit at that, and it was still hard to believe he was truly attracted to her. She was so used to mirrors showing her a girl too homely for anyone to love her.

Evidently mirrors could somehow lie.

If only Jordy had been wrong about the truth. If only ignoring it or not saying it would make it go away. But it wouldn't. She had to face the truth.

She'd been completely out of her mind to bring Jordy here to her hiding place. His tears had unlocked her heart. Now she'd fallen for him. Big time.

Worse, she was highly impulsive when she was this crazy in love.

Pure overwhelm slammed her brain. She froze right where she was and closed her eyes. "Jesus, I can't do this anymore. I can't figure things out all on my own. I need you to take over. I need you to be in control of my life."

I am the Lord. I am Your Healer. Be still and know.

Lord, it was you—you warned Jordy to stop, before we got too carried away, too soon. Thank you. Thank you that by grace we stand.

"... WE'LL HAVE TO leave without her," Susanna's dad said as she reached the edge of her camp site, coming from the crossroads. She stood beside their rusted, abandoned swing set. Her parents and sister faced off on the deck.

Cara crossed her arms. "I'm not leaving without my sissy!"

Did the dirt caking Susanna's clothes have invisibility powers?

Their mom patted Cara's shoulder. "Baby, I'm sorry. We'll just have to hope she shows up at the dance." She turned to Susanna's dad. "Why did you do that to her? You know how sensitive she is."

During that speech, Susanna crunched gravel as she walked to the deck's edge. Her parents and sister remained too focused upon each other to notice her approach. She stood right behind them and cleared her throat.

Her family members all jumped and looked up.

I wonder what Jordy would think of my family's normal? She headed inside the back door, locked it, and shut the curtains.

After she'd changed, she came out in new stonewashed flare jeans with glittery snowflakes on both outer calves. Her shiny green blouse matched her eyes. She entered the tiny RV bathroom and washed her face and hands at the RV sink. After quickly running her wet comb through her hair, she put on her cherry lip gloss and a dab of lavender perfume.

She scrutinized her reflection. *Still don't know what Jordy sees in me but I tried.* She swallowed hard. *Okay, Lord, please help me to be the friend Jordy needs tonight. I've made a fool of myself and hurt him quite enough.*

Back outside, she found her family where she'd left them, staring at her with their mouths agape.

Why hadn't they yelled at her? "What? Are we going or not?"

Her dad cleared his throat. "Yeah, let's go."

Soon, they entered the party house with the dance already hopping with "the Electric Slide" in progress. Susanna glanced at the DJ setup at the far end of the dance floor. Cool, the fiddler with the monkey puppet was back.

They grabbed a table at the front of the back section, near the restrooms and the snack bar. Krystal and Amy approached. Cara waved at them. "Hey, guys. This place is a blast. Let's go outside."

"Sure," Krystal said, "Are you coming, Susanna?"

Weird. Eyes narrowed, she followed them. "Why? Are you asking?"

On their way out the door, Krystal said, "Of course. You're my friend."

Something was up. Susanna stopped by one of stone pillars supporting the veranda and narrowed her eyes at Krystal. "Since when do you like me?"

"Fine, we're hoping to run into the guys."

Amy thrust out her lip. "And a certain guy from Chicago seems to always show up whenever you're around."

Krystal nodded. "It's so strange. He can't see anything in Susanna."

"Hey!" Cara folded her arms. "There's plenty to see in my sister. She's pretty, she's smart, she's creative, she's funny, and she's mature, unlike some people I know." Cara stuck her tongue out at Krystal.

Including yourself. Susanna waved. "Let her say whatever she wants. A twelve-year-old can't hurt me."

Growling, Krystal clenched her tiny fists and cursed. "I'll show you what a twelve-year-old can do."

"Ooh, a cat fight," one of the guys called from the shadows beyond the circle of light, likely Ty or Greg, she could tell apart the others' voices.

All six of the guys strolled into the light.

Jordy tossed the football up and let it fall to the ground. "Nah, it's just Krystal running her mouth. She can't be stupid enough to follow up on that."

Krystal sneered. "You're an idiot if you think I won't. She won't defend herself, nor will anyone else. Who could ever truly like such a gross cow?"

Face warm, Susanna sent a mortified glance at Jordy.

His eyes narrowed and he crossed over to Krystal. "If a guy insulted my girl like that, I'd beat him senseless. You, I have news for. In my eyes, you're a child headed down a dark road, one I want no part of. While Susanna is a beautiful young woman, tonight and every night, and I love her exactly as she is. Now stop your bull, or I will tell my family you're startin' trouble."

Did Jordy say what Susanna thought he said? In front of everyone?

"You! You jerk!" Krystal screamed as she backed away. "I'll tell them! I'll tell them what you did to me! You put your hands on me, and you liked it. I wish there'd been a cop around so he'd haul you off to jail! If I hadn't bit you, who knows what horrible things you'd have done to me. I'm gonna tell your grandfather! He's gonna send you to military school."

Wow, Krystal heard it, too. What innocent mistake was she exaggerating into attempted assault? Susanna would ask later, if she didn't wake up first.

Boo stepped up beside Jordy and glared at Krystal. "He didn't do nothin' to ya. None of us are stupid enough to take your bait. You're always prancing around, asking for it, just starvin' for a lil' attention. No one believes a word you say. I certainly don't and none of the other guys do either. Right guys?"

The other guys looked away. Ricky kicked up dirt.

Susanna's head swam. This all felt like a strange dream.

"Right guys?" Boo repeated sharply.

Ty sighed. "Right."

"Who, Krystal?" Nate said. "She's a pathological liar. We all know that."

"Guys, you can't do this to me!" She ran to Greg. "Greg?"

He laughed. "That spoiled brat will say whatever is convenient to her."

Krystal gasped. "Greg, no!"

He folded his arms and turned away from her.

Krystal grabbed Ricky's arm. "You believe me, don't you? You wouldn't betray an old friend for a new one. You believe me."

Ricky looked away from her. Crickets chirped and cicadas hummed.

At the hand on her shoulder, Susanna glanced up at Jordy, suddenly at her side, his jaw tight, his eyes torn between his fury at Krystal and remorse.

"Ricky?" the twelve-year-old girl whispered in a scared, desperate tone.

He shook his head. "You have told obvious lies multiple times, you do have a mean streak, and I've never known Jordy to hurt anybody. Further, you're the one we caught in the act of assaulting his girl. I'm sorry, but you've gone way too far this time." Ricky turned his back to her.

"Guys?" Krystal cried.

Everyone besides Jordy and Susanna turned their backs on Krystal, the glaring Cara and Amy included.

"No one deserves this," Jordy said in her ear. "We have to intervene."

Krystal was looking around, the panic on her face making her look like a child closer to ten than to her true age. "No. Please, Susanna, help me. It was all in fun. You know that. Tell them."

You have a strange idea of fun. Sighing, Susanna nodded to Jordy.

He spread his arms out. "Guys, we do appreciate you supporting us, but Susanna and I should really discuss this with Krystal in private."

Krystal gasped and fled toward the campgrounds.

The others stopped turning their backs. Jordy and Susanna jogged after Krystal. Jordy ran ahead and blocked her path. The young girl froze.

Huh? Susanna caught up to Krystal. "You can't truly think he'll hurt you. He would've hit you already, if he were going to."

The teary, big-eyed looks that Krystal sent them both did feel unsafe.

Huh? Susanna scrunched her brows together.

Jordy squatted, below Krystal's eye-level. "Kid, I never, ever would have slapped my hand over your mouth, if I had already known about why I think that did freak you out. I'd never harm a child. I'm so sorry a gross fat guy did. No one deserves what you were afraid was about to happen all over again."

"Don't tell. He'll kill my parents and people still won't believe me."

"I hear you. Real sexual abusers are often family or 'friends' or otherwise are members of your group that your group may side with. But you still need to tell a trustworthy adult, kid. You can talk to teachers, doctors, police, or to my mother. Any of such ought to believe you, make sure your parents will be safe, and ensure you get the help you need."

Wow. "Would you like to go talk to his mom?" Susanna asked softly.

"No. We're good now, thanks." Krystal wiped her face, held her head up high, and strode back to the other camp kids, who all looked confused. "We had a misunderstanding. We worked it out. Can we all be friends again?"

Cara, Amy, and Ricky nodded, looking relieved. The other guys glared at Krystal until she retreated inside the party house.

Jordy caught Susanna's eye and asked softly, "You okay?"

This all still felt too unreal. She nodded. "Thanks. You guys didn't have to get involved in the first place."

Boo shook his head. "It became our fight when Krystal attacked Jordy."

Jordy slapped hands with him. "Thanks again, man."

"No problem. Us country folk got to stick together." Boo winked.

A slow smile crossed Jordy's face. "Yeah, I guess we do."

Susanna bit back a smile. No more City Boy for Jordy.

Ty picked up the football. "Come on, Jordy, go long."

Jordy sent Susanna a silent apology and ran out to the lawn with Boo.

Cara and Amy marched toward Susanna. Amy looked like she was about to launch into jealous hysterics.

No more. Susanna returned inside and took several deep breaths. She flopped back at her parents' table, facing the crowd dancing to "Old Time Rock and Roll." She grinned. Jordy defended her—in front of all the camp kids. And he'd been right. The guys were on their side now.

Later, at the snack bar, Susanna and Jordy both reached for the last bag of cheese puffs. He smiled and grabbed a bag of chips. "I'll just have this."

Her cheeks grew warm. "Thanks."

She paid for the cheese puffs and returned to her seat.

Her mom said, "Aw, that was sweet of him."

Susanna swallowed. "Yeah, friends do that sorta thing."

Her dad took a sip of his Coke. "Friends, huh?"

"Yeah, friends. Got a problem with it?"

"Nope. You know, I was only teasing you earlier. I didn't mean for you to get upset and run off like that."

It was his way of apologizing. "I just needed some breathing room."

"That's one of the reasons we come up here."

Cara ran over and flopped down, breathing hard. "Sis, man, you really missed something out there! I had to come take a break."

The DJ with the monkey on his shoulder broke out his fiddle and started a line dance where each participant had their hands on the shoulders of the person in front of them. The fiddle was imitating the sound of a train.

"The train! Let's get on!" Cara grabbed Susanna by the arm.

Susanna yanked free. "Okay, okay, you don't have to pull my arm out of its socket." She followed Cara out to the dance floor and got in line behind her, who was in line behind Amy.

The hands placed on Susanna's shoulders had a masculine feel, plus she caught a whiff of musk aftershave. She had a fifty percent chance of getting paired with him in the tunnel, so it had better be Jordy. If not, Amy wouldn't mind switching partners and it might sidetrack her from crushing on Jordy. Susanna tried to count the people ahead of them in the line to figure out who she'd get, but lost track.

They circled the entire room once and the dance floor three times. The two people behind the fiddler stood across from each other and joined hands over their heads. The third person passed underneath their hands and stood next to the person on the left. A forth went through and joined hands with third and so on until their turn came.

Susanna followed Cara and Amy through the human tunnel. Adrenaline coursed through Susanna in time to the fiddle's imitation of a train. They did this at every dance, but it never grew old.

At the tunnel's end, Cara and Amy joined hands overhead. Amy spotted the guy behind Susanna and hissed, "Sue-Ann, switch partners with me."

Cara's hands tightened around Amy's. "You're with me, Amy."

Susanna crossed underneath Cara and Amy's hands and stood next to her sister, ignoring the pouting Amy. Jordy came through and joined hands with Susanna. In between the folks passing through the tunnel, Jordy's eyes shone like star sapphires. A smile tugged at his lips before he made a funny face at her. She couldn't help but laugh.

He laughed with her and flashed her his killer smile.

She blushed. If he ever tried to kiss her again, it'd be so hard to say no.

All too soon, the train ride's live fiddle music stopped playing. Everyone else headed back to their seats. Jordy held fast to her hands. Cara and Amy glanced back at Jordy and Susanna. Tears filled Amy's eyes. She fled out of the exit, shoulders heaving.

Cara smirked at Susanna and sat with their folks.

Susanna's cheeks burned—they knew. Amy would get over it, but Cara would tease her about her "boyfriend." She glanced back at Jordy. "Let go."

"Sorry." Jordy released her, but he came up beside her and put his arm around the small of her back. He said in her ear, "Stay with me."

"Why?" She glanced to her arm, around him without thought. Oh.

An oldie played, bringing families with young children out to the dance floor, but Susanna focused on him. "I still owe you a huge apology."

"For earlier?" He put his hands on her shoulders, facing her. "That was entirely my own fault. It all is. So I am sorry. I shouldn't have—"

"You were right," she mumbled. She'd put her hands on his hips. "I had no idea what 'someday' truly means. I was careless and selfish."

"I wrong to dump on you. Yesterday, too. When we met, you showed no familiarity at all with flirting, let alone with making serious romantic plays. I've merely reaped what I've sowed."

"Thanks for not being upset anymore, anyway." While still following him mindlessly into his barely swaying idea of dancing, she listened to the song playing. Her face burned. "We're supposed to be doing 'the Twist!'"

"So what if everyone else is going fast? We need to take it slow."

From his tone of voice, the expression in his eyes, he didn't mean just dancing. She bit her lip. "Doing 'The Twist' is fun."

"Figuratively speaking, we need to take it slow even when our culture and our own hormones are playing a fast song. We need to wait until we're ready, including morally and medically. I'll have to keep our relationship low key, whatever we are. Friends is best for now; I still need to get right with God. I can't expect the Lord to keep doing favors for a prodigal."

"Did your old church neglect to teach about God's grace?"

He laughed. "You and Sean both. Grace was just academic is all. Before I fell, I'd never truly grasped that I am a sinner in need of a savior. I had a far better grasp of what 'Jesus is Lord' means in my everyday life."

The DJ cut "the Twist" short and put on "Susie Q."

Ha, ha. Smirking, she slipped to Jordy's side, and said into his ear, "I'll be true, when you like the way I walk and talk with Jesus enough to join me in it. You bring the angry broken heart. Let Jesus bring everything else."

He pivoted and their eyes met. He grinned. "I love you, Susie Q."

"Oh, you." She hugged him, broke away, and fled to the women's room. She splashed cold water on her face then faced the girl in the mirror.

Her goofy grin lit up her plain features beautifully.

Chapter 19

SINCE THEY'D ONLY TAKEN Mom's car up to Glenshire, Jordy rode back with his parents on Monday afternoon. So far, he'd successfully avoided getting interrogated over Susanna, who he'd waited for outside the restrooms and just chilled with for the rest of the evening.

His mom turned onto the highway. "The dance last night was fun. I hope we have another soon."

"Sorry, honey," his father said, "That was the last dance of the season."

"What about you, son?" his mom asked. "Did you have a good time?"

He recalled Susanna's beaming face from the party, the fire in her eyes glowing brighter than ever. "Yeah, you should've seen Sue-Ann last night."

His father turned to face him. "So, son, how depressed are you today?"

Laughing, Jordy shook his head. "I've recovered so much, from the great view from up here, it's clear how accurate my diagnosis truly was before."

"Then can I raise the topic of the love life that you're still not allowed to have yet without you also breaking the rule requiring respectful behavior?"

Uh-oh. "Sir, despite my last ex-girlfriend's efforts to trip me up, it's been three months since I last did anything truly immoral with a girl. And, unless you want to go so old-school, you stone me to death, you need to give me the same grace my grandfather has given you, don't you?"

Pain and grief filled his father's eyes. "I hold myself responsible for what an abusive peer group did to you, and our chat about Vera this weekend will suffice on that one, but it's clear we really needed to talk about Susanna."

Uh-oh. "Sir, we're only friends."

His father raised his eyebrows, his eyes amused. "If you've truly bought that from yourself, I have some land on Mars that I'd like to sell you."

Uh-oh. Jordy cringed. "Why wouldn't we be only friends?"

"When was the last time you and a male friend spent a good two hours holding hands and staring into each other's eyes? And your hiding spot in the bush? I could see you two. I saw what you clearly had on your mind. And you spending half of the dance with friends who truly are just friends doesn't make how you spent the rest of it not really a date with your new girlfriend."

"Jordan, please leave him be." To Jordy, his mom added, "You're okay, sweetheart. For you, this is a huge step in a much better direction and I am so proud. Your dad and I honestly asked your grandfather to introduce you to a friend who'd be a positive influence, and he couldn't have made a better choice. Your dad simply worries a guy can't be 'just friends' with a pretty girl. Never mind that he and I were best friends in high school."

Jordy's father glanced at Jordy's mom. "I can't speak for women, or all men, but he is my son, and I couldn't be just best friends with an attractive girl since I fell in love with you. We also eloped during your sophomore year of college—and you dropped out a year and a half later because of me."

"We made it, and our son does have special needs to consider." Jordy's mom glanced at him in the mirror. "Can we discuss this in private?"

His father nodded to Jordy's relief. Jordan repeating one of his dad's old stories felt weird in a way his new therapist would want to hear about.

"But I do need to make one thing clear," his father said, glancing back at Jordy again. "'No dating until eighteen' *is* back in effect. If anything, son, the horror we've gotten you out of makes that more important, not less. And it is also against the rules to try to sneak around the rules by not calling it a date."

Don't panic. Jordy sucked in deep breaths. What a disaster. If he cut out every activity he was prone to view as a date, then he'd only get to see his girl in Chemistry class and when giving her rides to school and back.

Mom had better fix this. He was not only being set up for failure but for a downward spiral in his mental health. Last time, he had separated himself from his girl, for a few days, after only one hour of cuddling while sobbing. And it'd felt like he was in oxytocin withdrawal i.e. becoming love sick. Only love had never before had anything to do with it for him, and the pool tables he'd taken his violent moods out on before weren't available at home now.

Worse, Susanna's mental health might also go into a downward spiral.

Hey, you, the Jerk In Heaven. If you'd been there, my twin would not have died, and I'm still furious about that, but I need you, so let's talk.

Jordy braced for the sudden fatal heart attack he deserved and waited to be punished somehow another minute before he continued the risky prayer.

THE NEXT DAY, JORDY spotted Susanna at the end of one lunch line. Yay. Grinning, he rushed over and got in line behind her by standing beside her in the aisle between the round tables in Easthaven's cafeteria. As they talked, they periodically moved ahead with the line but they mostly faced each other.

"Are you okay?" Susanna chewed her lip. Worry shone in her eyes. "You were so quiet in study hall and you sat further away today."

Lord, help me, everything in me wants to go find my father and beat him senseless. He grunted. "A jerk I'm unfortunately related to has given me orders to stop seeing you—never mind that my parents like you. We can have some social interaction, like this, but I need to avoid even the appearance of us dating, until my mom persuades the jerk to let us decide what we are."

"Is this my fault?" Susanna asked, big-eyed.

"No, you've done nothing wrong. It's Jordan trying to be my dad again. That or he's being a jerk on purpose to prove why he hadn't been parenting me the way my dad did when I was twelve."

Sean tapped Jordy on the shoulder. "Dude, are you even vaguely aware we're standing in line behind you?"

"Huh?" Jordy said as he blinked at the school friends he hadn't noticed.

Mike waved at a girl with long hair in cornrows. "Natasha, come here."

The girl came over, smacking bubble gum. "Yeah?"

Mike waved at Jordy. "This is Jordy, he just moved here from Chicago."

Oh no. Mike was another Brandt, who'd also pulled this. Jordy glanced at the sick, green look on Sue-Ann's face. His stomach tightened into a knot.

The girl with cornrows visually assaulted Jordy, her lusting look far too familiar. She whistled. "Chicago's missin' one fine white guy."

"Uh, thanks," Jordy said, his voice breaking on him almost like when it had been still changing. *Stay here, we've got this.* He refocused on Sue-Ann's too-green face. *Please let us be still okay.* He cleared his throat and slid his sister's ring along his chain. "So, how did you do on the quiz in Chemistry? I can't believe that guy gave us a pop quiz on the third day of school."

The girl with braids smacked her lips then marched off.

Thank God. Jordy gulped down air. There would be more just like her.

Sue-Ann managed a smile. "I only got a 78, but it's just the first one."

Jordy laughed. "Hey, you did better than I did. We should try studying together again sometime. We were surprisingly productive. In Chicago, my study dates were only an excuse for an after party." Doh, she didn't want to hear about what he used to do on study dates besides study. "Uh, sorry. That is why I horribly misunderstood your intentions. It was my bad."

Green again, Susanna squeezed his hand. "By grace." She reached in her jeans pocket and slipped him a triangular note. "In case you ever do need to reach me as a friend. Be warned Cara hogs our phone line."

Peachy. He pocketed the note. "Thanks. Given how much I already miss you, I'll have to think of a reason to call you that can't be taken as romantic."

Once through the line, Jordy, Sean, and Mike took their lunches back to their table and flopped down with Jordy in the middle and the other two on his immediate left and right.

Mike glared. "Dude, Jordy, Natasha is hot and clearly didn't mind your jewelry. So why give her the cold shoulder? If I didn't know better, I'd think that sophomore was your girlfriend."

I wish. "She's not," Jordy snapped. "We're just friends."

"She's a girl who is a friend you wish you were kissing," Sean said dryly.

Mike took a bite of his French fries. "Yeah, come on, man, who are you trying to convince here? Me, or you?"

Face warm, Jordy sputtered. "Uh, what Sean said is the situation, with the big complication of my father grounding me from dating until eighteen."

Both guys whistled. Sean said, "Wow."

"You dog." Mike slugged Jordy's shoulder. "What did you do to get into that much trouble with your old man? You aren't actually complying?"

"For now anyway." Jordy forced his guilty grin. "I am hoping my father just needs to see for himself why Mom views Susanna like she's a drug I've become hooked on and thinks it's a mistake to demand that I give her up. So the most effective, rebellious thing I can do here is strictly obey and let Mom tell him 'I told you so' after he sees what 'Susanna withdraw' does to me."

Mike laughed crudely, like his mind was in the gutter.

Huh? Oh. Face still warmer, Jordy rolled his eyes. "Not what I meant."

"Call me when it gets bad, bro." Sean slapped Jordy's upper back. "I'll pray you through it." Sean's cold stare past him dared Mike to complain.

"Oh, so you two are ganging up on me." Mike rolled his eyes. "Fine, then from now on, you can join Jordy in spending Saturday nights doing whatever boring stuff Jesus Freaks do for fun."

Sean's grin wanted to annoy Mike further by praising God loudly in the middle of a public high school's cafeteria but his lips refrained.

Jordy laughed. Mike's idea of a punishment was Sean's idea of a victory.

WHY AM I SUCH A BOY scout? Jordy's stomach roiled. He scrubbed the dinner dishes harder than necessary as he and his father cleaned up for his mom on Thursday. She was exhausted from the move and from trying to be strong for him these last three years, but right now everything irritated him.

Once the dishes had dried, his father asked, "So, how's school?"

Growling, Jordy slammed three plastic plates into their cabinet. Would Jordan never stop riding him? "Fine. I don't know why you keep bugging me. I've barely spoken to Sue-Ann since Tuesday."

His father finished wiping down the counters, draped his dish rag over the sink's faucet, and faced him. "Okay, I've had enough. We need to talk. Something's going on and it has something to do with that girl."

"Jordan, 'that girl' has a name! I won't even think about talking to you again until you've used it!" Jordy felt like he was distantly watching himself. Lovesick combined with a history of trauma and clinical depression—when would his dad realize he did need his girl?

His father's face saw a sixteen-year-old acting like he was twelve. "Son, I have nothing against Susanna. She's a sweet girl. My problem is how you're acting. You're moody, you're aggressive, you're not doing your schoolwork, and you're out at all hours. What's going on?"

Jordy crossed his arms. He'd said all he had to say to Jordan. If the guy couldn't figure out what was wrong on his own, he was a moron.

His father sighed. "Like it or not, I am your dad, and you are going . . . ."

Not anymore you're not. Jordy made a break for the door.

His father got there first and blocked the exit. "I'm not playing tonight, Junior. Now—"

Fury boiled in Jordy's veins. He clenched his fists. "Move."

"Make me. Wanna test me on this? Be my guest. I'm still an Eagle Scout. If you start it, I will end it. Now you go sit down before I sit you down."

Where in the world did his father find his backbone? Jordy jerked out a chair at the table and flopped in it. "Happy?"

His father sat across from him. "Yes. Now what's going on?"

Jordy glowered. "You tell me what's wrong with me. Since you laid down the law, and I've obeyed it, I'm losing sleep again. My appetite's shot. I can't concentrate for long at school or on my homework. I snap at my teachers, my classmates, you and Mom. I keep viciously beating my bed while screaming into my pillow. I keep driving in circles around the block—"

"By her place, right?"

"Yeah, have to. It's right across the alley."

"Then, after you've passed her place you turn around and drive by again and so on until your dad finds you and tells you to go home before that girl's parents call the cops. You take a last look at her house and wish her parents would ever consider you good enough for their daughter."

Huh? Jordy blinked. "Are we talking about me or you?"

His father shrugged. "I used to do that to your mother, before she defied her parents and started dating her best friend, me, just in time for her senior prom. Our college was a short drive from home, so we were never far apart. Two years later, we became married college kids. A year after that, we had to choose between me passing up a high-paying job and her dropping out."

Jordy tensed. "And what does this have to do with me?"

"Plenty I suspect. Susanna's the first thing on your mind in the morning, the last thing you think about as you finally fall asleep, and consumes a good portion of your thoughts in between. Right?"

Heat spread over his face. "I am struggling with intrusive fantasies that have become shameful, but our therapist is helping me with that. So?"

His father shook his head. "You're falling in love. The negative impact it has on your mental health is why my rules are necessary."

A little slow, old man. Jordy laughed, shaking his head, his eyes weirdly wet. "My heart isn't going, going. It's already gone. Our bond is sealed, not just emotionally but spiritually—and I haven't even kissed her properly yet. Separating us now is putting my mental health into a downward spiral that could possibly end in my death. To reverse it, you must let me see her."

His father's jaw tightened. "Did your mother coach you to say that?"

"No, we both simply know how serious the issues I had overcome were, since we lived through it." He held up the ring on his chain. "Sir, this belongs to Susanna. My heart is sure of it. God had a reason for bringing her into my life now. If I can lay aside my anger at him long enough to consider trusting him again, why can't you?"

Sighing, his father lowered his head. "I'll talk more with your mom, our therapist, and seek God's counsel. I'll also need you to show me evidence this is a divine connection by it actually bringing you back to the Lord, son."

"Fair enough." Jordy slid the ring on his chain. "I am praying about it."

JORDY FLOATED THROUGH school Friday, going back and forth between his angry prayers and meditating upon anything that diverted his mind for even five minutes from the intrusive thoughts about his girl, the cuddling that he sorely missed, and where his body would like for it to go today, not someday. The compulsion came from his brain trying to self-correct, the fantasy gave a temporary relief from the returning, dark cloud of anger, hopelessness, and pending doom. But the illicit relief wore off fast and left him feeling worse.

It'd be so much easier and healthier if he could just hug her already.

Did she understand? Being near her, but not with her—to hear her voice, but to have to speak like they truly were just friends—it hurt too much.

At least Sir Flirtalot hadn't returned, and he remained free of endlessly repeating a traumatic experience, thank God. Still surprising, God answering his angry prayers. Not shocking that a new problem drove him to the Jerk, as did his fears that his girl was suffering, too.

"Jordan Durant!"

Why was his math teacher calling Jordan? His father wasn't here.

"Earth to the blonde boy in third seat of the center row! Hello!"

Jordy looked up. "Are you talking to me?"

"Yes and I realize—"

"Jordan's my father. I'm Jordy. I'm not a blonde, and I'm going to beat up the next person who makes that mistake. It's getting on my nerves."

His teacher smiled sweetly and used the voice of a mother soothing her crying baby. "You're new here, so I'm going to give you a break. Here, the bell at the end of ninth period means you can leave. Have a good weekend."

Jordy glanced at the clock. Two thirty-five. School let out five minutes ago. "Sorry, Ma'am."

At home, inside their cottage-style living room, he found his mother re-reading *The Power of a Praying® Parent* by Stormie Omartian.

Rage clenched his muscles. *Will she never let up?*

Okay, he needed to see his girl ASAP. Deep down, he was thankful that his mom never gave up on him.

She set her well-worn paperback down on the end table and rose from the couch. She patted his back. "How was your day, son?"

"A miserable, exhausting, losing battle. I need Sue-Ann, Mom."

"That father of yours—honey, you'll have to ignore him and do what you have to do to stay healthy. You were making such great progress. I appreciate that she was a key part of it. What I saw happening with you two was nothing short of a miracle. If you ever want to talk, I'm here."

Whoa, his mother, telling him to defy his father? That was nothing short of desperate. "Mom, if you want me to stop calling Dad by his first name, try respecting him yourself. The tension between us and him isn't good for me, either. Let's keep praying God shows him that we're right and his law truly is killing me and that I'll graciously be allowed to see her."

His mother gaped.

He spun and went downstairs to his room, his jaw clenched. He hovered by his double dresser, over his twin's gold jewelry box. Today, was Susanna's fifteenth birthday. Every time he saw her today, and followed the cruel rules, she'd been so sad, so near tears. He had to go celebrate her day with her.

But what was truly the right thing to do? He opened the jewelry box and stared unseeing. The pain he was in would've been good reason to not get so attached to her in the first place, if he'd been thinking clearly enough.

But he hadn't been. Dating her would be the emotionally honest course, but what if his jerk of a father was right? The man had lost everything three years ago. Likely, the jerk's rules were meant to avoid Jordy later suffering a nasty romantic split like his parents' split. And, on his own, what chances did

Jordy have of him dating Susanna never ending in disaster?

Later, would he be any better able to bear the pain of still another major loss? Just his twin's death had put him well on his way to clinical depression. But after what was stolen from him in his freshman year—he'd grieved like his girl had died before he'd met her, until Susanna's love comforted him.

And she should've died during her own freshman year but hadn't. His prayers for her at twelve-years-old had included asking God to protect her, to keep her safe from all harm, to hold her close to God's heart like his sister.

Ugh, I'm a lovesick fool, seeing connections in randomness.

No. Not going back there. Jordy growled. That was it. His faith had been re-emerging as the darkness had passed, like his old therapist had predicted. In fact, his new faith was made of stronger stuff. Before, he'd been unable to fight depression's lies. Still, he had to reconnect with Sue-Ann right away.

He refocused on the jewelry box open before him on the dresser. Half of the pieces were too juvenile for a fifteenth birthday present, but he had some great possibilities: sapphire earrings, one bracelet, and three necklaces.

Not to mention the engagement ring dangling from his chain.

That might be more efficient. It'd make an expensive promise ring, but it would work for that purpose, too. But what if that idea was crazy?

How had the guy he'd still been when he'd left Chicago fallen in love?

Mom said it herself. It was a miracle his new connection to Sue-Ann had replaced Sir Flirtalot's generalized connection to all of his abusive peers. The old had gone, the new had come, and he was free. What more did he need?

The Jerk in Heaven softly and tenderly calling for him to come home.

Jordy closed his eyes. He slammed his fists onto the dresser and hooked his thumbs over the edge. "Okay, I'm here. What do you want from me?"

The warmth of the Light he'd seen in Sue-Ann's eyes surrounded him, giving him the oxytocin he sorely needed, and prodded his big ball of anger with a wordless *hand it all over.*

Depression had lied when it had said he could hide from God as well as when it'd said that he must. Jordy sucked in his ragged breath. "You set us up, ultimately, God. Why? To torment me? 'Look, she's not dead, too, she's right here, son. But you can't keep her, not without me. Go ahead, try to have her without me. It'll end like it ended with Vera.'

"Do you enjoy rubbing that in? Or do you just want to put me up against a wall? Lure me back with a carrot named Susanna? That's your game here, isn't it? Well, good work, God. You've got me hedged in so the least painful way for me to go is back on my knees before your throne. But why Sue-Ann? She deserves better than me. Don't you think she's hurt enough? How can I ever be worthy of her? She loves you, but I hate you."

Deep remorse swelled. That was the least of the awful things he'd said to God when he'd ripped down all the churchy posters and tore them to shreds. Jordy snapped his jaw closed and trembled. Christine's jewelry box glared up at him like an accusation. She'd be horrified by what he'd become. Christine would want to see Sue-Ann rescued out of his monstrous clutches.

No, she'd run to him, sobbing, hug him, and beg him to come home.

Tears wet his eyes. He wiped them away. "God, I'm sorry. I didn't mean it. But I'm furious and I'm furious I have no right to be furious. And I am sick and tired of feeling this way. And what I became without you has left me so disgusted and ashamed and full of remorse—you have set me free from sin. You have given me new life, and I had to fall and you had to intervene for me before I truly understood the gospel. Or before I ever felt any different. I'm told that won't matter, if I do return to you. And I'm ready to ditch my fears that I've never truly been saved and can't ever be. So fine. Have it your way."

He fell on his knees and raised his arms to God in surrender.

Chapter 20

JORDY LAY HALF-ASLEEP on the floor where he'd surrendered all to Jesus finally. He'd also spent a solid hour and a half talking to the Father like his therapists only wished he'd ever risk opening up.

Better was one session here than a thousand elsewhere. It did help a lot that he had tons of experience with mortal therapists. But God worked for free, was always available, and it'd turned out he gave out doses of oxytocin.

And once Jordy was done handing over his big ball of anger, well, this holy "high" was so blissful, he was peacefully drifting off to sleep.

Someone knocked on the door at the top of the stairs.

Jordy pushed himself up from the floor and sat on his bed. "It's open."

His father came down. "I wanted to let you know, we'll be heading out in about five minutes."

Jordy nodded. "Sure, Dad. I'll be ready."

His dad started back up the stairs, stopped with his foot in the air, and spun around. "What was that, son?"

"Dad, do you know I love you?"

His dad's mouth and eyes both opened wide. "I love you, too, son. Are you serious? You've been closed off to me ever since Christine died."

Jordy stared at the floor. "I know. I blamed you, but that wasn't fair. You had an important deadline to meet. You had no way of knowing what was going to happen when you didn't pick her up. I was at fault myself, if any of us were. I should've gone to school and got my homework myself."

His dad came back downstairs, sat beside him, and put his arm around his shoulders. "Son, you were too sick to go anywhere on your own two feet. Don't you know we almost lost you, too? You had to be hospitalized for three days after Christine died. Don't you remember?"

Jordy shook his head. "They gave me something, that whole week is a blur. The entire first year after we lost her is hazy. At the end of eighth grade, I scared Mom by thinking it was my thirteenth birthday. I was confused and sad to hear I was fourteen." He drew a breath. "Anyway, I'm sorry for lashing out at you, Dad. I have been as difficult as possible. It was hard."

Tears formed in his dad's eyes. "I forgive you, son. We knew a lot of that was from your depression and suffering trauma at a crucial age. If you ever feel like you've missed something and need to go back and do it, that's fine."

Noted. Jordy swallowed. "Oh, and about the Junior thing . . . ."

"You were always bound to eventually ask me to call you Jordy, too. You had long since asked your mom to call you that." His dad laughed. "We ought to have confused you so bad. Me calling you Junior, your mom calling you Jordan, and your sister calling you Jordy. The way that you two were, it's no wonder you favor Jordy. The last time your mom ever called you Jordan, your sister got up and tapped me and said, 'Daddy is Jordan.' Then she hugged you and said, 'This is Jordy.'"

"I remember." Jordy hesitated. He might regret this. "Dad, could we all pray together at dinner? Holding hands?"

"Are you sure?"

"The wound still hurts, but it's important to Mom, so I'll endure it."

"We were going to eat on the way, but something can be arranged." His dad looked at his watch and stood. "Speaking of which . . ."

"Oh, yeah, we need to go." Jordy bit his lower lip. "But I have something else I need to talk to you about. Well, two things."

His dad settled back down. "Go on."

Jordy picked at a loose thread on his quilt. "Susanna, she truly loves the Lord, and that connection has strengthened both of us in the Lord so much, I've come home. But her family is fairly secular and is unsupportive of her faith. Could she go to church with us?"

His dad nodded, surprise registering in his eyes. "Us? Really?"

Jordy gulped. It'd been two years since the last time he endured parental nagging about him not going to church. "I talked things out with God."

"Oh?" His dad stared a moment. He swallowed and nodded. "Yes, you can invite as many friends to church as you wish, including Susanna. I'll talk to her parents and smooth things over if necessary. Hitting rock bottom did teach me how to talk to folk with harder lives and different beliefs and values than us." He stood again, turning toward the stairs. "Let's get going."

Jordy drew in another breath. "Uh, about friends. I've been praying, and

I believe the right thing to do is to commit to Susanna for the long haul." He played with her ring on his chain. "How impossible it'd be for us to make it on our own is what drove me to my knees. It'll keep us close to God."

Alarm filled his father's eyes. "We'll talk after dinner."

"'But if they cannot exercise self-control, let them marry. For it is better to marry than to burn with passion,'" he recited, making his dad pale. Jordy added, "With God's help, I hope we won't reach that point until we're out of high school, since her parents won't respect God's word on that point. But I'd appreciate your support, if marrying early becomes our only moral option."

"Again, I need to talk to your mom and pray before we finish this, but be prepared to confess what you're wanting to take her away from. Marriage is not a way to escape personal problems, son. Let your mom and I intervene."

Oh you do know me. Jordy sighed. "Okay. I'll be up in just a second."

Jordy returned to Christine's jewelry box, still open, waiting for him to decide. He closed it and fingered the ring. It had cost him two months' worth of memorizing Bible verses for a dollar each. Really, it was his to do with as he pleased. And, if Susanna said no, he owed her the Bible he'd promised.

And he already owned the perfect one for her. After he'd thrown a royal fit over Christine's clothes being given away, his parents had said he could give the rest of her stuff away himself, whenever he felt ready to part with it.

He opened the wardrobe. From off the top shelf, he grabbed Christine's NKJV girls' Bible by its shiny purple case's messenger bag strap. He slipped the strap over his shoulder and started upstairs, but he stopped at his mom's voice asking, "Jordan, what's wrong?"

His dad answered. "Marissa, well, first the good news. God just gave us our son back. He even called me Dad and said he loved me."

Jordy tiptoed the rest of the way upstairs and peaked around the corner. His dad had embraced his mom.

Sobs shook her shoulders. "Thank you, Lord, thank you."

Would Sue-Susanna be so happy? Jordy gulped. How would she react to how important his faith truly was to him? Would she believe him? Though, she showed no awareness of why he'd feared he'd been eternally damned. The theology debate that had sparked that might be over her head, and it no longer mattered. He grinned, glowing inside. Grace had taught his heart to fear—and grace had relieved his fears.

LEST THE PURPLE ROSES smudge, Susanna held her birthday cake with both hands by the van's side door as her dad drove on Glenshire's bumpy gravel roads. She bit her lip. She was not in a hurry to see Jordy. All she had to do was walk across the alley and ring the bell. Simple. No problem at all. And of course, she saw him every day in Chemistry, and they both had lunch the same period, and he still took her to school and back. Really, she could see him whenever she wanted. And by now his parents' misunderstanding about their relationship should be straightened out, right?

So, why was she thinking about this at all?

Why did dating him appeal the moment he wasn't allowed to date?

Okay, admit it you lovesick fool. Jordy has all but ignored you since lunch on Tuesday. And he no doubt had been violating a no-dating rule in Chicago, too. His dad is back, but he no longer respects his dad, so he must in truth agree we can't only be friends anymore, but he doesn't feel ready to be more than friends, either. For sure he has forgotten your birthday, and you're desperately hoping things will somehow be different here.

She sighed. At least it wasn't just her. Jordy had been down right rude to his classmates and even to his teachers. He was late to Chemistry Wednesday and when Dr. Vinoski questioned him, Jordy snapped at him.

At least she was too busy worrying about him and praying for him for her to do worse than cry into her pillow at night, missing him so bad it hurt. On Tuesday, at least, he had been universally following "thou shalt not date." Even to her, it'd been too clear what Natasha had wanted from him. And his brush off had sent a clear signal that he was only interested in Susanna.

Since then, Jordy had been courteous but distant. She bit her lip. What if he changed his mind? She hadn't seen anyone else trying to get with him, but that didn't mean shenanigans weren't going on behind her back. And the guy who once pulled off a five-timer had to be a master at hiding things.

The van rolled to a stop on the far left side of their camp site. Her dad glanced back at her. "Let's eat the pizza while it's hot. We can unload later."

After they had eaten and finished unloading the van, Susanna sat at the picnic table and admired the purple roses on her fifteenth birthday cake.

Cara ran over. "Can we cut the cake now?"

Their mom shook her head. "We just ate. Let your stomach settle."

Cara jutted out a pouty lip. "Can she open her presents, at least?"

"All right. I'll get them." Their mom went inside the trailer.

Cara sat across from Susanna. "I hope you like mine."

Susanna asked, "And where did you get the money for a present?"

"Mom paid for it."

Their mom returned with two gifts in red and green Christmas wrapping paper. One gift looked rather suspiciously like a book. The other appeared to be stuffed in a used pudding box. "All right, which one do you want first?"

Cara clapped her hands. "Open mine!"

Susanna rolled her eyes. "All right, give me Cara's."

"Let me." Cara snatched the larger, flatter present from her mom then handed it to Susanna. "Here, Sis."

Susanna opened the package. She stared at a nonfiction book on how to convince boys to date her. This had to be a gag. "Uh, thanks."

"I figured, since you like to read, you should read something useful. You only have a year before you'll be sweet sixteen and never been kissed."

Was Cara serious? Susanna rolled her eyes and laughed. "Just wait until you see what you're getting for your birthday."

"I can hardly wait."

Susanna's mom handed her the present that looked like it was in a used pudding box. "Now, open ours."

She tore off the Christmas paper and opened the pudding box to find a gray ring box. She peered up at her mom curiously. Her mom beamed back. Susanna pried open the rusted ring box and gasped at the blue star sapphire. She'd been hoping to someday be given this cherished family heirloom for as long as she could remember. "Aw, Mom! Your blue star ring?"

"Yeah, I bought it on my fifteenth birthday."

Susanna frowned. "You bought it?"

"My parents couldn't afford it, and I wanted it, so I split the cost."

"Thank you so much, Mom." Susanna hugged her.

Her mom's eyes moistened. "No problem, baby. I love you."

"I love you, too." Susanna slid the blue star ring onto her right hand.

Someone started clapping. Susanna jumped and spun around.

Just beyond the edge of their site, Jordy stood in the gravel road, with one arm through a present in a pretty floral gift bag. "Beautiful, people! Just beautiful!" He made eye contact with her mom. "Can I steal your daughter?"

Her mom smiled and nodded. "Sure. Behave yourself, Susanna."

"Don't I always?" She followed Jordy down the road. Wow. Who'd fixed Jordy? Still, underneath the confident strength he projected, she sensed he was nervous. Something had changed about him.

She fell in step with him. "Where are we going?"

"The ravine. The lake would be more fitting, but our favorite spot there might be too private, and I can be impatient at times."

"Who isn't sometimes?"

Jordy laughed. "You justify everything."

"I know. It's because I—" Her cheeks flamed. Best to keep him no longer so sure of her feelings for him. "I mean, sometimes, when you . . . care about someone, all you want to see is their good side."

Jordy held her hand. "It's okay, I know what you mean."

Her stomach churned. If he did, then that would explain why he'd truly backed off so much. But why was he so calm rather than angry at himself?

They reached the fallen oak tree down in the ravine. She climbed up on its back and sat sidesaddle. Her dangling legs kicked.

He stood next to her and handed her the gift bag. "Here. Thank my mom for finding a bag for it, but this is from Christine and me."

"Oh?" She reached in and pulled out what looked to her like a tiny, shiny purple purse. She slipped its black strap over her head and unzipped the case curiously. A Bible, as promised. She flipped through it, grinning. "Wow. This is perfect. Readable, beautiful, much harder to lose, way easier to find."

"Exactly. Christine managed not to lose it, and she would have forgotten where she'd left her head, if it hadn't been attached to her shoulders."

"Me too!" Susanna sniffled, her chest tightening. It felt like her real best friend forever had died before she'd met her. "Thank you so much."

"You're welcome." Jordy patted her back. Their grief shone in his eyes. He wet his lips. "What'd your folks get you?"

"This." She pointed to her mother's ring and told him about the gag gift that her sister sounded serious about. "I've got a goofy kid sister, don't I?"

"She's definitely not subtle."

"Thank you for your sister's Bible. It means a lot." She glanced at it and zipped it up tenderly. "It's beautiful, thank you."

He pulled her down from the tree and held her with his arms around her waist. "A beautiful girl's Bible deserved to be given to a beautiful girl."

Susanna's heart swelled, and her arms landed around his neck. Aw, him returning to her like this had to mean they'd both missed each other badly—but wouldn't he still get in trouble? Sighing, she pushed away. "Jordy—"

He placed his index finger on her lips. "I love you. I will never lie to you. When I say you're beautiful, I mean it."

The emotion filled his voice and shone in his eyes.

Her heart thudded. She whispered, "You really think so?"

Jordy studied her. "Why wouldn't I? Why are you still this self-conscious with me? Is it those extra twenty-five pounds?"

She gasped. The flatterer under-guessed by ten pounds. "How . . . ."

"You're the same size as Vera. My body has found your figure intriguing ever since hello. And discriminating over weight is against my principles. My sister was always plump, and puberty was cruel to her. In seventh grade, a girl named Kaitlyn had transferred from a prep school in the city; in Chicago proper, I mean. She tore Christine to shreds."

Susanna winced in empathy.

Jordy added, "Kaitlyn was appalled to learn she'd insulted the sister of the guy she'd set her sights on. And, at the time, I was the largemouth bass in a goldfish pond, and my twin was naturally my right-hand girl. Me, I always hated Kaitlyn, but Christine never held a grudge. She prayed for her enemy daily. My sister never met Kaitlyn's standard of beauty, but Christine walked with a grace that radiated from her. It lit up her eyes like an evergreen fire. I feared I'd never see that light again." He traced the line of Susanna's jaw with his index finger. "But, I did. In you."

She touched his cheek. "It's in you, too, Jordy."

He took her hand. A wry smile crossed his lips. "Only because God has awoken this sleeper from the dead and given me back the light of Christ." He snapped his fingers. "Speaking of which, what the Holy Spirit told you, that we are children of the light? It's from the Bible."

She arched her eyebrows. "Really?"

"Yep, Ephesians 5:8, 'for once you were darkness, but now you are light in the Lord. Walk as children of the light.' Since I knew that text, God was reassuring me that I am his child and telling me to get up and walk like it. I can't say I was surprised. He'd already used you to reach out to me before."

Susanna wrinkled her forehead. "When? Oh, at the lake?"

He squeezed her hand. "You mourned with me as if you were weeping the tears of Christ, as you loved me with Christ's love. That floored me, such compassion. What the Lord did for me through you was so amazing. My dad was as right to separate us as he was wrong. It drove me to go to the Lord directly. It took most of the week, but I've given over everything. He took all the anger. He's relieved my oxytocin cravings even. I've come home."

She put her hand up. "Meaning you got right with God, as you put it?" At his eager nod, she mirrored his grin and hugged him. "That's so cool!" She let herself gaze directly into his eyes. If only he was allowed to be here. "I missed you so much, I'm tempted to pick up where we left off, but we can't, can we?"

Jordy held her in his arms. "This week was an unpleasant taste of what me truly trying to be only your friend looks like when I'm head over heels in love with you. I already knew I'd been breaking the no-dating rule with you in spirit when my father called me out for it. And me seeing you like that was a remainder of Sir Flirtalot. So I had to stop it."

"You're here now, though," she said quietly.

"Hoping and praying it isn't for the last time." He traced her jaw. "That is up to you. By the way, the way you keep forgetting to say 'I love you, too, Jordy,' is on the list of adorable quirks that you share with my sister."

"I do love you, too." Face warm, she snuggled into his embrace. "And us not being allowed to date had this odd effect of me suddenly wanting that, if I understand the question you're dancing around, so don't be so nervous."

"So we're both rebellious like that." He kissed her on the cheek sweetly.

Whoa. She planted a wet kiss on his cheek. "What are we going to do? I don't want to get you in trouble."

"Hey, you let me worry about how I've convinced my parents to make an exception and allow me to see you and only you."

"Really?" She squealed. Wow. She could make that noise? "How?"

He drew her closer and murmured, "Oh, I twisted my dad's arm with an implied threat to lie about our ages on a marriage license tomorrow. So now

I'm not allowed to elope with you, but I am allowed to be your boyfriend, so I hope your sister saved her receipt."

Susanna laughed. "I'll give her gag gift back to her on her birthday."

Jordy swallowed. "Okay, now for the tough part. My parents' conditions regulate only my behavior, and I don't want it causing you anxiety, so please just trust me. For an example, you are allowed in our house, but I'm required to redirect us away from tempting situations. Make sense?"

"Kinda, but, um, can I truly trust you on that?"

Jordy winced. "Sir Flirtalot, not at all, but there's something you need to understand. When I make a commitment, I go all the way."

She jerked away from him. "Jordy!"

His cheeks turned crimson. "Sorry, that came out wrong. What I meant is, Christianity wasn't merely a Sunday morning thing for me. It was central to my daily life. And what God has done for me through you is so powerful, now that I've accepted that gift, I'm doing a rapid one-eighty. This includes me going back to church, and I'm hoping you'll go with me."

"Of course." She slapped him on the chest. "Don't scare me like that!"

He laughed. "Glad you're going. Wolves kill by separating the lambs and the weaker sheep from the flock. So you joining our flock is safest for you as well as reassuring to my folks. My mom was already desperate enough to see me recovering to support us, but my dad's a 'don't make me regret this.'"

Susanna blinked. "Dad, not Jordan?"

"Yes, Dad. I've reconciled with him, too. But, as I was saying, I can't risk not complying with the compromise that he and I have agreed upon. You and I will need my parents' support to make it."

To the altar? "Fair enough," she whispered. Was this really happening?

Jordy took a breath. "Do we have to discuss the 'all the way' that you're worried about? I'd rather not go into the specifics on what I have and haven't done or on what happened to me right in a high school auditorium. That day turned my life so dark, I'd violate your innocence just discussing it in detail."

Her face warmed, she stared down at the fallen oak tree. The world went fuzzy until she found her hand petting the tree bark.

Jordy sighed. "Yep. Um, first of all, I'm sorry for the wrong impression I've habitually given you. At my darkest, I wanted revenge on abusive peers that I collectively blamed for the loss of my innocence. Not to take that from anyone else. Vera was a virgin, too, and I did drag her down fast but not like you've imagined. I've never gone 'all the way' to vaginal intercourse myself."

What? The relief flooded her as she gawked. "You're still a virgin?"

He grinned sheepishly. "I was the sort of hypocrite who told myself what I wasn't doing justified what I was doing. That was one of the problems with my friendship with Brandt, too. We used each other's sins to excuse our own. Plus, that awful day in study hall, he was a leering face in the crowd that kept me trapped while they egged on the assault, and he always harassed me for refusing to go 'all the way.' In hindsight, he likely sicced Isabel on me."

"But you never gave in?"

Jordy shook his head. "I couldn't after I'd given girls a false impression that I'm more experienced than I am. I was also hiding this." He fingered his sister's ring. "Then, I wore it as a memorial to my losses, but it still held me back somewhat, an answer to my mom's prayers no doubt."

"If you're telling me the truth, that would be a miracle."

Remorse filled his eyes. "Not exactly."

Her breath caught. "What do you mean?"

"Um, the lewd conduct that I have engaged in was morally, legally, and medically equivalent to sex. What I did do was just as wrong and quite risky; I still could've been exposed to STDs. It's been three months since I stopped, and my tests came back negative, but I still feel unworthy of a girl like you. If I could take what I have done back, I would, but I can't. I can stay faithful to you now, and we can seek to keep our relationship pure with God's help, my parents' help, and couple's therapy. But all you have to go on is my word, and my word never meant much. I gave Vera my word as a scout. I broke it."

Susanna swallowed. "What about your word as a Christian?"

"I do have that. And this." He pulled the chain around his neck over his head and held it out by the ring. "This is yours. Please accept it."

She gasped, covering her mouth. "You are not asking me to . . . ?"

"Me getting engaged before eighteen would violate the compromise Dad and I agreed upon," Jordy said sheepishly. "But that ring is my property. And he didn't say you couldn't promise now to say yes when asked someday."

Susanna laughed so hard, she held her belly. "Oh you are a scamp."

"Yeah, well, pre-engagement promise rings are a thing, and I do need us to have some sort of long-term commitment headed toward marriage."

Christine's ring glint in the evening sunlight streaming through the tree tops. Susanna's heart thudded as she eyed it longingly. "You're sure you want to give your sister's ring to me?"

"Positive. Please say yes. I've never been more sure of anything."

Susanna took the ring and pulled its chain on over her head. "I have an idea of what we can do the next time the guys call me your girlfriend."

Jordy slipped his arms around her waist. "And what's that?"

"Something like this." She drew Jordy closer, let her arms hang from his neck, and their lips met in a gentle, sweet kiss.

Don't miss out!

Visit the website below and you can sign up to receive emails whenever Andrea J. Graham publishes a new book. There's no charge and no obligation.

https://books2read.com/r/B-A-EQLI-OSTHB

BOOKS 2 READ

Connecting independent readers to independent writers.

Did you love *Country At Heart*? Then you should read *Is There Life After Mars?*[1] by Andrea J. Graham!

[2]

On the Martian Frontier in 2084, a mystery illness threatens to kill twelve-year-old farm girl Gloria Patri Fowler Cruz. This provokes her dad, Mama's aristocrat ex-husband Peyton, to defy social class divisions that ripped him from his family. And Gloria's new, wearable medical device doesn't work without an artificial intelligence. She substitutes her entertainment AI, dressed as a digital dog, Jake. Her AI develops human qualities, thanks to magic that he believes comes from God. Gloria questions if she can trust her dad, Jake, or God. In the colony's capitol, Peyton's vice admiral father rules like a king, hates Mama's family, and will do anything to keep them out of the aristocracy. But politics is Dad's thing. Gloria would rather clobber her "bro forever," Holter Sloan. He has no time to play. He's too busy crushing on her fraternal twin!

Read more at www.christsglory.com.

1. https://books2read.com/u/3kpxAg

2. https://books2read.com/u/3kpxAg

Also by Andrea J. Graham

Argevane Series
Daughter of Kristos
Son of Kristos
Daughter of Eve

Life After Mars Series
Is There Life After Mars?
Life After Venus!
Life After Mercury
Life After Paradise: Into the Web Surfer Universe

Web Surfer Series
Web Surfer ANI
Nimbus Rider
Restoring: Web Surfer 3.0
Reconciling: Web Surfer 4.0

Standalone
Country At Heart

Watch for more at www.christsglory.com.

About the Author

Andrea Graham studied creative writing and religion at Ashland University, has been envisioning fantastic worlds since age six, and has been writing science fiction novels since she was fourteen. Bear Publications released her book, *Avatars of Web Surfer*, which she wrote with three co-authors. She is the wife of author Adam Graham and edits his novels, including *Tales of the Dim Knight* and *Slime Incorporated*. Her own publishing imprint, Reignburst Books, released the Web Surfer Series and the Life After Mars Series. Find her as an author at christsglory.com and as an editor at povbootcamp.com.

Andrea and Adam live with their dog, Rocky, and their cat, Bullwinkle, in Boise, Idaho. They're adopting their first child.

Read more at www.christsglory.com.

About the Publisher

This is the personal imprint of Andrea J. Graham, who dreams of turning it into a full-service publishing company along with partners who would share her vision for a company staffed by Christians willing to go beyond the limits of the CBA while being true to the God whose reign is ready to burst forth in unexpected, undreamed of ways.

CPSIA information can be obtained
at www.ICGtesting.com
Printed in the USA
LVHW031341111222
735003LV00003B/440